SIMONE BREAKS ALL THE RULES

DEBBIE RIGAUD

SCHOLASTIC

Published in the UK by Scholastic, 2021
Euston House, 24 Eversholt Street, London, NW1 1DB
Scholastic Ireland, 89E Lagan Road, Dublin Industrial Estate, Glasnevin, Dublin,
D11 HP5F

First published in the US by Scholastic Inc., 2021

Text © Debbie Rigaud, 2021
Photos © Shutterstock.com

ISBN 978 0702 31088 1

A CIP catalogue record for this book is available from the British Library.

Printed by CPI Group (UK) Ltd, Croydon, CR0 4YY
Paper made from wood grown in sustainable forests and other controlled sources.

1 3 5 7 9 10 8 6 4 2

www.scholastic.co.uk

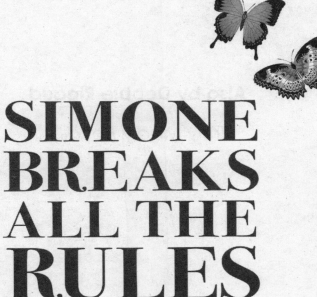

SIMONE BREAKS ALL THE RULES

Also by Debbie Rigaud

Truly Madly Royally

For Viviane Rigaud. Thank you, Mummy, for the many stories. You live on in them all.

PROLOGUE

(four years ago)

"Psst . . . Anne," I whispered out the side of my mouth as our car pulled up to Madame Honoré's house. "Make a run for it."

My older sister shot me an exasperated look. "That's not funny, Simone."

"I'm dead serious," I declared. "Would I joke at a time like this?"

Of course, both Anne and I had to admit that it was too late to fight this battle. Our bridge-and-tunnel journey over, we had arrived in Queens to meet Anne's arranged prom date.

Our mother set up the whole thing without Anne's involvement. She must have cast a wide net for this catch, no doubt activating her entire tristate-area network of Haitian mamas with teenaged sons.

I wished I could say that nothing in my sister's seventeen years had prepared her for this embarrassment. But the truth was, by then, Anne already held titles in the Overprotected Olympics. And at thirteen, I was being groomed as her successor.

"Ssssshhhhh," Mummy hissed from the passenger seat. She was in full arrival mode. Hushing folks was to my mom what getting seats and tray tables in their upright positions was to flight attendants.

My seat belt's metal clasp *ka-klow*ed as I unlatched it. Anne flinched at the sound, and that was it for me.

Anne was usually as composed as Beethoven. If the flouncy Sunday dress she wore came with auto-flip sequins, she'd *still* seem low-key. The girl was that unfussy—in personality, not in looks, for Anne was the pretty one. I was always flattered when people mistook us for twins. Our personalities, though, could not have been more different.

My mom once joked she should've named us Push and Pull. Anne, like her long, straightened hair, was pulled together. And every time she started to inch a toe over to the wild side, she'd pull herself back behind the line. Meanwhile, I subtly pushed boundaries the same as I pushed back on my parents' rules. Today, for instance, I had opted not to flat-iron my unyielding coils *or* to wear the corny outfit my mom had picked out for me.

"Are we seriously going through with this?" I asked my parents, leaning forward for urgency's sake. They both pouted in that intense way only Creole-and-French-forged lips can. "Isn't that famous Haitian restaurant nearby?" I continued. "We can order dinner to go and be back in Jersey before the food gets cold. The traffic going the other way is light—"

"That's enough, Simone!" Mummy whisper-screamed without

looking away from her sun-visor mirror as she freshened up her makeup.

"*Eh bien*, I'll wait outside," Papi said with one foot already out the car door. Poor guy. He was so overpowered by all the estrogen in his life.

After another minute of grooming (Mummy) and stalling (Anne and me), the three of us got out of the car and headed to the house with Papi.

Our host, Madame Honoré Fils-Aimé, met us at her front door with her cheek angled toward us, ready to receive our greetings. This was a cultural gesture she'd earned. To be sure, the kisser is of lesser status than the kissee. Madame Honoré was the senior woman as well as the host—not to mention (if you ask my mom) the lifesaver of the day—so it was all cheek out for her.

"Constance, Gérard, comment ça va?" She greeted my parents with a broad grin, setting a formal tone by speaking French instead of Haitian Creole.

"Allo, Madame Honoré," my mother answered, half an octave higher than normal. Her top row of teeth was so overexposed, I imagined them drying up.

The spicy aroma tickling my nose from the front stoop and the beads of sweat on Madame Honoré's penciled brow conjured an image of our host whipping up a tasty dish over the hot stove. It was enough to put me in a better mood.

"Allons, allons." My mother coaxed me and Anne to step inside. Her public voice and trained personality reported to duty in all their Francophone glory. "Ah, Simone, l'as-tu laissé dans la voiture?" she asked me.

"Non," I answered, stepping from behind Anne and showing my mom that I had not in fact forgotten the macaroni au gratin that stole my window seat.

After handing over the pan of food, Anne and I offered Madame Honoré the obligatory cheek-kiss greeting. We instinctively walked single file, following the foot indentations in the plush beige carpeting, to an ornate sofa that looked like a double-wide throne. We were careful not to bump the gilded coffee table that was mobbed with tiny figurines of white women in hoopskirts.

I felt so tense for my sister that my scalp throbbed, as if I were wearing too-tight braids. Our hands rested side by side on the velvety seat cushion, so I gave Anne's a poke and flashed her a grimace, minus the gross eyelid flip I'd learned from Gabby. Our cousin Gabrielle was the buckwildest person we knew. She was only eleven, but her talent for telling the world to shove off with a bawdy grimace, a well-timed belch, or the choicest Creole cuss word was the stuff of legend. Gabby would wreak the best kind of havoc if she were here right now. And Anne's lip curl told me she was thinking the same hilarious thought.

"Jude! *Vini'm pale'w*," Madame Honoré abruptly called out in Creole.

A tall, broad-shouldered teen boy barreled down the stairs and paused when he saw the small crowd in his living room.

Madame Honoré rattled off names in our seating order. "You

remember Madame Gérard, Gérard, and their daughters, Anne and Simone," she told the boy. "They came to your brother's communion party when you were eleven."

"H-hello," Jude reluctantly said without much eye contact. Shockingly, he didn't make the rounds planting kisses on everyone's cheeks as my sister and I would've been obligated to do had we been in his shoes. Nor did his mother reprimand him for not doing so. He just stood there nodding in greeting.

When Jude turned to take a seat, he exposed the one wireless earbud he had plugged in his ear. The shiny silver phone that peeked out of his front jeans pocket was probably cycling through a playlist. That would explain Jude's head nods.

Papi couldn't stop glaring at him. It was all he could do not to leapfrog the coffee table and scare some respect into the kid. Anne's expression stayed neutral, like she was in a Vulcan mind meld with one of the hoopskirt-wearing figurines. I wondered how she could be so still, so outwardly quiet when her fate was being decided by everyone but her. I squirmed in my seat to shake off the secondhand embarrassment. Mummy kept her feet crossed at her ankles and laced her fingers together in her lap. She spoke with a tight smile and a singsong voice in crisp Creole, as if she were being graded on etiquette.

"As we discussed over the phone, my daughter Anne needs to attend senior prom with an escort, and the good Lord pointed me to you," she told Madame Honoré. "Jude would make the perfect companion for this event. We would love for him to attend prom with Anne. If you agree to this, that would be a grand gesture on your part, and we would be very grateful." She smoothed down her skirt with splayed fingers to signal the end of her proposition.

I wondered if Madame Honoré would jump to her feet and kick us out, scolding us for perpetuating an old-fashioned immigrant stereotype and imploring us to get with the times.

No such luck.

Madame Honoré beamed, nodding in an I-agree-I-have-been-a-huge-blessing fashion rather than the general I'm-following-what-you're-saying one. She obviously delighted in her good standing. A properly vetted son to our family's dateless daughter was a gold mine to parents like Constance and Gérard Thibodeaux of East Orange, New Jersey.

Anne's shoulders were high and tense. She finally coughed up some flippant words. "Great, thanks."

"Of course, Anne," Madame Honoré said tenderly. "You two will make a gorgeous prom couple. Just let us know what color you'd like to wear and my boy will make sure his cummerbund matches."

Mummy gasped excitedly. "Oh, can't you just see her in something bright and eye-catching?"

"Mais oui," agreed Madame Honoré. "I was just about to suggest that—like a peach or even yellow—"

"Black," Anne interrupted with a confident nod. She leaned forward to look around Papi at Mummy. "I'm wearing black."

Battle line drawn, she momentarily froze in an eye lock with

Mummy. Anne was giving off such Old-West-outlaw energy, a tumbleweed might have blown by. The only motion in this stillness was Jude's head bob. Dude wasn't fooling anyone that he was paying attention.

"Eh bien, black it is, chérie," Madame Honoré murmured. Anne blinked in slow motion and then wedged back into her spot on the crowded sofa.

The particulars were then discussed—the date of the prom, transportation arrangements. It was agreed that after prom, Jude would sleep at a cousin's nearby house in East Orange.

The room relaxed after everything had been decided. Both mothers appeared happy. Anne looked resigned. All went as was expected.

That is, until a boy my age tore through the front door, reeking of grass and sweat. He was shadowed by an older man I assumed was Madame Honoré's husband, Honoré. The boy was gnashing on some gum and wearing a dirt-stained baseball uniform.

I sat up, because baseball's my favorite sport.

"We won!" the boy exclaimed to Madame Honoré, who raised her proud chin and smiled.

He scanned the room for another reaction, and his eyes landed on mine.

"You play?" he interrogated me as my parents greeted the older man, our host's husband.

The nerve. I felt exposed at a time when I was trying to fly under the radar. The neck swivel was a reflex I couldn't rein in when I spit out the only comeback I could think of. "Do *you?*"

Confusion crumpled every corner of the boy's brown face.

The sight of our interaction prompted Madame Honoré to break out in a gleeful chortle. "And when it is Simone's turn," she squawked, gesturing to Baseball Boy, "my younger son Ben will be ready."

Nope. Not gonna happen. No way was I ever going through with an arranged prom like Anne. With this vow ringing in my heart like a fire alarm, I glared at Ben. And the weirdo he was, he pleasantly smiled back.

CHAPTER ONE

(present day)

Plum lip stain with a hint of metallic gloss. Yup. It's working nicely with my deep brown complexion and my metal-frame glasses. Only, under the bus shelter's fluorescent lighting, the shade looks . . . extra. Way glossier than I'm comfortable with for 6:30 a.m. at a headlights-streaked intersection. What if I see Gavin on the bus? He'll think I'm trying way too hard. It doesn't have to be *that* obvious that I want him to notice me. I dab my lips with a square I yanked from Mummy's Marie-Antoinette-looking tissue box before I left the house.

"Typical Simone, dulling her shine," shouts a familiar voice. I close out of the camera mirror and brace for the storm that is my cousin Gabby.

"I knew all this quiet wouldn't last long," I call out to Gabby, who is powering up the flat city street like it's a hill. She heaves out a breath cloud when she reaches the bus shelter. The few commuters trailing behind her arrive with far fewer theatrics.

Despite the March chill in the air, Gabby's black puffer coat is unzipped and sliding down one shoulder. Her navy-blue uniform skirt is identical to the one I have on, except hers is extra crinkled. An early riser Gabby is not. It takes all the tools in her bag—including a bangin' morning playlist and bacon-scented candles—to get the girl up and out the house.

"Hey," she says, louder than necessary, because her earbuds are no doubt on full blast. I give her a wave.

Gabby nods across the street at the bus picking up passengers headed to Newark. "Just imagine! That'll be your bus next year."

I purse my lips and give my cousin a side glance. "*Hmmph*, no, it won't," I protest, not willing to concede that I'll be commuting to the Rutgers Newark campus for my freshman year of college.

"So you've spoken to your parents about living on campus?" she asks, and then leans an ear toward me to catch my non-answer. My silence rings loud and clear. Gabby gives a shoulder-bounce chuckle and plugs her earbud back in.

"For your information, I'm planning on talking to them . . . soon," I mumble to myself. The first and only time I brought up my desire to live away from home for college, things didn't go over so well. Thankfully, the paramedics had been called off in time, and blood pressures went back to baseline. For now, I'm letting things breathe for a while before I mention it again. It's only been a few weeks—*er*, months. Okay, fine. It's been a year, but who's counting?

Mummy's old-fashioned like oatmeal. If you don't believe me, check my life—it's sealed in a boy-proof container, down to the no-dating-until-college rules and the all-girls Catholic high school I go to.

At my ripe old age of seventeen, I've never had a boyfriend. And the only time I've kissed a boy was during the Christmas play when I was fifteen. Technically, Mary and Joseph weren't scripted to kiss, but the choir boy was so moved by the Holy Spirit, he went for it. No one noticed, though. A woolly lamb scampered in the way at just the right moment. If I'd known that would be my only lip-lock so far, I would've used more tongue.

A New Jersey Transit bus pulls up, but it's not ours. *Why is the number 60 always the last to come?* I guess it's a "perk" of going to a tucked-away school most people in our neighborhood have never heard of. Just because Anne graduated from St. Clare Academy, I'm expected to, too. And I will, in just a few months. My mother convinced her kid sister—Gabby's mom—that Gabby should go here as well, and I'm grateful for that.

Pretending to be unbothered by the long wait, I lean against the bus shelter's plexiglass. Instead of making contact, though, I fall right through an empty frame! Status update: The plexiglass is missing! My butt meets the concrete and my legs hang over the low metal bar.

That's when it goes off like a firecracker: the cackle and pop of Gabby's unbridled laughter. She is the last person you want around when something embarrassing happens.

"Ohmygod, I'm done! Bye!" she screams, stomping away, and then jogging right back.

"Really?" I hoist myself to a standing position, right my glasses, and smooth down the strands of my puffy blowout. Thank God I'm wearing my New York Mets boy shorts under my skirt. But I'm sure the sight of my spindly long legs slung over the hollowed-out frame is forever etched in my fellow commuters' minds.

"My bad," Gabby says. The vein on her forehead gives away that she's fighting another outburst. "I should've asked if you're okay first."

"Whatever," I mutter, dusting off the back of my coat.

"Aw, come here, my clumsy cuz," Gabby coos, walking over with her arms outstretched. I want to duck, but I don't trust myself not to trip over my feet because I'm feeling unlucky. My ego's too wounded to hug her back. My one solace is that Gavin wasn't around to witness my literal downfall.

My face still feels tight with embarrassment moments later when we finally board the 60 bus. I follow Gabby absentmindedly and almost bump into her when she stops halfway to grip a pole. No more seats. I grab the pole and stare neck-brace rigid out the window. I get so lost in the passing city scenery that I almost miss it when Gavin boards the bus.

I hold my breath and watch as he makes his way down the aisle. His broad shoulders, intense eyes, and the glistening waves in his hair instantly make my heart go *beat-beat-beat all through the town*. Gavin looks over my head, scanning the back of the bus. Not seeing any space there, he claims a standing spot. Right next to me.

I can't believe my sudden change in luck. As more commuters climb aboard and pile up behind Gavin, I mentally rehearse my intro.

Gavin peels off his backpack and rests it between his feet. He's wearing his Millwall Prep Lions jacket, which gives me an in. He may not be aware that I know he just started at Millwall this semester. His uniform and his bus stop have been dead giveaways. Plus, he seems to have a lot of friends—some of whom are loud talkers, which is how I learned his name. Thanks to his school jacket, it won't seem so creepy if I start a conversation with "Oh, cool—Millwall is our brother school." Maybe then he'll ask if I'm coming to the basketball team's house party tomorrow. (Answer: St. Clare's varsity basketball team is invited, so all the seniors plan to crash.) And then *bam* . . . love connection! Next stop: kissing.

Before I speak up, I let my neck go slack and do a tongue check for anything in my teeth.

"Step all the way in, people!" The bus driver is eagle-eyeing his ginormous rearview mirror like a detention monitor. "The sooner you make room, the sooner we can get going."

Gavin takes a step toward me, and we are now only inches apart. The dangling gold "G" pendant at the end of his necklace swings back into place.

I catch a wonderful whiff of coconut and argan oil, and recognize the hair product he must've used this morning. Does that mean he smells me, too?

I'm sure I'm funky from stress-sweating brought on by my epic fall at the bus stop. I keep my arms pinned to my sides. My mouth seals up, too. How can I make flirty conversation when I'm potentially a walking funk factory? This is a disaster.

The bus starts moving, and I'm forced to take the surf-ride stance—feet planted shoulder-width apart, knees slightly bent, toes gripping the bus floor. To grab the closest safety rail between us would mean raising my arm over my head.

I turn my back to Gavin and signal to Gabby. She frees one ear from her earbud to listen to me low-key ask her in Creole, "Do I smell?"

"Whose auntie?" Gabby asks, confused.

"No. 'Santi.'"

"I do?"

I give her a laser-beam glare, then point to myself.

"You?" she shouts.

I nod yes.

"You do? Whoa. Good thing I can't smell." She points to her nose. "Still stuffed up from that cold I had."

Forget it. Forget it. *Forget it!*

Gavin is hardly ever alone, so now's my chance. I take a belly-deep breath and switch arms so I'm holding on to the pole with my left hand. I pivot in Gavin's direction. *Here goes . . .*

Before I can say hello, the bus jerks sharply and Gavin lurches right at me. Quick as a reflex, I reach out and steady his shoulder. He seems impressed I'm as stable as the pole I let go of. He doesn't know I've been a bus and subway surfing champ since infancy.

Gavin's surprised eyes search my face. His sigh of relief warms my cheek and gives off a distinct hint of cherry-flavored gummy-bear vitamins. He gently taps one of my hands in gratitude. His touch is like a spark shimmying up my spine, and I flash him a heart-eyes emoji smile.

"Get it, Simone!" Gabby's whoop slams like a sledgehammer and shatters this crystalline moment.

The girl must be trying to stop my heart. I get the urge to leap up and hoist myself out the overhead emergency exit. Gavin's eyes slit in search of the disembodied voice coming from somewhere close by.

I don't even notice I'm taking a couple of paces backward, away from Gavin, until he says, "Simone is a nice name."

The happy startle that seizes me is only outgunned by my deer-in-headlights reaction.

"By the way, I'm Gavin Stackhouse," he says, as if I have no clue. As if I haven't noticed him on this bus for weeks. Like I haven't been trolling his IG page ever since Millwall Prep's account posted and tagged a picture of him. But his friendly half smile is an invitation.

"I'm Simone," I say nonsensically, before rushing to fix this. "Uh, Simone Thibodeaux."

The bus goes over a huge bump and I practically bounce right out my shoes.

"Hey, Simone Tib-*bounce*-doe," he intones in an unmistakably

15

flirty key. My stomach flips like my real last name is Biles. "My bad, I mean . . . Tib-bo-doe?"

"Yeah," I say. "It's French." This last part I say out of pure nervousness.

"You Haitian?"

"Yes." I smile with pride, even as my chin juts up defensively.

Here it comes. This is usually the point where people come at me with nauseating remarks about Haiti. As Mummy explains it, folks search for reasons to feel better about the scorn they harbor for a people. My toes dig into the soles of my shoes.

Please don't ruin this moment for me, Gavin. Be the difference.

I almost want to plug my fingers into my ears or change the subject, fast. Whatever keeps his juicy lips from forming the words "voodoo" or "poor" or "church group mission" or—

"I always thought Creole sounded like a pretty language," he says. "Can you speak it?"

Holy firsts! It takes everything in my power not to tip him backward in a big dramatic movie kiss.

"Uh-huh" is all I manage to say with the little breath I have left.

His eyes meet mine. "Nice."

No sense in killing the mood by confessing that I speak Creole with a thick American accent. "Creole weighs a ton when *your* tongue carries it," my fancy grandmother likes to tease me.

"*Sak pase* is all I know," he says, and my knees buckle. "But everyone knows that much. Can you teach me something else?"

"Um, *kouman ou ye* is another greeting you can use instead of that one," I say. My smile is stretched so wide, I can barely enunciate—sort of like speaking in below freezing temps.

"*Koumo yay.*" He juggles the words.

"Perfect." In lieu of squealing, I grip the safety rail and playfully tip away from it, shoulder bag hanging, before pulling myself forward again.

My head is buzzing . . . or is it my phone?

I've set up my phone to pulse in triplets when it's Gabby texting. Whether she likes it or not (not), Gabby's like my jailbreak accomplice in the getaway car. She deserves all the specialized rings and alerts necessary if I'm going to try to beat my parents' system and have a life.

But for now, I ignore my cousin's clowning even as Gavin takes notice of the distraction. "You're buzzing like a queen bee," he informs me.

The sound of my phone short-circuits my game. I can't even think of some witty response to the queen bee comment. And that stings.

"Uh, yeah." I break eye contact and reach for my coat pocket. "I better check that."

As low-key as possible, I nudge Gabby with my left elbow, like, *Don't.* She shuffles out of reach. The only reason I read her text is because I don't want to give Gavin the impression that I'd ignore my phone just for him. He may be cool, but I ain't no fool. I glance down at my phone and read:

Are you gonna introduce me, or shall I introduce myself?

It takes a lot for me not to react when I see Gabby's message. I look away from Gavin so my cousin can decode the private reply in my glare: *Foul play. For the last time: It was just a harmless prank and they were fake spiders.*

In her calculating smile is her unquestionable retort: *I told you I'd get you back when you least expect it.*

I stare Gabby down and she blows me a kiss. If I know my cousin, I better act quick.

But Gavin gets blessedly distracted by another wave of boarding passengers.

"I know you all love being near me," the bus driver quips. "But do me a favor—step all the way down, people!"

Gabby issues her final warning. *"Ahem-hem*, yo."

Gavin inches closer to me, and I take that opening.

"Oh, Gavin, this is, uh, my cousin Gabby," I say, gesturing to my left with my free hand.

He leans forward to look around me and nods in greeting. "'Sup, Gabby."

Gabby waves. "Hey."

Satisfied, Gabby plugs in her earbuds and transports herself back to her own world.

Gavin turns his attention back to me. "Simone, do you—?"

"Next stop, Millwall!" the driver calls out. Ugh. Just that quickly, we're almost at the town of Millwall, where Millwall Prep is located. Not to be confused with its snooty sibling town, Millwall Cliffs, where my school is located.

As Gavin turns away from me to press the call strip above the window, I wait for him to drop the unsaid word.

Do I what? Do. I. *What?*

But it doesn't come.

Just like that, I'm left drowning in the glistening waves covering the back of Gavin's head. Gasping for air quotes.

I ignore the emotional bowling ball rolling in my stomach as best I can and pretend to lose myself in my phone.

"See you around, Simone," says Gavin with a dip in his cheek. I mouth a weak *good-bye* because I'm caught off guard.

Gavin steps off the bus with a crowd of guys and I'm relieved-bereaved to see him go.

Ten minutes later, Gabby and I get off at our stop and walk past the people strolling the sidewalks. Millwall Cliffs is the type of town where people walk for leisure, not out of necessity. Folks out here are way more likely to ride in fancy cars than on the bus. But they do step out of their cars to stroll the small downtown shopping district.

Our uniforms give us away, so locals know Gabby and me and the handful of other Brown and Black student commuters are Academy students. But on the rare days when we come here in our regular clothes, there are more double takes.

After a fifteen-minute walk, we step through the door of St. Clare Academy. A sea of blue-and-gray uniforms pour into the halls, though there are more flashes of gray than usual. Looks like the gray skirts are making a comeback. I scan the scene, scouting for funky new shoes or other cool accessories. I can always find a few that inspire me. Because of the strict rules around uniforms, a lot of St. Clare Academy girls get crazy creative with the fashion choices they are free to make. For me, it's all about my glasses—I've collected a bunch of cheapie statement frames over the years.

There's something different about the school today. Decorative party poms in fuchsia and white dot the walls, drawing my eye to the new posters hyping the upcoming senior prom. It's a little over two months away.

Prom. I imagine Gavin offering me his arm as we glide into the splashy venue together, stunning onlookers with our sensational style and lovey-dovey chemistry.

Are you ready? one poster asks in sparkly lettering.

I nod confidently. *I will be.*

CHAPTER TWO

It was the youth of Cairo, I type feverishly on my laptop, *who sparked a political demonstration that inspired the Arab Spring. Heroic South African high schoolers pumped high energy into the anti-apartheid movement. And that's not even counting how many armies Joan of Arc led before her sixteenth birthday.*

Having the senior lounge all to myself on my study period is doing wonders for my writing flow. All seniors have to hand in a research paper on a topic of their choosing in a couple of months, and I may just finish mine early. Though sadly, not before the lunch rush kills the vibe in here in just a few minutes. This windowless room with its inviting beanbags, a work table, a comfy turquoise couch, and soft armchairs is a big draw for seniors looking to break away from all the commoners in the common areas of the school.

I pause to save my document, which I've titled "Teen Heroes in History." I'm devoting way too much time to this project,

21

considering I've already been accepted early decision to Rutgers University. But just like when you feed a stray cat and it keeps coming back, something in this paper is feeding me, and I can't stay away.

These years are for setting off something sensational, I continue. *That rebellious spirit in the heart of every teen stirs for a reason. A soaring independence and an urgency to live on our own terms to announce to the world that we will not be held back—*

"Let me guess—you're not allowed to go to the house party tomorrow."

Gabby plops down next to me on the couch, almost knocking my water bottle onto my laptop. Maybe I can scare her away with my tuna sandwich breath.

"No, I plan to go," I say. It *will* be a little tricky for me. But the party starts early enough that if I go just for an hour, I can still make it home before my parents do.

"That's what I'm talking about." Gabby beams. "You're finally starting to get out more, take more chances, even if there's zero chance of you going away for college."

I sigh. I guess we're having this discussion again. Gabby is like that one thumbs-down on your favorite YouTube video.

"That's a lie," I lie. "Where'd you pick up that rumor about my zero chances?"

"Uh, from your mom." Gabby stares squarely at me. "She'll tell anyone who asks that you're commuting next year."

Reliable enough source.

With each gum-popping jaw grind, Gabby triggers a release of artificial strawberry smell. "How did she put it?" Gabby ponders. "I think she said an unsupervised dorm heaving with *lusting vagabonds* does not sound like a place she'd send her girl."

I tap a finger on my chin and pretend to search the ceiling for answers. "Gee, if I had to guess, it wasn't just *anyone* asking, but *somebody* in particular who got her all riled up on this topic."

"Hey, I couldn't just eat her food and not make small talk. That would be indecent," Gabby protests.

"Sophomore in the senior room!"

My lab partner, Amita Nadar, shuffles in, crooning in time with the moody song humming through my laptop speakers. I like Amita. We operate on the same wavelength. Over the years we've partnered up on as many group projects as we can. Our mental synergy is epic when we work together to crush assignments. I guess it's like the chemistry that athletes share with their teammates. If school was baseball and I was the lead-off batter, she'd bat cleanup. Or vice versa. I'm convinced Amita and I could solve all the world's problems if we tried.

It all started when we were assigned as lab partners freshman year, so I still refer to Amita as my lab partner. Funny how the word *friend* never comes to mind. Beyond school, we don't know much about each other.

My best friend, Naya, and I were joined at the hip until she and her family moved all the way to Nairobi, Kenya, at the end of sophomore year. I missed her a lot, and at first, we tried to talk every day. But that eight hours' time difference is brutal. Eventually our WhatsApp response times lapsed longer and longer, and now it's to the point where we only check in with each other once a month or so.

Finding someone new to roll with in this school hasn't been easy. I'm cool with everyone, but close to no one—except Gabby, of course. Most of the other seniors aren't the most relatable. The ones who *are* relatable are sweet and all, and I have a good time hanging with them in the senior lounge. But I can only vibe with them until a trigger topic, like race, is raised. And then, suddenly, they feel like strangers.

As for the girls I catch the bus with—they are a little too loose-lipped with folks' business to really connect on a deeper level.

Gabby started as a freshman here my junior year, so I've mainly been hanging with my cousin these past two years.

Amita drops her lunch tray on the coffee table between my MacBook and Gabby's rudely resting feet.

"I can't leave because there's a life-threatening crisis going on," Gabby insists. "Simone is missing a backbone!"

"How are you two related again?" asks Amita, while swatting Gabby's feet off the table. I'm not sure if she realizes it, but Amita's face performs all the thoughts cycling through her mind. It doesn't help that her bangs remind me of stage curtains—a swoopy black arc draping across her brown forehead. Amita's face is now showing how perplexed she is by Gabby.

The truth is, everybody at St. Clare Academy knows

Gabby—if not for her mouth then for her killer hair-braiding skills. She has a side hustle doing hair, and word has gotten around. Ever since she was invited into the lounge this fall to braid a senior's hair, and then another's, no one really objects to her entering this sacred senior space.

"Our mothers are sisters," Gabby explains. She gives Amita some room but doesn't get up to leave.

"No, I mean how is it that you two are so different?" Amita's food and her words wrestle for dominance in her mouth.

I wonder the same thing sometimes. It kind of sucks when a sophomore knows more about life than you do. That suckage quadruples when that sophomore is Gabby.

Even though Gabby and I share a grandmother, her upbringing is vastly different from mine. That's because my mom is old-school in more ways than one. For starters, Mummy is fourteen years older than Gabby's mother. It's no family secret that my parents struggled for over a decade to have kids. My mom was deep into her forties by the time she got pregnant with me, her second and final child. Mummy claims she's overprotective because she's raising girls in a fast city and can't take any chances. I think it's because she probably spent her childhood policing other kids and saying things like *Ooooh, I'm telling!*

"The difference between Simone and me," Gabby's explaining to Amita, "is that I am immune to emotional blackmail. If anyone is 'disappointed' in me, that's their problem."

I suck my teeth. The girl expects me to kick in the front door and snatch what I want when it's much less messy for me to sneak in the back window. She has no idea the amount of tiptoeing and scheming I have to do just to get half as much freedom as she has. The in-your-face way won't work with my parents. Yes, it's true—my mom is an emotional peacock. If I try any dramatic moves, she'll just upstage them with a mesmerizing display of all her colors—from worrywart yellow and gloom-and-doom gray to scorched-earth red. If I do things my low-key way, it's easier.

Gabby is yakking so emphatically, I catch glimpses of the gum surfing her undulating tongue. "Simone." She now shifts to face me. "If I were you for just one day, all your problems would be solved. Believe me."

"Oh, really," I chuckle, picking up my laptop. "And by the end of that day, I for real, for real wouldn't have a bridge left to cross, you'd burn them all so fast."

"Whatever it *takes*!"

Those words burst out of Gabby in such a berserk way, it tickles my funny bone. My neck goes slack and my head tips all the way back in laughter.

Amita coughs out her chuckle, careful not to spew out her lunch. She knows nothing of this conversation's backstory, but she still can make sense of things.

"You two need each other," she says. "The yin to each other's yang, and it cracks me up."

Two ring tones chime out. Both Gabby and Amita pull out their phones with a quick draw.

"Hey," Amita answers her cell.

"Shoot," Gabby says at the same time, gawking at her screen. "I'm late for my next client. A junior's meeting me in the pink rest-room for a French fishtail braid."

"See ya," I call at her back.

I may be the late bloomer in the family, but Gabby's the one who's always running late.

"No, girl, I'll tell my dad I'm going to study at your house," Amita is saying into the phone. She walks to the far corner of the room, but I can still hear her. "And then you pick me up and come with me to this Millwall Prep party."

Something feels mad familiar about Amita's conversation. I'm intrigued to hear more. Eavesdropping without being obvious about it is like singing while playing an instrument; you've got to do both things effectively. I make busy work, tapping on my keyboard and tidying up my lunch tray, while tuning into Amita's words.

Her free hand charts points on an imaginary map. "If my dad asks why you can't stay over to study, just say that our project's equipment is too heavy to transport to my house."

A lie. Bingo. That rings the bell. Not so much the lie, but the lying. It's tough to live your truth when you have to weave tall tales just to protect the little freedom you do have. And things can get stressful when you're always looking over your shoulder, trying to get your story straight.

Amita hangs up, breathless and mumbling to herself. With my laptop speakers now silent, it's obvious I've probably overheard.

I feel a little guilty about paying attention to her call. Amita masks her embarrassment with a nonchalant hair toss before she walks back to her seat.

She takes a few nibbles of her lunch, and then abandons the effort. She slumps low in her chair like those dudes who drive up and down the main ave in my city, and she studies the old tiled ceiling.

I click "repeat all" on my playlist to drown out the awkward silence. Amita still doesn't budge.

"Is everything all right?" I ask, concerned she'll continue to sit here motionless if I don't do something.

She blinks out of her daydream and smirks at me. "Are you in peer counselor mode right now?"

Amita knows about my one-term stint as a peer counselor last semester. I'm the younger sibling in my family, but I'd always wanted to take on the big sister role to someone. Peer counseling helped me do that. But a lack of life experience has a way of making you feel woefully underqualified for the job. I decided to sit out this semester.

"That tenure is over. But I'm still a good listener." I immediately catch the irony of my words, but it's too late to unspeak them.

Amita points a finger at me. "That part. That part is totally clear."

We both laugh until we forget to feel guilty, awkward, or embarrassed.

Amita sits up and broadcasts her confessional face. "Between me and you," she starts. "I have a boyfriend and my parents don't know, because they don't approve of dating in high school. I have to come up with elaborate plans just to hang out with him."

I totally get it. Strict parents can lead you to "lye" like a cheap box of hair relaxer. A year ago when I told my mom I was considering going away for college, she asked me what I have against her living a long life.

Amita holds her phone up to me, showing a photo of a fly South Asian guy with a gorgeous smile. I lean in for a closer look and gape at the shiny-haired boy holding up two fingers. I don't know what's brighter—his teeth or his crisp white shirt.

"Is that your boyfriend? He's, like, model hot."

"Thanks. It would be nice if he were more than just a face on video chat," she says. "I hardly get to see him."

"That sucks—I'm sorry," I say, bummed for Amita.

"Pritpal is a sweetheart about it," she says sadly. "But I don't know how much longer I can keep this up."

"Sounds like we just might have the same parents," I say.

"I don't hear that every day." Amita drops her shoulders with a ragged sigh.

"Me neither." I close my laptop. "What I hear every day is more like *No*—or really *Non!*" I mimic Mummy's accent and lip pout.

"Ah, so you're about that immigrant parent life, too?" Amita picks up her sandwich and takes a healthy bite of it.

"Yup," I say. "My parents came from Haiti to Brooklyn to Jersey. Yours?"

"From India to Jersey City to Verona." After taking a beat to swallow down her food, she adds, "I didn't realize we had so much in common."

"Same."

There are very few people I know whose parents are old-school strict like mine. The daughters of immigrant parents, like both Amita and myself, are hit the toughest. And we don't have just any immigrant parents. We have traditional ones, who view the more lenient "American" parenting style with scorn. Amita's parents sound a long way from adopting the freewheeling styles I see in, say, Gabby's mom, who is also an immigrant.

Amita frowns through a chuckle. "Most of my friends don't know what it's like," she says. "I keep giving them excuses about why I can't hang out late or sleep over. And they wouldn't understand anyway. Imagine your only rule being, 'Don't burn the house down.'"

"Or my favorite: 'Don't get tied down in one serious relationship.'" I make a face.

Most girls at our school can't relate to a life on lockdown, so it's a detail you downplay, especially as a senior.

"And the embarrassing part," I add, thinking of Gabby's exasperation with me, "is that sooner or later, your friends start looking at you like *you're* as weird as your parents."

"You mean like Gabby?"

"Yup. She thinks a simple heart-to-heart with my parents is the only thing keeping me from going away for college."

"*Pfft*, right. Like that'll work."

"Reasoning? Logic? Girl, please. That's so not my mom's thing," I say, shaking my head. "She's not about the law, but the order. Like, spare her the whole impassioned speech to the jury, and get to the verdict."

"Exact same with my parents."

"Solidarity, sister," I tell her.

Amita throws up her hands up in *whaddyagonnado?* surrender. Our high school career has been parentally hijacked, and the only consolation is that we're nearing the end of it. Should I just throw my own hands in the air, too? I wonder. There are barely three months left of my high school life, and being a peer counselor dropout and experiencing a stage kiss have been the only highlights.

I slump back on the couch, ready to low ride and stare at the ceiling, too, when I catch the sight of my open laptop. My research paper stares back at me. The title: "Teen Heroes in History." And under that, a word jumps out: *activist*.

The mental image of teen suffragist Mabel Ping-Hua Lee riding a white horse at the 1912 New York City suffragist parade flickers in my mind. She wasn't the only one on horseback, but as a Chinese American, she boldly stood out. What an empowering sight to the women of color and immigrants marching in the streets or peering from apartment windows. Against all odds, activists act. I may not be an activist myself, but I value how people's passion for change *activates* others. One thing I've learned in my research is that it's all about taking *action*.

Solidarity is right. I glance at Amita.

Something has to be done. And that means we need to act.

I sit up. "We can't go out like this," I declare. "Doing all this research on teen heroes has got me thinking. It may be a reach, but what if we—"

A group of girls walks in, and Amita's expression flashes alarm and then relief. She's clearly relieved I'm as protective of my sheltered-girl secret identity as she is. A discussion like this requires discretion. I nod to the exit, and we gather our things and leave.

"Not the pink bathroom," Amita says.

Oh yeah, Gabby's hair salon. I think fast. "The white one, second floor."

As soon as we've determined we're the only ones in the white bathroom, Amita leans against a sink, crosses her arms, and turns to me. "What were you going to say?" she asks.

I stand up tall and face the mirror. Before I can tell Amita my idea, I notice a sneaky bread crumb making a mockery of my face. I grab a paper towel from the dispenser, wipe off the crumb, and launch the balled-up napkin across the room. It lands just short of the garbage can. But you better believe after picking it up and trashing it, I strut back to Amita like I'm marching on Washington. Mind focused, chin up, footsteps intentional.

"We should team up and form a united front against this tyranny," I tell her.

"Meaning what, exactly?" Amita clearly isn't signing on to any revolution until she reads the fine print.

I start pacing to keep that brain wheel spinning. "Meaning we take back control of our lives." I stop, because that's as unrealistic as the statements Gabby sometimes makes. *Read the room, Simone.* "Scratch that, and let me start over. I guess it's fair to say that once upon a time, we had a hunger and we knew how to powerfully express that until we got what we needed."

"When?" Amita asks with a frown.

"Okay, so maybe I'm describing our time as crying infants—that still counts."

Amita smirks. "It does?"

I nod. "It means we were born powerful and demanding. And now what's happened to us? We are not our parents' puppets, no matter how much they try and dictate what we do."

Amita stares thoughtfully. She slowly unfolds her arms and rolls up the sleeves of her light-blue Oxford shirt. A sure sign she's allowing herself to be intrigued by my glory, glory, lavatory speech. I can't lose her now.

"That umbilical cord was cut a long time ago," I continue like a preacher buzzed on communion wine. "That apple fell from the tree and *rolled on* some distance. That bird flew away from the nest. And as seniors, it's time we lead the resistance. Let's claim some level of independence before we graduate."

"I like the sound of that," she says. "Except, how do you propose we do all this?"

"Well," I start slowly. "If we band together, maybe we can find the support we didn't have before. It would be a way of resisting our parents' unrealistic rules, getting back some self-respect, and having a social life before we graduate. All without having to rope in the friends who don't fully understand our home lives. The less involved they are in our scheming, the better chance we'll be viewed as more than just our circumstances."

Amita slowly nods her head with an emboldened bounce. "I'm down."

I heave out an exhale. "Finally, an ally!"

"I think I know of one other person in our class who would be interested, too—Kira, that girl with the—" Amita's fingers run up and down the length of her neck.

I nod in understanding because, yes, Kira does wear lots of turtlenecks. "The more the merrier."

I grin in an extra-corny way. I'm hyped!

"It's weirdly a good feeling, right?" Amita hugs herself and giggles out her relief.

"Makes me want to do my slippers dance," I say, and I let loose the happy jig I'm family-famous for. My lanky build and long legs, I'm aware, make for good physical comedy. Thus, on occasion, I'm happy to poke fun at myself to amuse family or friends. My house-slippers tap-dance routine kills every time.

"Um, no-no, please don't—" Amita's hands swish side to side like windshield wipers.

A girl I recognize as a freshman walks into the bathroom. She takes one look at our wackiness, gestures like she forgot something somewhere that's *not* here, and exits quietly.

I stop dancing, and Amita and I crack up.

We decide to meet up in an empty classroom after school, and Amita says she'll bring Kira along to join our united front.

"And who knows?" I shout over the period-ending bell. "Maybe this will put us in a better starting position next year when we're freshmen again."

Amita scoffs. "I'm not fooling myself into believing that things will change drastically during college." She leads the way out the white restroom and we both hook a right.

"Are you going away for school?" I ask Amita. A girl from any other type of household would find my question silly. For most seniors I know, going away for college is a given. I'm glad Amita doesn't skip a beat or look at me sideways.

"The only reason I get to go away is because my dad is competing with this other Indian family whose daughter got to go away. But that girl is still under house arrest every time she comes home over break," she mutters as we walk past a student rocking cobalt-blue Doc Martens and a perfectly sculpted French fishtail. Another satisfied client for Gabby.

"I say we take what little battle victories you can get, soldier."

"Damn, Simone," Amita tosses over her shoulder. "You got me thinking I should've done my report on revolutionary teens and not on suspension bridge wonders."

"*Pssh*, everybody likes bridges," I tell her.

Amita smiles. "Not like I do. I feel like the luckiest girl in the world every time I drive across the Brooklyn Bridge. I write about it for my own selfish needs." She turns to head to her next class, then calls out to me, "But what you're working on is helping us all, my friend."

I continue down the hall, grinning to myself and testing my march-on-Washington strut.

CHAPTER THREE

Our welcome addition to our after-school meetup, Kira Gifford, slides into the desk next to Amita. I don't have many classes with Kira, but I sometimes bump into her in the cafeteria. She usually brings her own lunch. I've always thought of her as a super-reserved girl who wears her uniform skirt long and her Oxford shirts buttoned up all the way. I chalked that up to personal style, but now that I know she's one of us, I'm guessing it may be because she's got helicopter parents.

Outside of her fashion choices, she's not your typical over-protected kid variety. Kira is a white girl with American-born parents.

I know this because news junkie Gabby never forgets a face. The moment Gabby saw Kira's dad during drop-off one morning last year, she'd called out loudly, "On my sweet Grandmère, that's Hurricane Priscilla girl and her lawyer dad!"

I'd lowered my cousin's arm, hoping Kira hadn't caught Gabby pointing. Everything Gabby had said was confirmed a few seconds later when I took out my phone and Googled.

Priscilla. When I was in the seventh grade and Gabby in fifth grade, Hurricane Priscilla ravaged a large expanse of the South. From then on, the name came to strike terror in everyone's hearts. Incensed with the bureau in charge of naming storms, a local New Jersey attorney made national news when he filed a lawsuit against that agency. I still remember the lawyer's sound bites arguing why the agency would be better served using only antiquated and rarely used names like Mortimer or Gertrude. Those clips of his complaints started popping up everywhere. It wasn't long before the memes and hilarious comedy parodies started. The whole thing had to be beyond humiliating for Kira, who always seemed quiet and understated. I'm still not sure how she got away from the media circus without the help of some crisis management expert, but no one seems to realize that Kira is her middle name and Priscilla is her real name. The students at our high school (besides Gabby) have never made the connection. I'm just grateful Gabby listened to my pleas and dropped the subject.

Looking at Kira now, I wonder if she's been able to disassociate herself from the girl named Priscilla, who was no doubt chillin' before the incident. Thinking back, her dad's ride didn't look too shabby, so I'm guessing her life's been pretty comfortable, at least financially.

"Hi, ladies," I greet both Kira and Amita. There is so much I want to find out from these girls. Judging by Amita's flashing eyes and Kira's quiet determination, I can tell we've got that mental synergy thing going.

Though this classroom is empty, it feels weird sitting on the teacher's desk. Plus, I don't want them to get the impression I'm naming myself team captain or anything. I drag a desk closer to theirs to form a circle.

I wish I could cough up a speech stirring enough to activate us. I'm not nice on the mic like Naomi Wadler or Greta Thunberg, but I give it a weak try.

"Thanks for coming. I had no idea we'd been dealing with the same, uh, situation—"

"Plain and simple," Amita translates. "We're all on lockdown."

"That!" I erupt, stretching out my arm to point at Amita, then holding that pose for a few goofy seconds. Kira's shoulders bounce in quiet laughter. I'm grateful for Amita's presence. She's coming through with that freedom fighter flex, bringing the type of passion this discussion needs. I drop the formality and lean forward, anchoring my elbows on the desk.

"And at seventeen, life on lockdown is downright embarrassing," I continue. Still so curious about the story behind why Kira is so sheltered, I glance at her. "What about your parents, Kira?"

Kira's tearing into a sleeve of vending machine lemon cookies. She holds out the stack in offering, and Amita and I help ourselves.

Kira shrugs. "My parents are weird," she starts in a crystal clear voice. I don't have to strain to hear her like I expected to, since she's pretty soft-spoken in class. "Ever since they made national news a few years ago and got brutally clowned by the media and Twitter, they've been paranoid and sort of went underground. They try to keep me off social media and everything. If my dad had his way, I'd never draw attention to myself or talk to anyone—especially not Alexa or Siri. I mean, they didn't even let me have a phone until, like, sophomore year. It would be halfway hilarious if this wasn't my *life*. So many dorky rules.".

"Ugh, don't get me started on the rules," I grumble, the bitter thought nicely balanced out by the sweet lemon treat.

"Let's see, there's . . ." Amita says, keeping count and pointing her now crescent-shaped cookie to each fingertip as she goes. "No boyfriends, no dates, no sleepovers."

"Add no going away for college to the list for me," I say.

"And the list goes on," puffs Amita.

"We deserve to play before graduation," I declare. "Maybe we can put our heads together and formulate a plan of action."

"Yes," gasps Kira, her hazel eyes as bright as the imaginary light bulb over her head. "A senior year bucket list to help us get all the play we missed out on."

"Ha. A *playlist* to stunt on our parents' forbidden list," I say.

"Everything on the forbidden list would go on my playlist, because that's what I'm missing out on," says Amita.

"So why not do that?" I challenge. I'm on my feet now. This is too exciting to take sitting down. "Let's create our own Senior

Playlist and try to check off every item before graduation!"

Amita wags a new cookie in the air. "A playlist. I love it."

"Because we want to leave high school on the right *note*," I crack.

Kira claps. "I see what you did there."

Amita is all business. She opens the notes app on her phone, ready to get the list going.

"Wait." I reach into my bag and feel around for my notepad. "We should handwrite this. It's more intentional and powerful to write things down with pen and paper." I open the notebook to a neat, clear page. Kira and Amita watch me in reverent silence. "At least that's what I learned from this Netflix reality show."

Kira and Amita's faces hang in disappointment.

"What, you thought this was a Haitian thing?" I smirk at them. "Nope, but trust me, having a Haitian on board can only help this effort. My people might be the most psychic-dream-having folks on the planet." I double-wink, then hold out the notebook. "Who wants to do the honors? No one can read my scrawl."

Amita reaches for the notebook. "How about we each write down what's most important to us, and then we can each take on whichever challenges we want."

"Or them all," adds Kira with a sneaky smile. "Here, I've got a cute gel ink pen in purple." She sniffs the tip of the pen. "I mean grape!"

"Super cute!" I coo at the sight of the sparkly unicorn at the pen's top.

The unicorn's wiry silver tail swishes as Amita writes. When she's done, she wordlessly holds up the notepad so Kira and I can read for ourselves. Right under the all-caps title *Senior Playlist* Amita has written two goals:

> *Go to a REAL house party*
> *Go clubbin'*

A mischievous grin sneaks onto Amita's face. She explains that she's already crafted a false alibi (seeing her best friend) for the house party tomorrow. Kira and I are both hoping to make a quick appearance. But going to a *club* is going to take double-oh-seven-level preparation.

Kira curls her fingers, beckoning the notepad her way. She writes something down, then holds the notepad up to us. "Okay, but how will one or all of us do *this* before graduation?"

"*Cut class?*" I shriek out her words, and we let out a sugar-rushed hoot and holler into the lemon-and-grape-scented air.

"I've got one!" I say, raising my hand, classroom etiquette game strong. I hold the notepad at an angle on my desk and rein in my pen strokes, keeping them steady and deliberate. *Go on a date*, I write, thinking of my swoony encounter with Gavin. And just in case this list is magical, I whisper to myself: "Tell parents I'm going away for college."

Amita overhears me and snaps a few times in the air. "Ambitious. I like it."

"Grant me a real college experience, yes, Lord!" I lift my arms, windmilling them like the praise dancers at church.

The more we write, the more raucous and hilarious the mood gets. We get to work calling out all the things we yearn to do, no matter how minor.

"My favorite childhood memories were of bike riding with my family, but for some reason, we don't do it anymore," Kira says.

I learned to ride a bike only recently, but I enjoy it. I want to keep at it, only my neighborhood is like an obstacle course of double-parked cars. Plus, I don't actually . . . own a bike. Still, I encourage Kira to add it to the list.

"I like that you're thinking about your happiness, because that's definitely important," I say. "We should all make sure that something we love doing is on the list."

"For years I've been obsessed with wanting to switch up my style," says Amita. "And now that I'm eighteen, I can't wait to do it." She adds *Switch up style* to the list.

"Dancing makes me happy, so clubbing covers that," I say.

And as the list keeps building, we share more stories and ask one another questions to assess what else needs to be a focus on the Playlist.

"I'm telling you," Amita says at one point, using her phone as an extension of her hand gestures. "My best friend Chloe has cussed out her parents for way less. Imagine if she had to keep *her* boyfriend a secret."

A thought occurs to me just then. I peel off my glasses and sit them on top of my head, my face suddenly itching to go naked with this announcement. "Y'all. What if we call this crew HomeGirls? Not only are we literally always expected to be at home, but it sounds old-school hip-hop cool, and doesn't make me feel like a complete loser."

"I like that," Kira croaks. Her vocal chords are strained from laughing so hard. We all titter like schoolchildren when we hear it. Kira is much more fun than I'd imagined she'd be. I love that she's now rocking hard-partying voice and hair. Her short auburn strands are dented from all the hair wringing she's been doing every time we wrote or said a cringey, surprising thing.

Amita's brown eyes are sparkling, and she uses the notepad to fan her flushed face. "That name kinda makes me feel better already."

At the end of our meeting, we all admire the page, a patchwork of different—but, thankfully, all readable—handwriting styles unified by a sweet-smelling purple ink and our desire for fun.

SENIOR PLAYLIST
1. *Go to a REAL house party*
2. *Go clubbin'*
3. *Cut class*
4. *Go on a date*
5. *Hang out in NYC*
6. *Sneak a boy over to your house or go over to his house*
7. *Ride a bike*
8. *Switch up style*

We tear out the page, and each take turns holding it. "I think Simone should hold on to it for safekeeping," suggests Kira.

"Agreed; and not because she's Haitian," asserts Amita. "Though it can only elevate our situation."

"It would be my honor," I say, folding up the paper and sticking it into my wallet, right behind the see-through slot that houses my monthly bus card.

We plan on refining our Playlist strategy at our next meetup. For now, the three of us have one goal already: Make it to that house party tomorrow.

CHAPTER FOUR

Go big or go home. Or in this case: Go big or stay home for college. If I load the bases for my next at-bat against my parents, maybe I'll put some numbers on the scoreboard. That's the strategy I hatch on my bus ride from school later that afternoon. Inspired by meeting with the HomeGirls, I decide I'll approach my parents *today* and broach the subject of going away for college once more.

By the time I'm in my bedroom and see my parents' car pull up in the driveway, I can almost hear the baseball stadium organ playing those fanfare notes. *Duh-duh-duh-dum-duh-dum* . . .

Batter up, I think.

It helps that Constance and Gérard Thibodeaux are in a good mood. Could be the Holland Tunnel traffic was light or that nothing had been out to get Papi this time—not those trickster potholes or the racist red lights. There's a buoyant lilt to their Creole, which triggers that excitable Pavlovian response you get when you hear the crackle of a candy wrapper. I give them a few minutes to unwind and then head downstairs to the kitchen to greet them.

They're posted at either side of our makeshift kitchen island—Papi is pouring himself a tall glass of water, and Mummy is leafing through mail, still mid-conversation.

"And then, right in the middle of performing surgery, Dr. Bumanglag stared down Dr. Gibbons and shouted, 'Puck you!'" My mother can barely get this out between bursts of laughter.

"Thank goodness for surgical masks, otherwise the venom in his words would've dripped into that poor patient's body." Punch lines don't land for my father as effortlessly as they do for my mom.

"After that, Dr. B was too angry to ask for anything, so I just kept handing him the instruments he needed." My mom wipes the tears of laughter from her eyes.

"That's 'cause you're the most brilliant nurse the operating room has ever seen," I chime in. It hits me then that I get the trying-too-hard gene from my dad.

My mom checks the pot of mushroom rice she's been warming up.

"Oh yeah?" She forces herself not to smile, but her ebony cheeks swell anyway. "Well, now this brilliant mind is telling me that my daughter must want something from me."

"More like *doesn't* want something from you," I answer, grabbing a barstool at the kitchen island. I'm already dressed down in

47

comfy joggers and an oversized tee. "One thing in particular."

The playful smile wipes clean off Mummy's face. "What?"

In this moment, the whole course of my life can change. The person I'd become if I go away to college might be so much more in charge than the person I'd be if I stay home. And that independent, can-do person could very well save Mummy's or Papi's life one day, I realize. Or both their lives! I imagine *that* Simone would think quicker on her feet than poor, stay-at-home Simone, with her sorry panicking self, wasting precious moments when she'd need to act quick and save a life or two. So, for the sake of future Constance and Gérard, I come out with it.

"I truly appreciate you wanting me to stay home for college, but I'm applying for a dorm room, and there's a good chance my loan can cover it." There—I said it. And I keep the statement as light as the mood, trying hard not to make a huge deal about it. I take a sip out of Papi's glass of water. "So what were y'all talking about that's so funny?"

Mummy glares at me, then crinkles up her forehead and asks Papi, "Sa blan an di?"

"Good one, Mummy." It cracks me up when they use that popular Haitian phrase, "What did the white person say?" In this case "white" meaning me, the foreigner in their eyes. Neither of them is laughing with me.

"Look here," Mummy warns. "Don't tell me what the donkey told the rooster."

Oh boy. I stop sipping . . . and gulp. When my mom starts

48

talking in Haitian folktales, she's suiting up for battle. I look away and mentally steel myself to stay focused.

"I'm not sure what that means, but I just wanted to tell you that I'm taking care of things," I reply with restraint.

She doesn't blink.

I reach over the counter to touch her arm in an effort to unfreeze her, almost like playing tag in reverse. "You won't be disappointed . . ."

"Simone, don't play with me," Mummy lays out in Creole.

"I'm not playing," I continue in English. It takes mad focus *not* to pour the whine, as Gabby and I say. "I just want to save you the trouble."

My father loosens his tie, looking exhausted. I can't tell if it's from his long day in hospital administration, his Yankees baseball withdrawal, or from this imminent mother-daughter clash.

"Eh-eh?" Mummy is clearly revving up her engine. "Trou . . . ble? You, save *me* from trouble?" she asks with a sarcastic chuckle. "I'm trying to save *you* from it. Trouble is losing yourself to strangers and false people you call *friends*."

I guess it's too late to make up some prophetic dream I had about college life. Besides, dream messages are too highly respected in this family to toss out on a whim. That's an emergency move I probably could only make once in my life—and this isn't that moment.

I heave out a sigh like I am manually pushing the number 60 bus up a steep hill. An immature reaction, I know. But I am just so over the same ol' sermon. Mummy didn't specially call them out, but it's clear this is just another version of her boys-are-the-ruination argument. It's her favorite bop; her one-hit wonder.

Top three on Mummy's list of "bad" are as follows:

1. *Men—she doesn't trust any of them, and yup, she'll say that right in front of my dad.*
2. *Criminals—this category is mostly filled with men. (Mummy is a New York City nurse who's seen victims of all sorts of horribleness.)*
3. *Tarnished Reputations—as a mom of girls, she's determined to stay a go-hard protector of Anne's and my reputations.*

Imagine if she knew I was sneaking off to that house party tomorrow. It's not hard to guess what she'd have to say about me going to a *boys* party at a *boy's* house.

And here comes the long, wailing note to wrap the song up in alarmist style. "Bondje o, what is this child telling me?" she beseeches the heavens. Then, as if she's caught me eavesdropping on her celestial convo, she barks, "Are your studies done? Why don't you go take care of that instead?"

Reflexively, one foot lowers to the floor. I'm ready to stomp away in frustration, but I stop myself. No. This has to be handled with a mature, level head. My reaction will either prove my point or hers.

This is the way I have to play it if I want to Playlist. I can't keep kicking this can down the road. Besides, this is the only unlisted goal I'm tackling. If I can get my parents on board with at least hearing me out, every listed goal will be much easier to reach.

"I'd love for you and Papi to tour the dorm with me."

Mummy turns to face the stove. She picks up a large cooking spoon and begins vigorously mixing the rice. A few black grains stumble into the fire, and a burning scent reaches me, reminding me of my revolutionary dreams in flames.

"This was never a problem with your sister." Mummy belts out another played-out refrain, no doubt trusting wholeheartedly that Anne is really at the college library right now. She'd never for a moment consider Anne and her nerdy college sweetheart, Max, are not as boring as they look.

"Maybe if you see for yourself how secure and convenient it is," I continue, careful to keep my tone as even as possible. "It could help ease your mind."

I look to my father for his reaction, but he has quietly exited the kitchen undetected. *Ti-bounce-doe.*

With the clang of her metal spoon dropping to the stove, an exasperated Mummy spins around to face me. She swipes her palms against each other as if she is wiping the slate of this conversation clean.

"That's it!" she announces. "Next weekend, we go to Queens to arrange everything with Louise!"

Not wanting to overdo things, I back out of the kitchen and

head up to my room. I have no idea who Louise is, but I have a strong suspicion she's one of those prayer warrior aunties.

Apparently, my sister was an alarmingly late talker. She didn't utter a single, solitary word until a spiritual squadron of Haitian women got to praying over her. She was close to five, so she remembers the drama of prayers raining down on her. The way Anne interprets it, this was an Anne appreciation party of Christmas-meets-birthday proportions. She assumed the women had been fretting that Anne was jealous of her new baby sister (*moi*), and this was their response to that. Oddly, it's Anne's happiest childhood memory.

Well, there will be none of that for me. I don't need a bunch of judgy aunties praying away my right to have a social life. Louise or whoever can save their rosary beads for a real emergency.

Someone must've talked my mom off the ledge, because—*poof!*—the tension between us has mostly vanished by dinner. I heard Mummy speaking on the phone before we ate, so I guess I owe her best friend, Terrence, a debt of gratitude. She trusts his judgment better than anyone's, and thankfully, he's a lot more reasonable than she is.

By the following morning, I take it as a good sign that Mummy and I are back to clowning each other for fun. This time we're calling out Anne's Type A operations. My sister is the reason I'm dressed this early in the morning. She's offered to give me a ride to the bus stop.

"Hurry up, Simone," Anne calls from downstairs. "I'll be in the car."

"Have a great day, darling," Mummy singsongs to Anne. Her tone immediately switches to gossip mode when she steps into my room. "You're messing with that girl's tight schedule?" She grins. "Ou brav!"

"You're the brave one for wearing those colors together," I tease, looking her up and down. "That shade of brown with that shade of green? Mummy, that doesn't match." It's a good thing the woman changes into hospital scrubs the moment she gets to work.

"I thought you said this top goes with these pants." She takes a peek at my full-length mirror leaning against the wall.

I touch her shoulder. "Yes, that style top, but the white one," I say as faux-gently as possible.

Mummy playfully swats my hand away. "Nobody tells the brown tree trunk it doesn't match the green leaves. And who do you think dressed you before you could dress yourself?" she asks. "And stop walking around in one shoe. Don't you know that means you're—"

"Killing your mother and father," we say at the same time. "My bad." I shove my foot in the other black Oxford and yank my backpack off the desk chair.

"Oh, and Simone? Let me know as soon as you find out when your school prom is." Mummy says "school prom" like it's a mandatory class event. I don't correct her because I know it's the only reason she's supportive of my attending.

Of course, I already know the exact date, day, time, and location of prom, but I flex like I don't. I crouch down to the floor where my laptop and books are and pack them up, all while keeping my head low. Her unexpected request puts me on quiet alert. My mom poking her nose in anything that involves me going anywhere alone with a boy is never a good thing.

"Why, are you going to rent me a slick ride? If so, I'm partial to Corvettes." I stand up and wink. If there's anything that can distract Mummy, it's a good joke.

But, apparently not this time. "Do you remember Louise in Queens?" she asks, looking serious.

I sigh to myself. There's that name again. My parents are always asking me if I remember this person or that person. It all sounds like a jumble of fuddy-duddy French names to me.

"Should I?"

"*Oh-ohhh,*" she heaves in that distinctly Haitian response signaling exasperation. "Louise Fils-Aimé!"

Like shouting it will make it click for me? Still don't know who she's talking about.

Mummy gathers her thin lips and delivers a crisp chupee. This reflexive act of sucking one's teeth to show annoyance is a universally understood sound in my family. Most of us kids do it with discretion, though, because it's considered rude by elders.

"Lou-ise from *Queens.*" Mummy is gaping at me, frustrated that my mind is detouring into chupee analysis.

Still nothing.

"Honoré's wife! Her son was Anne's prom date."

"You mean Madame Honoré?" *Why in the patriarchy does she go by her husband's name?*

"Oui."

My nose tingles with emotion. *Oh no. No, no, no, no, no!*

I mentally scroll through my memories of the trip to Queens four years ago, when I was thirteen. The arranged prom discussion. Anne's blank gaze. Her zoned-out date. The creepy Victorian figurines. My vow to myself. And—*gasp*—the younger brother in the baseball uniform!

Red. Frickin'. Alert.

I take a breath. I'd almost forgotten about that day. I knew that Anne's prom was arranged, but I thought that tradition had fallen out of fashion for my mother. I'd even imagined she'd regretted doing that.

Okay, play it smart, Simone, and calmly get ahead of this, NOW.

"Mummy—"

"Her younger son is seventeen and graduating this year, too, so he will be perfect as your date."

"Just because we're the same age?" I'm heating up; my skin is dampening. My tortoiseshell glasses start their slow descent down my sweaty nose.

Mummy nods and gently pats her chest. "And because he's from a good Haitian family that I respect and trust."

"I can't believe this!" I say.

So much for keeping cool.

"Simone, don't play with me," she says.

"Mummy, don't ruin prom for me," I snap back, wondering what will become of my prom daydream—Gavin and me making an elegant entrance, arm in arm.

"You think I could ever fix my lips to say that to my mother when I was your age? I had to trust that she knew what was best for me."

I give her a look. "Did you even have a prom in Haiti?"

"That's not the point." She dismisses me, waving her hand at the pesky logic mosquito buzzing its way into our conversation. "Trust *me* when I tell you it's not as bad as you're making it out to be."

"Uh, this is *exactly* my idea of bad."

"Anne took the older son to the prom and she had a perfectly fine time," Mummy continues.

I roll my eyes. "Well, I'm not Anne."

Mummy crosses her arms as if to seal off the entrance to any more rebuttals. Argument closed. The creases in her forehead deepen. That telltale Haitian pout to her lips is back. Another chupee is a few heartbeats away.

But this is not over. I find a calmer tone. "I don't understand why—"

Honk!

"Your ride is leaving," Mummy says dismissively before turning on her heels and heading out the door.

CHAPTER FIVE

Anne and I ride in tense silence. She's pissed I made her wait, and I'm pissed she hasn't pulled her weight. If only she took a stand once in a while, I wouldn't be in this predicament. But instead of blazing trails, she's been all, "Yes, I'll go to an all-girls high school," "Yes, I'll go to prom with the date of your choosing," and "Yes, I'll stay home for college."

Anne swings out a protective arm to safeguard me when she stops short at a yellow light. I'm wearing my seat belt, but her reflex says *Just in case*.

"Sorry," Anne breathes. "Didn't want to chance the yellow light—not at this corner."

Suddenly I feel like an unmasked villain on *Scooby-Doo*, except I'm the guilt-ridden kid sister inside the ghost costume. "No, *I'm* sorry," I say in all sincerity.

Anne shrugs, turning the steering wheel with more ease than you'd expect for someone driving with her coat on. The girl is always cold. I'm grateful she hasn't cranked up the heat today, no doubt remembering the nosebleed this habit gave me the last time I was in here.

"It's all good," she's calmly telling me. "I make it a policy not to hold an after-lecture funk against you—especially one from Mummy. What was it about this time?"

I suck my teeth. "Your mother is lining up an arranged prom trip to Queens for me."

Anne's sleek strands swing like a co-wash commercial when she whips around to glance at me.

"No way. I thought she got all that out her system," she says.

I make a popping sound with my mouth. "No such luck."

"I'm sorry this is happening to you. You're way cooler than I was in high school, so I can't understand why Mummy can't tell that you can get your own date to the prom."

"It's not that." I swallow down my hurt feelings. "It's that she doesn't trust my judgment like she does yours."

"Well, her judgment is way off a lot of times. I told you how charming my prom date turned out to be, right? He was on his phone the entire time and barely talked to me all night, except when they named me prom queen."

An amused laugh knocks my head back. "I still can't believe you were prom queen. That's kinda dope."

Anne sits up and nods delightedly at the lived facts. The guy waiting for the light in the neighboring car beams, assuming that gesture was meant for him. None the wiser, Anne leaves him behind at the green light.

"That was back when faculty used to be able to vote for prom queen," I say. "They stopped that nonsense."

"What can I say? Adults just love me."

"Including Mummy."

"I know it doesn't help you, but once you get to college, she doesn't ride you nearly as much anymore. Look how much she loves Max."

"Yeah, but what if you and I do college differently?" I say. "You've been with Max since your freshman year. And you forget—Mummy had me tag along on your first date with him."

Anne's face pinches. "Ugh, I forgot about that."

"*Mmm-hmm*, I think you're on the brink of moving out the house, so all your Thibodeaux family memories are looking rosy."

"Could be. But prepare yourself for that trip to Queens anyway, because there's no use resisting Constance."

Come next Saturday morning, rain, shine, or meteor shower, we will be heading to Madame Honoré's house.

But for now, a tiny victory. I can make that house party without any complications. This miracle was made possible by the unseasonably warm weather we're having. Over the course of an afternoon, all of North Jersey has ditched our coats and sweaters for long-sleeve tops. So Millwall Prep's basketball team decided to turn their house party into a backyard barbecue with a mercifully early start time. That means I can hang out for about two whole hours before heading home.

After school, Amita, Kira, and I change in the pink bathroom. As much as I don't want to kill the happy buzz, I can't stop thinking about Mummy's threat of an arranged prom date. Not even my excitement over potentially seeing Gavin at the party is enough to get my mind off it.

I'm over by the glazed window's ledge, carefully folding my uniform into my bag, Amita's at one mirror refreshing her already-perfect eyeliner, and Kira is at another mirror trying on different headbands. Amita and I pause to witness Kira's polka-dot selection.

The tiled walls amplify Amita's voice. "Kira is switching up her style, and I love to see it."

I nod. "Yes, Kira!"

Kira smiles at her reflection. "Aw, thanks. I figure this is more fun, like my jumpsuit."

"I need some polka-dot fun in my life today," I lament.

Kira winces. Amita reads my face in the mirror. "Uh-oh, what happened," she states instead of asks.

"No big deal—my parents are just forcing me to take their friend's son to my prom, that's all." I look down at my sneakers.

Kira lets a shout get past her inner censors. "Yay!" she squeals.

"Is that a good thing?" Amita asks, turning from the mirror.

"I'm sorry," Kira says, giggling. "It's just that sometimes

misery loves company. I'm kinda in the same predicament. Except my parents expect me to go solo. They try to frame it in some woke message about not needing a date to have fun, but I know it's because they think I'm too naive to handle a date."

"The condescension," says Amita. She makes a gagging motion.

"Right?" Kira cops a Jersey girl attitude, and I can't help but giggle.

"*Do* you want to go with a date?" I ask her.

She nods. "I do. I'm not crushing on anyone in particular, but I'm not picky. As long as the guy is a nice person."

"There, the universe heard you loud and clear," I say.

"If only my parents could hear me," Kira sighs. "I don't know how much you guys remember, but my dad went on a media tirade over a hurricane being named after me."

I nod sympathetically.

Confused and clearly unaware of Kira's hurricane-gate history, Amita asks, "There was a Hurricane Kira?"

"No, Kira's my middle name, which I decided I'd go by since then, because Priscilla would blow my cover."

Amita looks on the verge of asking, *Sa blan an di?* so I blurt out the first thing that pops to mind.

"Pun intended," I point out. The girls stare at me blankly. "Blow my cover? As in hurricane-force winds—ah, never mind."

Kira chuckles, and then lets the joke lighten up her mood. "The real funny part is," she says, "my dad can't stand my mom's mom, Kira, who I was middle-named after, and I won't let him call me Priscilla. Kira fits who I am way more than Priscilla anyway."

I nod in understanding. "Well, at least we can count on Amita to do prom the way it was intended."

"Um, no," Amita confesses. "Having a cousin as your prom date is not exactly the night of my dreams."

Oh man, I can't believe what I'm hearing.

"My parents don't even know Pritpal exists, and they act like they're doing me a favor by insisting I take my cousin Krish," she explains.

"That's it—doing prom our way is officially added to the Playlist," I announce, walking to the windowsill to grab my wallet from my bag. I unfold and smooth out the Playlist.

"Here, you should keep the special pen with that," says Kira, handing me the grape unicorn pen.

"Thanks!" I say, positioning the list on the cool stone of the windowsill. I add *Resist arranged proms* with intense satisfaction. Next, I pass around the list for the HomeGirls' inspection and they nod with approval.

"We have less than two months to make this right," says Amita. "We got this."

"Yes, we got this," echoes Kira.

Crickets from me.

"Seriously," I say to my HomeGirls as I stow away the list in my wallet. "Any ideas for how I can get this Queens meeting canceled? Asking for a desperate friend who wants to take her Millwall Prep crush to the prom."

Kira's bottom lip puffs out with intrigue at the mention of a crush.

"Hold up," Amita says. "Before we get to the whole Queens business, I want to know who this crush is." She mimes sipping tea.

"Right?" adds Kira, laughing.

I smirk. "His name is Gavin, and he's this gorgeous new transfer at Millwall Prep. We've only spoken once—on the bus. But he's on their basketball team, so he'll be at the party."

Amita nods approvingly. "Nice. Sounds like a cute potential prom date. But as far as this Queens trip . . ."

"Don't go," mic-drops Kira.

Amita and I look at Kira like she has two heads. Kira is obviously not as well-versed in the nuances Amita and I have had to learn and navigate.

"What?" Kira asks. "What did I say?"

"You don't just *not* go to something that's been preplanned and set up between two families," Amita explains.

"Why not? It has nothing do to with the adults and everything to do with Simone," says Kira.

"It has *everything* to do with the adults and *nothing* to do with Simone," says Amita. "That's the whole problem."

I rummage through my bag. "It's so much about my mom— she stars in a one-woman show called *Afflictions I Suffer Because of Simone*."

"Oh, my dad's in the same show," Amita says. "Migraine. Sinus headache."

I list some of Mummy's greatest hits. "High blood pressure, heart palpitations, vertigo . . . plus, she can out cry you any day."

"I think the best thing to do is to just go to Queens," says Amita. "Go with the flow, and when you get a chance, speak to this guy in private. Tell him you have other prom plans."

"Maybe," I say. I decide to stop worrying for now, and I pull out a few choice accessories I brought from my collection at home. "Okay, ladies." I hold up a pair of large hoop earrings, a printed headscarf, and a pair of interconnected metal bracelets. "It's just a laid-back barbecue, so we're going for casual cool, but with a bounce. Any takers?"

Amita goes for the earrings and Kira takes the bracelets. I tie on the headscarf, rocking a 1940s vintage look that goes great with my red lip shade and my denim jacket.

"Looking good," Kira says to our reflections before we exit the school and make our way to Amita's fancy car. I call shotgun-slash-co-navigator, and we all hop in.

Amita's ride is a Honda, like Papi's car, but a way newer model. I downplay my surprise. St. Clare is not known for its bus-riding students from urban centers, like Gabby and me. Well-off kids like Amita and Kira are the norm. My family wasn't awarded financial aid, but we are on a payment plan, paying tuition in smaller quarterly installments. I see how much my parents scrounge and save to keep me at the Academy while also paying

Anne's undergrad fees. It's obvious when they fall behind on my tuition, because the reminder letters start rolling in. Once, I was denied my grades at the end of the term. Them St. Clare nuns don't play.

Getting accepted into NETWORK two summers ago has helped. It's an enrichment summer program that feels more like a paid internship, and because of it I've been able to save pocket money for irresistible accessories. But most important, I've saved money to pay Auntie Victoria, the Ghanaian seamstress I've always wanted to hire to make my prom dress. She used to live in my neighborhood, and I miss all the creations she'd model up and down the block each time she walked to the corner store. I've kept in touch with her, and found out how much she'd charge to custom-make my prom dress. The only thing left to do is for me to visit her workroom to pick out my favorite printed material, called cloth or African wax print, for the dress.

The burst of Amita's bubbly voice startles me back to the moment. "We are not just on our way to an actual house party thrown by actual BOYS," she's saying. "We're on our way through our Playlist!"

She's right. My hands in the air, I snap over and over. "HomeGirls, we are *manifesting*!"

"More women should team up like this—it's powerful," says Kira, a tinge of awe in her voice. "We even changed the weather pattern!"

We holler and high-five. Amita turns up the music and we

keep the vibe going until we pull up to the house party. It looks like we're not the first to arrive. The upscale suburban street is lined with parked cars, and a whiff of smoldering charcoal permeates the spring air. That's when I decide the party will be worth the lecture I'll get if I decide to stay longer than expected—especially if I stay later because of Gavin.

We enter the house and follow the sound of thumping music and clinking glasses down a long hall. When we reach the gleaming gourmet kitchen at the end of the hallway, the scene is totally not what we pictured. There's a tall blond boy balancing jars of condiments in his arms.

"Welcome, ladies!" he greets before zipping past us to the sliding glass doors leading to the smoking grills.

Kira, Amita, and I head through those sliding doors and check out the scene on the wraparound deck. There's a lively game of cards in play at a table, and a set of stairs leads down to partygoers hanging in the backyard.

I wonder if Gabby is here yet. Since my cousin is on our school's basketball team, she hitched a ride with her teammates. This being her first year playing, it's her chance to not only get to know the St. Clare players but the Millwall Prep ones, too. Gabby crushes everything she sets her mind to—sports, hair styling, people's feelings. It's amazing to see her in action, even when it's not.

After the HomeGirls and I grab burgers, waters, and sodas, I lead the way down the stairs.

"Damn, girl!" It's Gabby. I don't know where she just popped up from. My cousin reaches out and unbuttons my top button. "Gavin Stackhouse is looking right over here."

I glance over for confirmation. Gavin is swirling the soda in his plastic red cup and watching me like my face is ESPN and I'm airing game highlights. I hope he can't tell I'm squealing inside. I try to channel Anne's calm vibe, but for some reason, I can't get this goofy smirk off my face.

"You need to get his number before somebody else does. Now's your chance." Gabby moves behind me. I can feel her knuckle poke the small of my back, nudging me in Gavin's direction. Amita and Kira couldn't look more entertained at my current situation.

Is that him? Amita mouths, and Kira widens her eyes waiting for my answer. I give both Amita and Kira the slightest head nod as confirmation. They back away like they're expecting Gavin to join me.

Gavin is standing with the blond boy from the kitchen. I'm guessing this must be his house because he's playing host like he's being graded on it. The blond boy moves on, distracted by another guest to his right.

"You gonna stand there and stare, or meet me halfway?" Gavin calls out as he casually strolls toward me. He is empty-handed now. Behind him, his plastic cup teeters on the edge of an Adirondack chair's armrest.

"Looks like you're covering ground just fine—you don't need my help," I reply. Thank goodness I've inherited some of that quick wit Haitians are known for.

There's a glint in Gavin's dark, dreamy eyes that can only be interpreted as amusement.

He plays along when he reaches me. "I was raised to go the distance, so doggonit, here I am."

We both laugh for a moment, and then fall into a semi-awkward silence. I stare at his army-green shell-toe sneakers, noticing how they're almost camouflaged in the grass.

Can I get your digits? My tongue is a springboard that these words are ready to dive off of, but I don't dare let them. I swallow the question down with the last of my water.

"Every time I see you, you're on the move," says Gavin.

"On the move?" I question, unsure what he means.

"You know, because the bus . . . it's on wheels."

I can see now that Gavin's eyes dance when he's teasing. Everything else about his mannerisms seems serious. He can joke with a straight face.

I kinda don't recognize the sound of my own laughter. It's more of a flirty titter than my trademark cackle. Gavin doesn't know the difference or seem to mind. He's studying me again, and it makes me feel like a goddess.

"How did I go seventeen and a half years on this planet without ever hearing that joke?" I ask, feeling on top of the world. Gavin's dreamy brown eyes are fixed on mine, and I—

"You mean *you're* older than *me*?" Gavin looks incredulous. "I could've sworn you were a sophomore. You seem so . . . young."

I can feel my face melting. There's no worse gut punch than

when someone points out that your late bloomer is showing. When it comes to experience level, sometimes it feels like some people can read my cluelessness like rings on a tree.

"Are you a sophomore?" I ask him. I'm afraid to hear his answer.

"Naw, naw." Gavin almost looks offended. He juts his chin out a bit more. "A junior."

Simone Thibodeaux, robbing the cradle.

There's the sound of a text alert and Gavin rapid-draws his phone from his back pocket.

He points to his screen. "Oh, I gotta—"

"Sure, sure. Go ahead," I say.

"See you around!" He waves, gives me an apologetic smile, and walks off, texting.

By now there's probably a melted pile of face pooling at my feet. I suck it all back in as best I can and rejoin Amita, Gabby, and Kira. Amita and Kira are talking to a few other girls from our grade. Gabby's face is beaming like a New Jersey diner at midnight.

"You see? You never give yourself any credit," she says, already assuming I've exchanged numbers with Gavin. "Girl, it's time you get in the game. Nothing's gonna happen for you if you stay on the sidelines."

If Gabby were in my shoes, Gavin would still be standing here, chatting and flirting, instead of making up an excuse to cut our conversation short. I look down at my feet. No matter how many times I change them, I seem to be stuck in the same shoes. It's like I'm programmed to walk the narrow path my parents and other people draw out for me. Even Dorothy had the freedom to veer off the yellow brick road now and then. But try as I may to shake things up, in the end, I always end up toeing that straight line.

Suddenly, heading home early tonight is fine by me.

CHAPTER SIX

I usually wake up mildly grumpy, though I try to keep it under wraps. But when my sleep is cut short by the loud chirping of my early bird parents—on a Saturday, no less—that grumpiness can't be contained.

WINS news time 5:41, and it's time to check traffic . . .

The radio volume is up so high in the kitchen, the reporter might as well be a DJ asking if Brooklyn is in da house.

. . . and here's what you need to know about the Hudson crossings . . .

Despite my best efforts to cling to the dream world a little longer, my senses switch on and commence processing real-life signals—the aroma of fresh-brewed coffee, the clinking of stirring spoons, and, of course, loud-ass conversation in the kitchen.

"Did the Yankees pitcher really get traded?" Mummy asks in Creole. She's probably the one who just lowered the volume a bit. My dad bleeds pinstripes—I'm all about the Mets.

"Aah, those bums," Papi spits out. "I wish I could take out an ad in the *Daily News* to say no one should come to their opening game. Let them play to an empty stadium."

"Wey," says Mummy emphatically. I've learned that *wey* or *ouais* is to *oui* what *yup* is to *yes*.

Impossible to fight it any longer, I open my eyes. It's still dark out, but the moon is full and super luminous. It's like I got pulled over by God, who's pointing a flashlight on my face and saying, "Do you know how slow you've been going, miss? You'll never get prom poppin' at this rate."

Ugh. No wonder everything is so loud—my door is wide open. Why did I leave it like that? Time to scrounge up my will-power and push past my drowsiness. I get up, drag myself across my room, and swat the door shut. I'm careful not to open my eyes too wide and kill my sleepiness, which I plan to resume once I get back in bed. The door slams louder than I anticipated.

"Simone! See-mone!" I hear Mummy shout for me, though she sounds muffled. Until she doesn't . . .

"Oh good—you're up." Mummy cracks open my door and pokes her head in my room.

"I'm not up," I groan, letting my body flop onto my bed.

"Then who shut the door, BO!" Mummy's Creole sound effect for all varieties of door shutting is always the same. If it were an object of any kind falling to the floor, she would've gone with *BEEP*.

"Constance, who are you talking to?" Papi's voice reaches us, but he stays downstairs. "Did you wake the girls?"

"Simone is already awake," Mummy says.

I bury my head in my pillow.

"Bonjour, Simone," Papi calls out pleasantly. And then, "Simone, did you hear? The Yankees traded another star relief pitcher."

I growl in response. Being a hard-core Mets fan in a Yankees family has its drawbacks.

"Okay," I say, defeated and surrendering to no one in particular. "I'm up now. I'm up." I cross the carpeted hallway to the bathroom. My father turns the radio back up in time for the game recap, and Mummy answers an incoming call on her cell phone. She's the only person I know who gets crack-of-dawn phone calls. It's ungodly.

I feel refreshed after brushing my teeth and washing my face. But the minute I step out of the bathroom, Mummy's waiting patiently.

"Here," she says, pointing her phone at me. "Talk to Ben Fils-Aimé."

"Who?"

"*From Queens.*"

Nothing is pinging in my brain's name recognition department. Mummy narrows her eyes in frustration at my blank expression.

"Your prom date." She uses her in-the-presence-of-company voice, but her face is menacing.

What? Why? I mouth silently and back away from her.

Mummy presses the phone against her chest and whispers through strained lips, "I called his mother to discuss things for our visit next Saturday and she called me back. I didn't expect her to put him on the phone."

I want to scream.

"Simone is being shy," she says sweetly, fake-laughing into the phone. "Just a minute, Ben." She gives me that look again and thrusts the phone into my hands. I can't believe this.

"Hello," I say through clenched teeth.

"Hi, Simone?"

He sounds wide awake. What is he, some kind of freak?

"Yes." I'm seething. Mummy knows this, so she stalks away to chat with Anne, who's just stepped out of her room.

"Hi, Simone, um, I'm Ben."

"Okay."

"Uh, yeah. I'm really just hearing about all this, but, um, my mom has all good things to say about you and your family."

"Uh-huh."

I think he's getting the hint. He's suddenly silent. And it's a loaded silence. I know I'm directing my frustration at the wrong person, but it's too early in the morning to be mature about this.

"Well," he finally speaks again. "I'm about to head out for a run, so I can give you my number if you want to text me or—"

"Not necessary," I cut him off.

"O-okay, well, then I guess I'll see you next week?"

"Or not," I say.

"That works, too," he says extra politely. It's like, the nerve of this guy. The more polite he acts, the worse it makes me look, and I resent that. "You have a good day. And, uh, good luck with everything."

"You too," I say, because it's the most pleasant response I can muster up.

I give Mummy her phone back, go to my room, and slam the door behind me, *BO!* On purpose this time.

CHAPTER SEVEN

Exactly one week later, I stare out the rear passenger window, fuming.

Queens, New York. Being here feels like a betrayal of the vow I made to myself four years ago. Not to mention the commitment to prom on my own terms.

The advice I gave Anne back then to make a run for it echoes in my head now.

I look at Anne and something inside softens a bit. Anne's already been through all this. She didn't have to come today but decided to out of solidarity. Or maybe she's here for damage control.

Thanks to our parents' strict rules, Anne and I have been in more than a few downright humiliating positions. One thing we've learned along the way is that cringe-worthy moments are better shared. Like when I tagged along on Anne's first movie date with Max. No question, it was embarrassing for the both of us. But at one point that night, when Max high-pitch-screamed during a scary part of the film, my sister and I realized we weren't the only awkward ones. It didn't cure our embarrassment, but the universal awkwardness took away the sting.

Mummy glances at me in her visor mirror. She's worried, I can tell. I'm getting a salty *Don't you embarrass me today* vibe.

Meanwhile, a tall pot of road rage is heating up in the driver's seat. "It's supposed to be alternated merging—*this* car and then *that* car," says Papi, pointing accusingly at vehicles closing in on us. You'd think he's choreographing a synchronized performance. He sucks his teeth, then delivers what's become his personal catchphrase. "If I was police, I would ticket that guy."

"Sometimes people have to take risks, take chances, and not always be policed," I say.

Papi's bulging eyes question me through the rearview mirror. "What are you talking about?" he asks. "We need balance. We need laws."

"Well, sometimes the laws are overreaching and create mindless followers. And all these followers could be why everyone's stuck in this traffic." I cross my arms. "If more people decided to go off the beaten path, not everyone would be clogging up life's highways."

"Simone," Mummy says. "I know what you're trying to do and it won't work. We said we were coming and it's too late to turn back now."

"No, Mother, *you* said we'd be coming."

I absorb the icy stare Mummy gives me and think of my

options. I need to be clever and outsmart the adults like civil rights teen activist Barbara Johns, who, in the 1950s, tricked her principal into leaving school so she could stage a mass student walkout.

My only hope is that Ben won't actually be around today. If he's anything like his big brother was four years ago, he is unbothered with all of this. My parents would get offended when they realize Ben isn't there. I hope they'd find it highly disrespectful. I'll be sure to remind them it's a slap in the face. I mean, if Ben can't show up for me today, he's got no decorum. And who knows? The boy is liable to act a fool at the prom. Maybe this will prompt them to call this whole ridiculousness off. I literally cross my fingers like I'm a fourth grader.

As we approach the house, Mummy turns down the radio and checks her look in the visor mirror. She grabs her black mascara and runs the tiny wand through the gray tufts along her hairline, and Anne titters to herself.

Nope. I will not so much as crack a smile at that. There will be no laughter from me.

Our car comes to an abrupt stop, and the platter of food on the floor slides against my ankle boots. Our offering this time is griyo, tasty fried pork cubes. Admittedly, you can't chew when you're pouting so hard. In any other emotional state, I would've snacked on a few of them.

A boy walks out of Madame Honoré's house. He's wearing glasses and looks about my height. He's the type of guy who could play an extra in a movie. He doesn't stand out, but his features are pleasant enough. My dad taps the horn, and the boy gives a casual wave and nods a greeting.

"Bonjour, Ben," Mummy calls out, lowering her window. I slide down my seat a little, hoping the tint in my window holds up in this light.

I was hoping he wouldn't be here. What was this kid doing? Keeping watch for us? If he's trying to pass off his lucky timing as pure coincidence, he's failed. How desperate must he be that he's working so hard to make an impression on us?

"Bonjour. You can pull into the driveway." He gestures to the spot next to the SUV already parked in the slightly sloped driveway.

This place looks different than how I remember it. Before, it blended into the neighborhood, and now it stands out. I can't decide if that's a good or a bad thing. The driveway looks newly redone, lined with stones. The house's roof is covered in terra-cotta tiles, and the front stoop is crowded with what look like mini palm trees. I almost check Google Maps to make sure we're not at some villa in Tuscany.

Papi's voice vibrates as he drives over the bumpy pavers like he's talking into a portable fan. "I wonder how they shovel this driveway after a snowstorm."

"Wow, this is something." Mummy's voice rattles in reply.

I'm not sure if Mummy is referring to the redone home or Ben's driveway invitation.

Ben walks over to the passenger side of the car, and I slink a little lower. He takes off his Mets cap, and I detect the shift in the atmosphere. Mummy gives him a look of respect. She appreciates old-school gestures like that.

My brilliant father reaches his arm across my mom to give Ben a handshake. Ben has to practically climb in the passenger side to accept it.

"Allo," they repeat to each other. With this greeting, I take it my dad approves of the star treatment Ben is already giving us.

"My mother will be happy you're here," Ben says in Creole.

Unlike my American-accented Creole, his sounds as native-born as his English. He focuses his attention on the back seat.

"Something smells good back there," he says.

Great. We smell like griyo, because Anne kept opening up the foil to steal pieces.

"Oh, that's just something we made for you to show our appreciation," Mummy says.

Ben backs up a little and pulls Mummy's door open so she can step out into the sunlight. She holds out her cheek for Ben's air kiss. He obliges, showing her all the respect she requires and more.

"Ready, Simone?" Anne softly asks me. She's being delicate with me, and I appreciate that. One sharp tone from anybody and I just may let loose a chupee from hell.

Anne gets out of the car, then comes around to meet me when I step out a moment later.

"Oh no, it's not a problem," I hear Ben tell my mother in a

reassuring tone. It doesn't take a genius to know what they're talking about. And I hate it.

"I present to you my daughter, Simone," Mummy says, beaming.

At first I glance away and cross my arms. Then I force myself
to be courteous and look at him. When I do, he seems to over-
look the ice in my stare. I don't see pity there like I expected. Good
thing the air kiss greeting isn't a kid-to-kid requirement.

"Simone hasn't been feeling well today, so please excuse her
mood," Mummy tells Ben. "On y va, Simone, Anne," Mummy
says to us in French. *Sigh. Not with the French again.*

I freeze. I'm not ready to go inside the house. Once that train
leaves the station, it'll be impossible to stop it. I need some space to
think.

Mummy and Papi go inside the house without us. They probably want a head start to warn Madame Honoré about my attitude.
Anne stays with me, maybe to shield me from Ben as much as she
can. Or to shield Ben.

But I don't want to hurt Ben. It's not his fault. He's just a pawn
in this dictatorial regime. In any case, he turns away and grabs a
grocery bag out of the trunk of the SUV we're parked next to. I
take it this means Ben wasn't waiting around for us and staring
out the window. He was simply in the process of fetching a bag of
groceries.

Ben looks like he has every inclination to walk straight back
into the house, but his manners stop him. Are his parents paying
him to do this or something? Are *my* parents?

"So, you're a high school senior like Simone?" Anne asks Ben, probably to make up for my lack of greeting.

"Yeah," he says simply.

"I hear you got accepted into all the schools you applied to?"

How does she know that?

Ben nods pleasantly and shifts his weight from one sensible brown shoe to another. He's playing humble, I guess. I'm locked in position. Not that I want to leave. It's either be out here or in my parents' presence inside.

Anne keeps the questions coming. "Have you decided yet where you're going?" she asks Ben.

I tense up and Anne gives my arm a gentle squeeze, as if to reassure me she's got this under control. I'm not questioning her tactics . . . yet.

"It was a tough choice picking between a few, mostly New York schools. But Rutgers is where I'll be going."

I feel Anne glance at me but I ignore her. *Big whoop.* Rutgers is a vast institution. Most people go to the main campus in New Brunswick, so there's no point fretting I'll bump into him in Newark next year.

"Cool. I go to Rutgers–Newark," Anne says, a smile spreading across her prim face.

"Me too," answers Ben, before catching himself. "I mean— not officially yet. Next year."

Future college-freshman me just winced—I could feel it.

Honestly, I don't know what's up with that matchmaker glint in my sister's eyes. I try nonverbally messaging her that Ben ain't it. But Anne ignores my laser-beam stare and continues questioning him.

"What are you thinking of studying?"

"Economics or something related, I think."

"I've taken a few econ classes here and there," Anne says. "It's not as dry as I thought."

It could be my imagination, but the more Ben answers Anne's inquiries, the more curious he seems about me. He glances my way more than a few times. I wonder if he's looking for me to put an end to Anne's interrogation. That'll be tough to do since I still can't bring myself to stop pouting and speak.

"And what about you?" Ben asks Anne, even though he's looking at me again.

Anne answers. "Oh, me? Well, I'm about to graduate with a degree in biology. I'm headed to med school in the fall."

"That's impressive. Congrats," Ben says sincerely. Then he asks, "What about you, Simone?"

I feel like answering, "I'm going to places you're not—like my prom." But that would be unnecessarily mean. I think of the HomeGirls and I hold back. They've been so thoughtful today, texting their support on our drive here.

Amita's last message was *Don't go in there embarrassing your parents. It'll make things worse.*

This is what you call a conundrum. It's not just that Ben is unbothered that he's a mail-order date; his kindness is charting sky-high at the precise moment mine has taken a dive. "Um, I'll be going to Rutgers, too," I say. "Newark campus." *Because, as I'm sure you've figured out, I'm not allowed to go away for college.*

"Oh wow." He smiles and nearly upstages the sun. "I guess I'll be seeing you around in the fall."

I can't believe what smiling does to his face. It's a drastic change, and I'm curious to see it again.

"My mom is waiting on these drinks, so I better bring them inside," says Ben, holding up the shopping bag.

I look down at my phone. A new text has come in from Gabby. *I just bumped into Gavin! He says he can't wait to see you again!!!!*

"You coming?" Ben calls out.

Anne and I follow as Ben leads the way to the front stoop of his home. With each step I absentmindedly climb, I feel like I'm growing wings.

Gavin said he can't wait to see me again?

I feel giddy. I feel free. I feel like I've found my dream prom date. *I'll ask Gavin to the prom!* It'll be my coup. My prom emancipation. My promancipation!

"I forgot something in the car," I tell Anne before I can cross the threshold into the house.

"Okay," she says, heading indoors. So proud she is of the third degree she's been giving Ben, she doesn't suspect a thing.

The minute I'm back at the car, I don't even open the door. I turn around to make sure Anne and Ben have entered the house.

That's when I take off running.

CHAPTER EIGHT

I'm pretty sure the main ave, Linden Boulevard, is a straight shot from Ben's house. All I need to do is make one right turn and head down a few blocks, and I should run into it. If there's one thing I'm glad I inherited from Mummy, it's her sense of direction. The woman is a homing pigeon.

I speed-walk down the calm street, passing modest front lawns lying like welcome mats before small brick homes. The jumbo jets overhead, preparing to land at nearby JFK Airport, give this part of town a low ceiling. Even without my glasses on, I could identify the airline logos on their tails.

I wonder how I look from the sky. Before I was born, Anne had flown to visit my parents' island nation of Haiti, but she'd been too young to recall the experience. In all my seventeen and a half years, I haven't ventured beyond North American shores.

I make it to Linden Boulevard and see that it's lined with every convenience you can picture—bakery, bookstore, butcher shop, storefront churches, medical offices, art gallery, visa services center, salon, barbershop, restaurants. But one thing it seems to be lacking, and that I'm desperately needing, is a subway stop. I feel like climbing up the pole of a streetlamp just so I can get a good enough survey of a three-block radius. I check a subway map on my phone instead. Nope, there is no train that runs to this neighborhood.

Ain't that some crap?

How am I supposed to get home? I can't even spot those dollar vans that pick up passengers during rush hour. Probably because it's not rush hour. What this street *does* have are bus stops; they seem to pop up every few yards, like sidewalk merchants. But it's not going to be easy to figure out which bus to catch in which direction—not to mention, which transfer. I wish I knew Queens as well as I know my grandmother's neighborhood in Brooklyn.

I just start walking. Almost every business in this area is a Haitian business. I can't believe my eyes. The sheer amount of culture—my culture—all around me gives me a moment.

"Yo, I can't believe li pap vini!" The mishmash of Creole and English rolls off the tongues of young passersby. Creole rings out in the street. Even the young people speak Creole well. I can understand Creole and some French, for sure. But speaking it is another thing. My accent is heavy, and my tongue trips on itself. My parents don't object when I speak to them in English, and they speak English to me most of the time.

Taking French these four years in school has helped with my

pronunciation a bit, and listening to konpa music helps some more. There's something about singing lyrics in another language that gets you to slow down and learn how to form the words more clearly. I learned that from Tatie Nadine.

A street vendor selling 1804 Haitian Independence T-shirts and cell phone cases is shouting to no one in particular.

"Wear your pride, honor their sacrifice. First Black Republic of the West. 1804, baby," he calls out while holding up the merchandise. "All a' them rappers wear the same-ol', same-ol' revolutionary heroes on their tees. Nobody's reppin' Toussaint, Dessalines, Anacaona, or Boukman, n'amean?" I'm mesmerized by the vendor's passion, and my attention only fuels him. "Let's show 'em we single-handedly beat Napoleon's goons and the baddest in the game—the British Royal Navy—so that everybody could have freedom, in every country. *We* did that. Period!"

"Straight up," I echo, wishing I had money on me so I could give him more than a soul sister nod.

I keep walking, but pause at an art gallery. I let myself be drawn in by the vibrant hues jumping from its interior. I don't want to stare too hard, or I'll be invited in. And I couldn't afford to buy even a bookmark in a place like this. There are a few white folks here, examining the original pieces neatly lined on the walls. They look like they've traveled from gentrified Brooklyn to get here.

I wonder if they caught the bus. A ferry?

My buzzing phone jolts me back to reality. Anne is calling, so I answer.

"Simone, where are you?" she hisses.

"I'm fine."

My sister sucks her teeth. "I didn't ask *how* you are. I asked *where* you are. Mummy thinks you're hiding in the parked car."

"I'll meet you guys at home."

"Oh, no you won't. You're gonna come right back here, and quick!" Anne is whisper-screaming. "I don't know how much longer I can cover for you. Mummy is suspicious."

"Good. Let her worry. She brought this on herself. I told her I wanted no part of this."

"Is this really the best idea you could come up with? Bouncing?"

My eyes start to sting, but I hold off any tears by forcing out a laugh.

"This whole thing is a show. It's Mummy's stupid show."

"So you play into the drama with more drama? Nice going."

A reflection joins mine in the glass. It's a fellow window browser, and I wish they'd go away. I claimed this spot first, and I intend to occupy it until I figure out my next move.

"Did you really walk this far out just to take a call?" asks Ben. *Oh great.*

"Um, can you go away?" I say through gritted teeth.

"Is that Ben?" Anne asks. "Good! I'll just let everyone know y'all are out on a walk, getting to know each other a bit."

"Wait, no!"

"Okay, I'll wait," says Ben, smiling facetiously.

"See you soon," singsongs Anne.

"Not you." I flash Ben a look. "Anne? Anne?" She's gone.

Ugh.

For a moment, Ben and I are toe to toe, staring at each other. He blinks first.

I want to see him as a stand-in for my standoff with Mummy, but something about him is too distracting. He's like a puzzle I can't solve. None of the pieces of my expectations seem to fit into his personality.

A woman pauses on her way into the gallery. "Sak pase, Ben?" she greets him. Then, upon seeing my tight face, she asks, "You okay, sister?"

"I—yes, thank you," I answer, easing the tension in my jaw. These two people aren't who I'm angry with.

"Ben, are you here to show your friend the gems you've dug up for the gallery?" the woman asks in a melodic Haitian accent.

"Like, actual gems?" I say, my eyes darting from the woman to Ben and back again.

"Ben helps raise tuition money for teens he's met in Haiti by selling their artwork," says the woman. As she speaks, she gestures emphatically—her hands like a conductor's wand as her musical words play on. "And you should see how talented these young people are. A beautiful ironwork piece sold just yesterday. *Bravo!*"

She pats Ben on the back before heading into the gallery.

"That's cool that you've been to Haiti," I tell him.

"You haven't?"

My silence screams out my answer: Nope. My parents have

gone back a few times, but they've never taken me. Anne doesn't remember going. On that one visit when she was little, Anne got really sick. The way Mummy tells the story, Anne vomited half her body weight. This incident became Thibodeaux legend, retold different ways hundreds of times. Depending on who narrates, Anne got sick because of the water, suspect fruit, or a hex from a jealous heart. And also depending on who's telling it, Anne recovered after she saw a top Port-au-Prince doctor, got prayed over, upchucked a goat, or laid a dinosaur egg. Nevertheless, Mummy has been too shook to ever go back to Haiti with her, or to take me.

"You'll go one day when you're ready," he says. I appreciate him not making me feel some kind of way over this. Too many people are quick to point out how messed up it is that I haven't visited. It's like they question my pride in my culture. But I love being Haitian. I love the history, the food, the culture, the people. I'm feeling totally at home right now in this neighborhood, even on this messed-up day that Lord knows I will pay for.

"I really like this area," I tell Ben. "If Haiti is anything like this, I can't wait to visit."

A car pulls up alongside us. A man wearing shades and a newsboy cap is behind the wheel. "Rantre non, timoun!!" he says, telling us to hop in.

I've dealt with these predator types on my hikes to the bus stop before school. The only response is a loud one, because they don't like scenes.

"Hey, ale ou vouzan, vagabon!" I bark.

"Hey, chill—that's my dad," says Ben.

Yikes. "Oh. *Pardon.*" I apologize and wave awkwardly. Monsieur Honoré nods respectfully in response, but I can tell he is not impressed with me.

"Listen, that's my ride," Ben tells me. "You don't have to come back to the house if you weren't planning on it."

With that, he turns and walks toward the car. Without a care in the world. What is that? Is it his way of calling my bluff? Or could he just be that unbothered by all of this? Seriously, who is this guy?

Ben never looks back. He's buckled in and seconds into scrolling through his phone when he realizes the car isn't moving. His dad is too busy gawking at me. I've seen that disapproving parental look before.

I allow myself one last glimpse of Linden Boulevard, and then make my way to the car.

Welp, I guess this is the end of my great escape.

CHAPTER NINE

In the car, Ben and his dad discuss the artwork that a traveling relative is flying in with on Ben's behalf. I'm grateful for their chatter. It gives me a moment to calm down and pull myself together.

I read through Gabby's and the HomeGirls' texts. Their advice lands on opposite ends of the spectrum.

Gabby's messages can all be summed up in one sentence: *Girl, you need to wear your big girl pants and tell everybody to vouzan.*

Amita and Kira are more low-key. They know the score. Their messages are more: *Stick with the plan. You'll get through this.*

But what's this? How did I not notice Anne's additional texts? *Mummy knows you bailed.*

I don't think I'll ever be able to trust Anne again if she snitched. But the next text refutes my assumption. The more I read, the more my stomach twists in knots.

Ben's mom figured it out. She said it's not like her son to linger when he's expected home. She called Ben just as he spotted you on the ave.

The next update comes a minute later.

Mummy is losing it—crying and the whole nine. You better get here, quick.

They sent Ben's dad to come get you. Look out for him!

When Monsieur Honoré pulls into the bumpy stone driveway, he doesn't cut off the engine. Instead, he pulls fingerless leather gloves out of a center compartment and puts them on. Now I'm starting to understand the hat and aviator sunglasses. At first I was so caught up in thinking about Mummy killing me that I thought he looked like my undertaker. But I see now that dude's got driving gear. And he's serious about it. The addition of the gloves must be for highway drives, because he tells me he's heading to the airport to pick up the relative who's flying in from Haiti.

While Ben gives his dad a few instructions for handling the artwork, I take a deep breath and step out of the car.

Time to face the music.

No one hears me walk inside the house. There is konpa music playing on the speaker, plus Papi and Anne are tinkering on the upright piano that separates the living room and dining area. They share a bench and a few weak laughs as they play "Ayiti Chérie," the Haitian folk song we all love. It must be their way of easing the tension.

Our host is seated in a dining room chair and Mummy is sitting right next to her. Although they're facing the piano, they are looking at each other, deep in conversation.

The living room is almost exactly as I remember it from four years ago. The rarely used couches, the empty aquarium, the creepy figurines heralding a Victorian past that did not belong to us. Even the expectant look on the haughty host's face hasn't changed . . . much. When she finally looks up at me, there's a disappointment filling it now.

Because of me.

I didn't realize until now that Madame Honoré looks about a decade older than my parents. That explains her décor and love for all things old-fashioned—not to mention her husband's driving gloves. She could pass for Ben's grandma. A fancy one at that. She's rockin' her Sunday best. Hair done up, accessories on point, fierce makeup application—down to the wingtip eyeliner flow.

And yes, just like four years ago, there is Mummy—back in her old role, playing extra grateful and as reliably deferential, even as she dramatically grieves my actions. When I see Madame Honoré place a cold compress on Mummy's forehead, my toes grip the floor in preparation of the wild emotional ride I'm about to take.

I greet Madame Honoré with a cheek-to-cheek air kiss. Her damp skin again shows signs of being over a hot stove all morning.

She immediately asks where I've been. "Simone-chérie, où étais-tu chérie? Your mummy was worried sick."

I glance at Mummy, who looks like a battered boxer resting between rounds. Her whole essence seems wounded, yet she's still got on her boxing gloves.

Papi stops playing the piano, then rushes over to me. Anne

twists around but stays seated on the bench. There's vexation etched deep into my parents' faces. The whole room crackles with godawful tension.

It's hard to look anyone in the eyes.

That's when Mummy's vigor returns. She leans forward, her hands throwing jabs into the air. "How dare you walk out like that? Without so much as a word!" Her voice hitches to my heart and sinks it below the belt. "Are you trying to make me suffer to my core?"

"Constance, be calm, be calm." Madame Honoré softly coaches her back into the boxing ring corner. "You don't want to raise your blood pressure."

Every transgression I make always boils down to me handing my mother some mortal injury. It must be why she wants me and Anne to be doctors.

"I'm sorry," I finally say. "I didn't mean any disrespect. I just needed time to think."

"You should've called me or your mother," Papi chimes in, his voice measured but strained. "If it weren't for Ben, we wouldn't know where you were."

Anne looks guilty for keeping silent about my whereabouts, and I feel horrible for putting her in that predicament.

"Never have I even been so humiliated by a child," Mummy continues. She's holding the cold compress in her hands and shaking her head.

"This wasn't her intention," says Madame Honoré. "She was

just caught up in one moment. We were young once and remember that feeling."

It sucks that Madame Honoré seems to understand me better than my parents. And it hurts when it takes an outsider to convince your own mom to think better of you.

I know Mummy wants to stretch this fight out, but she chooses not to look worse in front of Madame Honoré. "What do you have to say for yourself?" she asks me.

There's a harsh edge to Mummy's tone and Papi shoots her a sharp look. But it's too late. That did it. The room has already gone blurry.

Everyone in the room looks thrown by my reaction. Mummy's face softens and Papi sighs with regret.

"Let's just move on," he says. "We'll talk about this on our way home."

But before I can wipe my tears, Ben walks in. My back to him, I escape to the bathroom before he can see the state I'm in.

When I return, fresh faced and composed, Ben is gone. Madame Honoré says she's sent him to grab the last bag from the car. As Mummy and Madame Honoré resume competing in their compliment Olympics, I walk over to the window that faces the street. I'm relieved they're as desperate to move on from the drama as I am.

"Your home renovations are lovely," says Mummy. "The driveway looks so . . . unique. We were almost afraid to park on it."

"Merci, merci. It's our first big renovation since we moved here in 1998." Madame Honoré eyes me hovering by the front door and smiles. "Oh, but your girls—they're beautiful young ladies now."

"Thank you," says Anne, on behalf of the both of us.

"How about Jude? I see he has someone special," says Mummy. I turn to see her gesture to the framed photo on the mantel. It's a picture of Anne's prom date and a girl who looks as porcelain-skinned as the tiny figurine women in hoop skirts. "They make a lovely couple."

"Yes, they do. And she's a kind young woman, from a place they call Maine. Jude is there visiting her now."

My mother pretends to be interested, but moves on to the son she really wants to discuss. "Ben gave us such a gentleman's greeting earlier. I'm only sorry for what happened not long after—"

Catching my cue to tune out of their conversation, I look out the window again in search of the actual Ben. His dad's car is gone, and I spot him talking to a pretty neighbor. The guy is so nice and easy to talk to, I'm not surprised by the look on the girl's face.

"*Eh-heh*," Madame Honoré is saying when I tune back in. "The first in his class, Ben is."

"Se sa m konnen," says Mummy supportively.

"He got an early-early college acceptance, too."

"That's wonderful. So did Simone."

I find myself watching out the window to see if there's anything else I can pick up about Ben and this girl's relationship. They are definitely not relatives, judging from their body language. She seems far more confident than I am.

Ben looks up and catches my eye. He says something to the girl to excuse himself and heads up the walkway toward the house. I quickly shift my focus down to the lace doily covering the window seat. I was only checking on them out of curiosity. I hope he knows that.

"And he's going to be running in a race this weekend."

"Oh really?"

"You should see them—even when it's cold out, they're running."

Madame Honoré stands up with renewed energy when Ben steps in. Her stacks of gold bracelets jingle as she beckons us over to a dining room table.

"Come eat, come eat," she says. "Everything is ready—mushroom rice, fried plantains, legumes, pikliz."

Hearing this menu, my stomach wants to pen a truce letter to my parents. But I remind it who's boss and muffle it under my crossed arms.

Thankfully, our host isn't making us eat all together at the table. Everything is buffet style, and we're invited to eat, plates in hand, in the living room.

Anne and I sit on the long couch, Ben is across from us in a dining chair he pulled over, and Papi, who never needs seatback support, is on the cushioned piano bench.

I'm surprised we all can eat after such an emotional last few minutes, but the food is bangin'. The spices are a perfect blend of *slap yo' mama* and *hug yo' mama*. Mummy's griyo and Madame

Honoré's djon djon rice need to just stop playing and run away to the prom together. These two are this gathering's real stars. A perfect pairing. There's no fitting world where these two dishes should ever be apart.

The flavor has me swaying to the syncopated rhythms filling the room. Just like at home on a Saturday, Haitian music plays on the speakers. But in this house, the sounds are more contemporary than my dad's eclectic remix of jazzy big bands from the eighties and Cuban classics from the fifties. As everyone eats and talks, I notice that Ben is more patient with his mom than I am with mine, but he doesn't let her fawning or nagging go too far. He kinda shuts it down in a low-key way, and his mother seems to respect the hint. There's a decidedly measured yet friendly way about him. He doesn't seem like he does anything out of obligation, but rather because he wants to.

Ben even indulges my father's long-winded questions about sports. When Anne hears where the conversation is going—she's not a huge baseball fan—she gets up and joins Mummy and Madame Honoré at the dining room table. I on the other hand pay closer attention—not because baseball's my thing, which it is, but to curb my dad's potential oversharing.

"The year I came to this country was the same year the Mets were in the World Series," explains Papi. His posture kingly, and his long legs elegantly folded, he holds his plate at chin level and pauses to scrape his rice grains into a neat pile. "I was missing my family, missing Haiti, and even though I could understand

English on paper, I couldn't understand when it was spoken. I thought every other person on the subway was named Agathe—you know the French name for Agatha? It was a popular Haitian name back then. So, I kept hearing *A-gathe* this and *A-gathe* that. It took me ages to figure out people were saying 'I got.'"

"And then the Mets went on to win the World Series, right, Papi?" I nudge. I've heard this story many times before, but I'm trying to politely steer it to its conclusion.

"Oui, they did! And, mezanmi-wo, it was so thrilling, it made me forget my troubles and love the sport."

"So you became a lifelong Mets fan." Ben sighs with satisfaction.

Papi blinks away the nostalgic gleam in his eyes. "No, I root for the Yankees."

"Oh." Ben looks unsure whether he should laugh, so he wipes his mouth with his napkin. I think I spot his slight smile before he does.

"You get to Shea Stadium often?" Papi asks Ben.

"Shea?" he asks.

"*Agh*," puffs Papi. "Simone, what is Shea called now?"

"He means Citi Field," I say.

"Oui," Papi says, turning back to Ben. "You don't live too far from the stadium. Do you go often? The season is starting soon."

"Not as much as I want to, but I follow every game," says Ben. "Once my summer internship starts, I'm hoping to be able to buy tickets more regularly."

"Okay, okay," Papi says, seeming to approve of both Ben's love for the game and of his nabbing a paid internship. He glances at me like he's calculating something. Maybe it's because I'm a huge Mets fan. Big whoop.

Sure, a lot of Black folks aren't baseball fans anymore, but that doesn't mean Ben and I should be instant buddies.

"Wasn't it shameful how the Yankees lost their season ender?" Papi starts that up again.

Ben, if you know what's good for you, just nod and agree.

"Yes, that was pretty shameful," says Ben.

"At least Simone's Mets earned their respect. How about the new pitcher everyone is talking about?"

"It was a good trade," says Ben.

I shovel another pile of rice into my mouth and try to withdraw from the conversation. But *ohmigod*, who would say that was a good trade? That guy hasn't proven himself yet.

I just want this to be over. When are we going to get on with the business of this?

"Do you play?" Papi asks Ben.

"I never played with the school team, and I kinda regret that."

I humph. "I guess no one's gonna ask me if I ever wanted to play. Women may not have the MLB, but Marisol Gutierrez's killer pitching skills are about to disrupt thangs," I say, unleashing the activist in me in the hopes it shames them into changing the subject. But that only makes Ben more interested.

"How do you spell her last name?"

I tell him, and he types a note into his phone, saying he plans to read up on her later.

"Are you following the Women's Baseball World Cup?" he asks me. "I watched a few of the games online; they're incredible."

Is he trying to impress me or is dropping interesting trivia on brand for him?

I leave this question unanswered because, to me, it doesn't matter either way. He can be as interesting and impressive as he wants, and I still wouldn't take him to prom. I may not have avoided the trip to Queens, but the vow I made to myself four years ago still stands.

Once my mother has daintily wiped the last Haitian cake crumbs from her face, I know it's time for the prom-arranging portion of the evening to commence.

Mummy clears her throat. "Please pardon our earlier incident. We really are grateful to be here. Thank you so much for having us over," she says, her eyes momentarily lowered in an embarrassment that I feel to my core. With a blink, she looks up with a shining face. "The last time we came here, we were so honored to have Anne go to prom with your older son. We still look at the pictures today and marvel at how wonderfully everything turned out. You have good boys."

Anne fidgets beside me, and I hear the couch cushion's squeaky protest. Jude was a lousy date, but Anne never shared that tidbit with my mom. That's the opposite of what I'd do. I'd remind my mom about the prom date fail every chance I got. And then Mummy would be the one squirming now, not Anne.

As good a boy as MC Baby Killah? I want to ask but don't. Mummy once pointed out a photo of the rapper, saying he seemed like a "good boy" just because he had clean-cut hair and no earrings or visible tattoos.

"And with Ben being such a fine young man," Mummy is saying, "I know he and Simone will have a nice time together, and I would like him to accompany Simone to her school's senior prom."

Madame Honoré sits up. "Oh, well, thank you for saying so," she says. "Jude said it was a nice time."

Anne and I exchange a look and almost bust out laughing.

"Ben is different from my older boy," Madame Honoré goes on. "He's a very busy person, but he's ready and prepared to do this favor because he loves to help out his mother."

"Amen!" says Mummy.

"Aw, man," I say under my breath.

Ben is quiet, studying my expression on the low. He gives me an apologetic half smile, and I look away. A tiny firecracker sparks in my belly, and I tune back into Mummy's voice until the spark fizzles out.

"So, we can work out the details," Mummy is saying. "I know you have a cousin that lives near us, and they may be willing to take Ben overnight. If you need me to call them and arrange for it, I'll be happy to—"

"No need," says Madame Honoré. "That's my husband's family. We're very close. And Ben is there often because he's been taking classes at Rutgers–Newark. You know he's getting college credit for that? Yes, so he sleeps there over the weekend sometimes, so it's not necessary."

I wish I had an out-of-state getaway crib to escape to. I should start knocking on doors in this area and make some friends. I hold in the chupee rising in my chest.

Madame Honoré looks at me with grave concern. "Simone, are you okay? You have a toothache, chérie?"

I nod and fix my face. Mummy seethes at me.

That's when I laugh. I can't help it. Mummy and I have been exchanging gnarly frowns back and forth like we are some relay track team at the Grimace Olympics. How anyone can stand to be around either of us today is anyone's guess. Mummy's expression breaks and she shakes her head and chuckles. This laugh is our shared awkwardness.

A slow smile opens up Ben's face as he studies me with curiosity.

"I'm fine, Madame Honoré," I offer apologetically. "Everything's fine."

And really, that isn't an all-out lie. After all, *Gavin wants to see me again!* I can picture us at prom now—Amita with Pritpal, me with Gavin, and Kira with—

Kira.

Kira doesn't have a prom date.

Which means . . .

I let myself entertain the thought. It isn't half bad, but I'd need Kira's permission first. If she agrees to it, Ben would make the perfect date for her. As much as I hate to admit it, he seems like cool people. And the logistics are in our favor. He's already expected to spend prom night in Jersey. What better way to give me a cover for Gavin while scoring a respectable, kind date for Kira?

Yes. Everything is fine.

The parents seem satisfied to see Ben and me exchange phone numbers. I didn't bring my yard of African wax print because I was saving it for my true prom date, not Ben. Gavin in a matching wax print bow tie and pocket kerchief would be killer. I'll just have to bring my second-choice wax print to Ben when we meet up again. It's plain and can pretty much go with any dress his date (Kira, hopefully) decides to wear.

"Thank you," I say to Ben, hoping he gathers that I'm grateful he came to find me earlier.

"Hey, no worries." Ben puts his phone in his pocket. "I get how you must feel."

"I'll text you," I cut him off, not wanting to have a conversation about feelings. "When I'm ready to meet up with a swatch of my prom dress."

"That works," he says, a smile in his eyes.

"Good," I reply.

I really hope this does work.

CHAPTER TEN

On Monday afternoon, Amita and Kira and I find ourselves standing outside a tattoo parlor called Ink It Over.

None of us have ever hung out in this town before. Here, the views of the Manhattan skyline are killer, and the shopping strip is wall-to-wall with cool, one-of-a-kind stores.

"Are you sure about this, Amita?" I ask.

Kira eyes each person that walks by, even though there's little chance we'll run into anyone we know. We didn't tell family or friends that our school had early dismissal today.

"I'm positive," Amita answers with full confidence. "Let's go in!"

If my trip to Queens taught me anything, it's that it's time for the HomeGirls to take things to the next level. But Amita is raising the stakes even higher with today's stunt.

"Number eight on the list, baby!" Amita shouts. "I'm switching up my style!"

We give her a high five and follow her in.

Inside, Ink It Over looks exactly how I'd imagined. Thick velvety drapes hang from the tall ceiling. Inspirational typography like *Be the Change* and *Persist* are pinned all over the walls. A steady but dull buzzing wafts from an arched corridor leading to back rooms.

Kira and I try to make ourselves comfortable on the black couch in the entry area. There's a huge gilded mirror hanging on the wall facing us, and the butterfly barrette in my updo is having a moment. Reflective sunlight is bouncing off the wings, giving it a stained glass effect. The translucent colors complement my dark brown skin and jet-black eyebrows, and I'm reminded again why shea butter is my faithful ally. My skin looks so moisturized on this chilly, windswept day.

The butterfly and I have an understanding. I felt like I busted out the chrysalis when I ran through the Queens streets on Saturday, and I feel like I'm taking flight being here with my HomeGirls today. Taking flight with wings made strong by my prolonged struggle to break through.

I guess late bloomers are tougher than people realize.

Amita is showing her ID to a receptionist with flawless, shimmery makeup. They take walk-ins here, and at eighteen, Amita meets New Jersey's minimum age requirement for body art. Kira and I watch Amita point to an item on the service menu. She taps her finger on that item a few times for good measure.

The receptionist smiles his approval of Amita's choice. "Got it.

One belly button piercing," he confirms. "Have a seat. It'll be about a twenty-minute wait."

Kira and I raise our eyebrows and glance at each other.

Amita is wearing a huge grin when she squeezes in between us, throwing her arms around our shoulders. "Ha, you guys thought I was getting a tattoo, didn't you?"

We scoot away from her, laughing off our initial worry that we'd be hunted down by Amita's parents..

"I still can't believe you're going for it so hard," I say, impressed. "Full style switch up."

"I know." She dances in her seat. "It feels good to be eighteen and doing things my way."

"Next, you'll do prom your way!" says Kira, pivoting to face Amita. "Hey, do you know what you're wearing to prom yet?"

"That'll be a surprise." Amita winks.

Kira's curiosity will not be satiated. "Will it be something that'll show off your new piercing?"

"Okay, fine, you got me. I don't actually know what I'll be wearing, but I wanted to keep my fearless eighteen mood going for a little longer."

I perk up. "I think I know too much about prom dresses, so I'm totally here if you'd like a free consultation."

On the ride home from Queens, our HomeGirls text chat was nonstop, with the girls showing support and trying to make me feel better. I'd rather talk about prom fashion than arranged proms any day.

"Oh yeah," asks Amita. "What look are you going with, Simone?"

As I pull out my phone and show the girls a few of my inspiration looks, I can't help but wonder how I'll approach the topic of Ben to Kira.

A young woman and man walk into the tattoo parlor and they're led to the back rooms almost immediately. They have appointments, plus they look like VIPs. The clothes, the flawless hair and makeup. I'm guessing maybe actors.

Seeing the couple reminds me of one of our Playlist goals. "We need to come up with a cover story for our clubbin' night," I say.

"You know what?" Amita says while digging into her cross-body bag. "This is perfect timing, because Teen Tuesdays start this week in Millwall." I don't know if Amita meant to pull out her eyeliner pencil, but she's poking the air with it as she breaks things down. "Every place from the bowling lanes to nightclubs will lower their age admittance to sixteen Tuesday nights from now until the end of summer."

"Well then, that should be the night we tell our parents we're working on our 'group project,'" I say.

Kira winces before speaking up. "This may sound weird, but it might help our cause if our parents meet our 'study group' first."

"To anyone else that sounds weird, but you're talking to the HomeGirls." Amita points her eyeliner pencil at Kira and then me. "If you're going to meet my parents—which I agree will boost the perceived veracity of our cover story—I'm going to need to email you both a document detailing what to say and what to avoid saying."

I tip my head and wave my hand with a royal flourish. "And I shall study said document."

"Let's do this!" Kira says.

I'm glad we had this extra time to catch up. We've practically turned this place into a lounge. Amita starts taking candid group selfies of us, and Kira's already leafing through tattoo magazines. It feels amazing having a spot to just chill with my HomeGirls.

An aqua-haired woman with a large mermaid tattoo wrapped around her arm comes over and introduces herself as Lena. "Let's go on back and do your piercing."

"Come on in with me." Amita gestures to us, a little aggressively. Do I smell fear?

As bold as Amita always seems, it surprises me when, the minute she lies on her back, she admits to having low pain tolerance. The girl starts wincing from the moment the mermaid woman swabs Amita's belly button with cleansing wipes. When she raises her knees like a tent and starts tapping her feet, Kira and I report to her sides and try to keep her mind on anything else.

"Tell us more about Pritpal," I prompt.

"Okay, so I don't tell everyone this," Amita starts prattling as she stares at the ceiling, dampness forming at the corner of her eye. "But Pritpal was just cast in a TV show! He's making the switch from singing to acting."

"Whaaat?" I shout, reenergized by this juicy bit of news.

Amita stacks her hands over her smile.

"Ohmygosh, that's so cool!" Kira says, pumped. "He's an actor? How did that happen? And which show? Will he be starring with anyone famous?"

I giggle with the realization that Kira talks the way she texts. One bubble per thought. On the drive back from Queens on Saturday, my phone kept going off back-to-back in the span of seconds, and I had to mute the conversation or else Anne was going to make me walk home from the Holland Tunnel.

"He's got to keep most of the details secret for now," Amita explains, "but it's for Netflix. He says it's an ensemble cast of teen newbies, and it's shooting here in Jersey."

I give Amita a soft high five. "Word up!"

"Where did you even meet Pritpal?" asks Kira.

"At some fancy relative's wedding. They paid a boatload of money for Pritpal to perform there."

"This story just keeps getting better." I swoon, careful my slight bunny hop doesn't unsettle Amita.

"At one point, he sang to me and jumped offstage to ask me to dance. Everyone thought it was just part of his act."

"He sang to her!" Kira sighs, her face etched with emotion.

I need someone to take my picture right now-now because I'd be surprised if there weren't stars in my eyes. "That's the dreamiest thing," I gush. I wonder if Gavin can sing. Naw, that would be too much flyness wrapped up in one. The brotha is already beautiful, charming, funny, popular, a talented athlete, and super smart—according to Millwall Prep's IG. What of the Haitian proverb that says something like *God is plenty generous, but He doesn't distribute evenly?*

"Okay, now breathe in," instructs Lena the Mermaid Lady. Reflexively, Amita grabs our hands and squeezes. "You're going to feel a pinch, so I need you to exhale it all out. You're doing great."

"Did your parents freak?" Kira asks even as she winces from Amita's strong grip. "When they saw you dancing with Pritpal at the wedding?"

"You see? It wasn't so bad," hums Lena. "Now just hold still while I adjust and clasp your belly button ring."

Amita nods and takes a shallow breath. "My parents? They actually laughed along with everyone else, not taking it seriously. They never brought it up again, but Pritpal and I exchanged numbers. Pretty soon, we were talking every day." Her hands go slack and she sighs happily. "I even met his parents a few times. They're cool. When they offered to meet my parents, I shot that idea down."

"Yeah, I get that," I say, trying not to look at the menacing tools hovering close to my friend's skin. My eyes catch a vintage-looking poster on the wall.

"Thanks," Amita replies with a wind gust of an exhale.

"Is that all for today?" Lena asks.

"Actually, no," I respond before Amita can. My friends look perplexed when I point to the poster that's caught my attention. "I'd like to get one of those tattoos."

Kira peers around Amita to meet my eyes. "So, Simone, how would you compare *your* Queens trip to your sister's?"

I appreciate the girls trying to keep my mind off the butterfly artwork Lena the Mermaid Lady is creating on my right upper arm. But I'm not squirming because of pain.

"That tickles," I say.

"Good," says Lena, who's using black temporary ink to free-hand outline and shade in the art left by the tattoo stamp. "Temporary tattoos were made for fun."

"Queens was . . . different this time," I answer Kira. "Ben was different."

"The butterfly is looking amazing!" Amita trills. She's absolutely giddy now that she's on the other side of her piercing ordeal. "Lena, you mermaid goddess. And it's so cool this'll last for two weeks!"

Lena's laugh sounds like a deflating tire, which tickles me as much as the ink application. My shoulder bounces slightly as I chuckle.

"Uh, uh, uh—easy there," says Lena, pausing the inking until I'm motionless again.

"And . . . done!"

I thank Lena for capturing my butterfly spirit. But then I re-thank her with much more oomph after I walk to the mirror for the full view of the tattoo. It looks so vivid and I love it.

After we pay and leave, we go to a nearby restaurant for lunch and are seated right away.

I anchor my elbows on the red gingham tablecloth and ask, "Ladies, how about we claim our promancipation?"

"Promancipation." Amita falls back in her chair, as if the impact of the word blew her there. "I like the sound of that."

"Tell us more," Kira says, leaning forward.

"Ever since Saturday, when I temporarily dipped out on my family, I've been thinking about how prom is an American rite of passage. It could be our last stand—that defining high school moment when we finally declare our independence. Every teen hero in history I've researched has had that defining moment. Why can't this one be ours?"

Amita and Kira both nod, letting the rhythm of the thought move them. A server stops by with a warm greeting and takes our lunch order.

Once we've ordered, Kira raises her glass of water. "Here's to our promancipation."

I beam and clink my glass to hers.

"To our promancipation," echoes Amita with a proud tap of her glass to ours.

"Kira, I'm gonna throw something out there," I say once we've all taken a pact-sealing sip. "And I want you to be totally honest with me."

It's fascinating to witness Kira's mouth shift so far to one side of her face. "Anytime someone leads with something like that,

I know I'd better listen extra carefully for the words *not* being said," she says without bringing her mouth back to center.

"A-ha, your momma didn't raise no fool," I tease. "So hear me out. I know you mentioned that if given an opportunity, you would like a prom date."

"Uh-huh."

"Well, with my arranged date and all the logistics around it, I figure, it would be messier to ask Ben *not* to show up. In order for me to get away with it, he'd still have to spend the weekend in Jersey, come up with a lie to tell his family, and blah-blah-blah."

Kira anchors an elbow on the table. "So, you're thinking Ben could be my date?"

Amita watches us, waiting for my reply.

I'm so grateful Kira's making this easy. "Yes." I pause when Kira looks off in the distance. "Only if you're open to that, of course."

"Maybe Ben can be like my cousin Krish, a good ally in all this," offers Amita.

"Ben *is* unexpectedly cool," I tell Kira. "And I'm not just saying that because I want you to agree to this plan. I would never tell him or my mom this, but I genuinely dig being around him. Let me see if I can find him online," I add, already searching Instagram. *Bingo.* "That's him."

The girls lean over my phone screen. "He doesn't have too many followers," says Kira, sounding a little wary.

"Unlike Gavin," I say. "Oooh, but these pics are amazing."

I scroll down a few rows. His profile is loaded with vibrant photos of different types of artwork—vivid folk paintings, detailed wood carvings, intricate ironworks. Each photo is taken from an interesting angle. And what's extra cool is they're all set in tropical locations, both urban and natural.

"He took all these in Haiti," Amita says, impressed, as she notes the location tags. "Simone, you recognize any of these places?"

"I've never actually been," I admit, excitement and pride stirring in my chest. "But these make me want to go even more now."

"Hmmm . . . let me do a quick profile read here," says Amita. She reaches out a finger and scrolls down until she comes across a photo of Ben himself. He's on a train staring into the lens and smiling broadly. Earnestly. "He's pretty cute," Amita says. "And it's not even a selfie. What'd he do, get someone on the subway to take his pic?"

"Apparently," says Kira.

"What do you think?" I ask Kira.

"Can I see his non-selfie up close?" she asks. I pass the phone to her. I know she doesn't have a social media account, but I don't realize how clumsy she is with the interface. That is, until she double-taps when she wants to zoom into Ben's face.

"Oh, um, I think I just hearted the pic," Kira confesses.

"Oh man, you just *liked* it?" I ask.

She holds up the phone. Sure enough, the heart below Ben's picture is shaded in red.

"Oh no! Unlike it, quick!" I say in a mini panic.

"How do I do that? I'm afraid to touch it."

"Calm down. I'll do it." Amita takes my phone, but it goes dark. Locked screen.

But then, in an eye blink, an alert dings.

Amita's eyebrows jerk. "Too late," she says. "Ben's requesting to follow you."

Huh? For a second I want to scream out a long "Nooo!" But that would be stereotypically dramatic for a Haitian. So, I scream it internally as I reopen the app.

"I'm so sorry, Simone," says a grimacing Kira.

I can't answer her because my internal "Nooo!" is still trailing.

"Just follow him back, and then unfollow him later," says Amita like it's no big deal. I think about unfollowing this advice, but I click, and the status between me and Ben changes. I place the phone back on my lap and try to forget what's just happened.

The familiar ding we hear next tells me all I need to know.

Kira leans forward and reads the alert on my screen anyway. "Ben sent you a direct message."

"What'd he write?" asks Amita.

"You can't ignore it. He knows you're online," Kira points out.

I sigh and read the message to them with the least emotion possible. "Hi."

"You have to respond," Kira tells me.

I send back the waving hand emoji, because maybe there's a chance he'll interpret it as "Bye, Felicia."

Amita leans in to read Ben's response. "If there's anything you need me to get or prep, DM anytime," she says, giving Ben a little voice.

"In no way does he sound like that." I belly laugh.

I give him the "Bye, Felicia" wave again.

He sends it back.

I glance at Kira. She winces. "Can you unfollow him now?" she asks.

"Not yet. It would be too obvious," instructs Amita.

If it weren't for the Kira prom plan, *too obvious* would be exactly what I'd be going for. Kira nods wordlessly but looks from the screen to my face.

"See what I mean about him?" I ask, proud of the awesome package deal I'm offering her. "And I'm sure you guys will get along. But you have time to think it over. If you want, you're welcome to meet him when I see him for a swatch drop-off next weekend."

"I'll be out of town visiting family," Kira says. "But I've made my decision."

Aw, man. I knew I shouldn't have sprung this on her so suddenly.

"I'll go with him," Kira announces.

She will? "You will?" I exclaim.

"Yup. I trust your judgment," she says. "Your mama didn't raise no fool."

I smile, reach for her hand, and give it a happy squeeze. "Well, then I have one last question. What color do you want to wear for prom?"

Amita offers to come with me when I meet up with Ben at Penn Station this weekend. I'll hand off a more muted African wax cloth that could match both my dress and whatever dress Kira chooses to wear. And while Amita and I are there, we'll determine if Ben's an ally . . . or a mole.

Our food arrives then and we dig in, feeling in charge of our destinies and relishing our metamorphoses into social butterflies.

CHAPTER ELEVEN

"First you escape into Queens and now you got a tattoo?" Gabby shouts over the rattling of the bus. We're on our way home the next day, at the part of the route where we cross into the town of Millwall like we're on a runaway train. As we careen down the steep hill that Millwall Cliffs residents hope keeps out the riffraff, nearly every seat and window squeaks. This hill accelerates our exit from the snooty town and hampers our entrance into it. Makes perfect sense.

My blue cardigan is tied around my waist and the butterfly is visible just below my short sleeves. Gabby's staring at it, stunned.

"It'll only last a couple of weeks," I shout back to her. Our seats in the rear of the bus are facing each other. "I went with some friends to get it done."

"Which friends?" Gabby's eyebrows slant.

"Amita and Kira."

Gabby points her chin at me. "What are you guys up to? I figured you were onto something yesterday."

I shrug one shoulder. "We just realized we have more in common than we thought, so . . ." I keep playing with my phone, though the laughing emoji I texted to the HomeGirls' chat has already been sent. I guess I'm bracing for Gabby to clown me about my switched-up style, switched-up friends, switched-up everything.

But all Gabby comes back with is "Oh."

A familiar laugh catches my attention. That would be Yadi Gonzalez, a junior at our school. She's in another verbal spar with her friend Ella Hopkins. They're talking about a businessman who chased down our bus, and it sounds like they're just getting warmed up.

"Wow—he barely broke a sweat," Ella shouts like she's impressed. "Yadi, you need to get the name of the deodorant he uses."

A St. Clare freshman and two sophomores bust out laughing.

"How 'bout I just get that info from you. Ain't that your daddy?" Yadi snaps back, pretending to sound seriously concerned. Everyone *oohs* and *whoas*.

Ever since freshman year, I've laughed my butt off on the 60 bus. It makes our forty-five-minute ride from the cities of Essex County into the affluent suburbs of Millwall Cliffs—and back—fly by. Catching the bus daily, you come across some pretty interesting characters. The amateur comedians can't help but point them out.

The aroma of bacon and eggs suddenly grabs my full

attention. But before I can spot where it's coming from, Ella cracks the case.

"Shannon, you brought enough for all of us?" she calls out to the freshman sitting a few rows ahead of us.

"Why are you always in my business?" Shannon says between chews of her bacon, egg, and cheese on a roll. But as bold as she seems, Shannon makes sure her comeback is delivered sweetly, in a singsong voice. She knows the deal. A freshman can't show up an upperclassman—especially not on the bus.

"For a second, I thought I was smelling plantains," says Gabby, rubbing her stomach.

Yadi points at Gabby. "I know, right?"

"Not even close," retorts Ella. "That must be that Haitian-Dominican same-island twinning kicking in," she adds, looking from Yadi to Gabby.

"It doesn't work that way." Yadi rolls her eyes.

"Who says?" Ella knows her argument is weak, but she can't help but tease. "Ain't that like being from the same womb or something?"

"Yeah, if the twins come out speaking two different languages," says Gabby.

As silly as the conversation is, it's entertaining.

But I'm pretty sure Yadi and Ella don't carry on like this when the bus enters the hood. Downtown, Yadi (rocking a blue polyester uniform skirt and bench-pressing a bulky backpack) would be labeled a nerd, but up here she becomes that bold city chick.

"What about you?" I ask, turning back to Gabby. Now that I've stopped hiding from her opinions about my recent moves, I get to enjoy her company. I missed that face. "What have you been up to? Bonding with your teammates?"

Gabby shrugs. "They're cool and all, but a lot of them are only about the game, and I want to talk about more than just basketball. But ohmygod, I got your text—did you really try and flee the scene in Queens? My mom didn't want to admit it, but I think she approves." Gabby makes a pouty face. "Aw, my little innocent girl is growing up!"

Not the "innocent girl" thing again. And oh no, have I become a hot topic among the Haitian aunties? It would crush Mummy if she knew her name was ringing out for the wrong reasons.

"At the end of the day, there was no harm done," I say. "It wasn't as dramatic as you may—"

"Good," Gabby cuts me off. "Now all you need to focus on is asking Gavin to the prom."

"Yeah, but how can I be so sure Gavin will say yes when I ask him?" Now I'm having serious doubts. Yes, Gavin and I finally introduced ourselves, and even flirted. But we'll have to skip our first date, second date, and first kiss, and go straight to the promposal?

"Not a problem," Gabby says all casual. "Things can turn in a snap."

I grin. It's something Gabby's mom always says, punctuated with a sharp snap like Gabby just did.

Maybe a magical gust of wind carries Gabby's words straight

into the heavens because when we reach the Millwall Prep stop, Gavin boards the bus.

I don't see him at first because I'm texting the HomeGirls. Kira's just discovered there's another day off coming up on the school calendar and suggests that we make that our NYC hangout day (number 5 on the Playlist).

Agreed, I type. *NYC Day has got to be epic. I have some ideas.*

But just as I send the message, a balled-up silver gum wrapper lands on my phone. Gabby, seated across from me, threw it to get my attention. I look up to see the corners of her lips stretch like elastic bands as she soundlessly yet clearly mouths *GAV-IN*.

It's too late to pat down my wayward twists or cute-ify the way I'm sitting because Gavin is already making his way down the aisle. The ride is bumpy but Gavin keeps his balance—as well as that smooth dip in his step.

I busy myself with my phone. Amita's response text has just come through. It's a cute pic of us HomeGirls at the tattoo parlor.

"Tib-a-doe, koomo yay?" Gavin greets me like an old friend. "Hey, Gabby!"

"*Okay.*" Gabby is all kinds of impressed. "Extra points for the *Kreyòl*."

"Nice!" I offer as casually as possible, despite the fact that my heartbeat is sped up like a Miami bass song. Somehow, even my glasses are fogging up. This brotha is bending science right before my eyes.

Instead of grabbing the empty seat next to me, Gavin remains standing and holds on to the pole. His other hand is stuffed in the hip pocket of his khaki uniform pants. His body is like a curtain blocking Gabby out of view. I can't see around him, but I don't mind. It's nice not having Gabby communicate her every thought with those crazy expressions of hers. Her face can be as rubbery as her chewing gum. This way, I have the freedom to do things at my own pace.

"Ti-ba-doe, Ti-bounce-doe. Now you see her; now you don't," Gavin says. "You left the party early last week."

He noticed.

"I had to be somewhere," I answer almost under my breath.

Translation: Slipping out of the backyard unnoticed was my way of avoiding having to explain my early departure.

"Whoa—that sounds stealth. You the governor's daughter or something?"

"If I tell you, the secret service would only erase your memory," I reply after a beat.

"It's cool." Gavin smirks. His lips are so smooth and shiny, I can practically see my reflection in them. "I like a girl with a little mystery to her."

You like her enough to go to the prom with her? I could seal this deal right now if I had the guts. But instead I just shrug playfully, like I have a secret I don't intend to share.

Gavin bends over to peer out the window behind me. His face is just a few inches from mine, and the tiny stadium audience in my stomach starts doing the wave. As he leans in, I can smell his minty breath. It's easy now to notice the gleam on his shiny black eyebrows and the curl of his lashes. I don't mean to stare at him, but there is nowhere else to look. Still, I find a safe focal point—the swinging bold "G" medallion on the end of the gold chain, which is dangling away from his body.

"Have you ever been to Karl Pool?" Gavin breaks into my thoughts.

The bus passes by the popular billiards and arcade spot every afternoon, and there are always kids hanging outside, but I've never been.

"Oh, everybody knows Karl Pool." I answer around his question, hoping he'll buy it.

"Cool. Are you and Gabby free to get in a Karl Pool game with me and my boy Rashod today?" he asks me.

"Oh, really?" I say, exposing full-blown goofiness without meaning to.

Gavin chuckles and nods his head. *You seem so . . . young*, I remember him saying.

"Yes, really," he says. "Or are you on some secret assignment right now?"

"I think we can swing by for a bit," I say, which is true because my parents don't usually get home until two hours from now.

"Cool." His smile is sending me. "We're gonna get off here, but we'll meet you there in like ten minutes."

When Gabby and I jump off the bus a few stops later, we're a block away from Karl Pool, but we take a detour stroll because we have a lot to excitedly rehash.

"He's clearly interested in you," she says. "Or he wouldn't have asked you to hang out."

"Maybe or maybe not," I counter, doubt seeping in. "I barely know him, but I'm pretty much running with this as if he'll be my prom date. Am I crazy?"

"You know as much about him as you do about the guy your parents want you to take," she says. "Familiarity isn't an issue."

"What about his age?"

"Girl, you're lucky he's a junior." Gabby is clearly amused. "I hear the senior boys at Millwall Prep are messy."

I stop in my tracks and face her. "How do you know these things?"

Gabby cackles, strutting ahead of me for dramatic effect, swaying her hips hard left and hard right. Her uniform skirt swings like a church bell at high noon. I do not chuckle along with her . . . at first.

"Okay," I continue when I catch up to her. "But he could have a girlfriend and just want to hang as friends."

"Rashod said Gavin's not seeing anyone," answers Gabby.

"What? You mean you talked to his boy about me?" My words echo out and the German shepherd at the bus stop goes from napping to yapping.

"Slow your roll." Gabby holds up her hands to calm me down. "At the house party, Rashod and I spoke casually about a lot of boring things—not just about y'all two."

I don't protest when she puts her arm around my shoulders to get me walking again. Embarrassing as she can be, she's only trying to help. If I weren't such a punk, she wouldn't have to step in and work her magic for me.

Gabby knows the score. I'll never forget the time in the fifth grade that my cousin had my back when I needed her the most. We'd entered the school talent show together, and seconds before showtime, I got cold feet. I'd realized too late that signing up for the show was not just about wearing the sparkly dance outfit—I'd actually have to perform. So Gabby jumped into action and said, "I'm your girl." Watching her take center stage solo gave me the courage to join her moments later.

Now is no different. I don't know what I'll say to Gavin. But like I did back on that talent show stage, I figure I'll jump in once Gabby warms up the crowd. Just watching her interact with new people calms my nerves. Her straight refusal to bow down to anybody, and her dismissal of any formality or protocol, makes everyone a lot less intimidating. I've been trained to be so obedient. Gabby's approach to new experiences diminishes what I find so scary.

We're just a block away from Karl Pool now, so Gabby starts hyping me up. It's like she senses the hesitation creeping up my spine. Gum popping, neck swaying, Jersey accent raging, she gives it to me straight. "Here's what you do—go in there and act like you know," she says.

"Right about now, I don't *know* anything."

"Stop telling on yourself, okay? Nobody needs to know you've never had a boyfriend."

"Are you kidding me? People can read it on my face."

"Let them." She sucks her teeth. "They're not fluent in *Simone*, so they'll question whether they read you right. Just follow my lead."

Yup, it's humbling to let someone younger take point. But if I'm going to do prom on my terms, this is part of the plan.

The smell of fries assaults us the moment we arrive at Karl Pool. And when I say *assault*, I place an emphasis on *salt*. Karl Pool's fries must be legendary for being over seasoned. Hanging outside Karl Pool is a giant shingle of a fry with eyeballs, holding a pool stick in its hands.

"Mmm, now I need fries," Gabby says.

We walk inside and it takes a second for our eyes to adjust in the dim lighting. The majority of the crowd gathered around the classic pinball machines is Millwall High boys.

I scan the crowd and spot Gavin leaning on a pool table, like an eight ball in the corner pocket of my heart. He must have gone home first and changed out of his uniform. He's wearing a gray graphic sweatshirt and dark jeans with a shiny "G" belt buckle.

Gavin's friend notices us—or rather, he notices Gabby. He walks over carrying a tray of crumpled napkins, a few stray fries, and empty food cartons. "Hey, Gabby."

"Hey, wassup—" Gabby looks at his chest as if she's hoping to see a nametag.

"Rashod," he reminds her.

The musk of discarded leftovers alerts us that we're standing right next to the trash. Rashod clears the tray and stacks it without losing focus on Gabby.

"Hey, Rashod," Gabby autocorrects with an apologetic smile. "You remember Simone. You guys about to hit the arcade?"

"Naw, we're about to set up for another game here," he says, pointing his thumb back to where Gavin is chatting with another guy. "Glad you can chill with us."

Gavin looks our way. His eyes are shining, like he's still laughing at a joke someone made a minute ago. "Step on up and be our next victims!" he shouts to us.

I look behind me because I'm not clear who he's talking to. He seems so laid back and familiar with us.

Gabby practically nudges me with her protruding eyeballs, like, *Say something.*

"Victims?" I chuckle nervously.

Couldn't there have been a joke in there? Is there a reason why I'm suddenly humorless? Maybe it's because Gavin is checking me out, and I know there's not much cuteness I can pull when I'm wearing my school uniform and knee socks.

But Gabby makes up with attitude what we lack in fashion. "You guys playing for keeps?" Gabby asks both Gavin and Rashod. "Because I'm a shark at pool."

What does Gabby know about pool? The girl barely knows how to swim in a pool. But Gabby fakes it till she makes it until the power of illusion turns everyone into a believer.

"How about you, Simone?" Gavin flashes a smile when we

reach his pool table. "If you're both good, you can't double up on the same team."

"Oh," I say. "Is that your way of asking me to be on your team?"

Nice, Gabby's eyes tell me.

"You can say that," says Gavin, handing me a pool stick. "I'm glad you guys came by."

I smile and instantly imagine Gavin and me in a cheesy romantic scene. What's the likelihood he'll lean in close behind me, his arms enveloping my waist, his cheek next to mine, as he points my pool stick and teaches me how to strike with precision?

"Go ahead—break!" Rashod calls out.

That's literally my cue. I'm pointing the chalky end of the stick to the white ball when something on my arm startles me, and I jerk. It's too late to control my reaction the moment I notice it's not a bug on my arm, but my badass tattoo, and I give the ball such a clumsy *thwack* it careens right off the pool table and rolls away.

"Now *that's* when you know you've got too much power," I fake-brag and then dramatically release my cue stick like a mic drop.

My joke lands, and everyone busts out laughing *with* me and not *at* me. I can't stop smiling.

"Wait, hold up," says Rashod. "You're even better than you claimed to be."

"Too late! She's all mine!" says Gavin, and I melt a little inside.

I strike a pose with the white ball I've retrieved and then take an elaborate bow.

My cousin's eyes sparkle with approval as she steps up to the table.

"Clickety-clow!" Gabby shouts, in case any of us miss the balls she sends to the pockets.

Amused, Gavin starts adopting her sound effects, with a twist. "Clackety clack-a-lack!" he flows like he's rapping over beats.

They go back and forth with this, and I can't stop cracking up every time. Rashod keeps watching Gabby with wide-eyed wonder.

"Hey, you guys ever check out LowKey?" Gavin asks me.

I have no idea what he's talking about. *A rapper's latest album?*

"LowKey?" I echo, because—stalling.

He nods. "I've seen a few Academy girls there before."

Oh, it's a place, not some album.

"That's because Academy girls know what's up," I say, wondering if I sound like I'm trying too hard.

"Let me know the next time you both are going. I'll meet y'all there." Gavin beams.

"Uh, okay," I say, wincing inside.

Gavin and I don't get the chance to have any more side chats. Once we start playing, he and Gabby mostly banter, and I'm grateful I don't have to answer any more questions about my non-existent social life.

With the game-ending *thwack*, Gabby raps, "All I do is win win win," into her cue stick, swinging her ponytail of ropey braids. "And dats on dat! I run this pool house. They might as well add braids to that fry mascot outside."

132

"Yeah, I'll give you that, Queen," says Gavin. "Respect."

"Well, we better head out," I say. "Bus."

Leave it to me to be watching the clock like a harried hare in Alice's Wonderland. But I'd rather not get home after my parents and have to explain where I've been.

I'm glad Gabby backs me up. "Yeah. It's been real, dudes."

That it has. My awkwardness aside, it was a good time. "I'm so glad we came," I say to Gabby as we walk out.

On the bus ride home, I replay the highlights in my mind. Gavin is not only fly, but fun! And it's clear he wants to hang out again. At LowKey, which—I learn from both Gabby and Google—is a local club that throws weekly teen nights.

But *would* Gavin want to go to the prom with me? Is it too soon to ask?

Sometimes thinking about teen heroes in history gives me pause. I need to take a moment to shake my head and let the "wow" marinate. Later that night, I'm on my bed with my laptop, rewriting a page of my senior thesis, and thinking about how mighty a spirit fifteen-year-old Claudette Colvin had to have to sit firm when she was ordered to move to the back of the bus in 1955. And this was nine months before Rosa Parks's arrest. Man.

The Playlist is opening my eyes to different ways of taking action, and I want my paper to reflect that. I've started including heroic innovations, too. It's a win for teens that Louis Braille was fifteen when he developed the tactile reading system for the sight-impaired that's named after him.

I'm so invested in my rewrite that when my phone dings, I don't jump to check it. Only after I've finished a few minutes later do I see that Gavin has messaged me!

He's sent a video. Before I view it, I double-check that this is not a group chat. He's sent this only to me. I bounce on my knees and break the sound barrier with my squeal but then quickly calm down in case Gavin somehow has an open video chat connection with me or something. I hit play and see him showing me his new car—well, "new" to him. It looks like some retro race car, complete with the fat tires and spoiler. But if anyone can pull off driving a shiny metallic-blue whip, it's Gavin.

Forget the car, I'm just amazed Gavin's hollered at me! His dimples and juicy lips are on full display in his selfie video. And he's in the best mood. He never says my name or anything in the video. It looks like a clip he could've sent out to different people.

"What's all that squealing about?" Anne walks in wearing a Rutgers sweatshirt and carrying a huge bowl of popcorn. She eyes the Word doc on my laptop screen. "You forgot about our *Creepside* date?"

Anne and I are currently obsessing over this old paranormal show, and we have a weekly ritual watching it together. I love these nights with her.

"Look at this!" I tell her, replaying Gavin's message. I know she won't approve of Gavin because she's not into smooth guys, but I'm too excited to keep this to myself.

"Oh boy, he looks like a real winner," she says with an eye roll. "What are you going to say to him?"

What *am* I going to say? THIS is my chance.

I type my response. Anne looks over my shoulder.

It looks like my perfect prom ride.

"Simone Thibodeaux, you are not going to send that!" Anne shrieks, but she is amused.

Send.

We both squeal, for two different reasons.

"This is juicier than *Creepside*," says Anne.

And then, nothing. Motionless, we stare at the screen until it fades to black. Oh. Hmmm. Darn. Cringe doesn't even begin to describe what I'm feeling. Anne rubs my back and I drop my head to her shoulder.

And then, the sweet sound of an alert rings out.

It's from Gavin.

Bet. We're all set for prom then.

Bet! I message back.

Anne spits out her popcorn in disbelief. My head spinning like the ceiling fan, I free-fall backward onto my bed. I cradle my cell on my chest and let out another squeal.

CHAPTER TWELVE

I bet Gavin's ankles are never ashy.

I don't think I'll get the chance to sneak a peek at them on the bus this morning, now that he has a car. But maybe his ride's not ready for the road yet and he'll hop on and take the seat next to me. It's empty for now as I scroll through #promstyles on social media.

I'm on the early, early bus so I can meet up with my HomeGirls for breakfast before school. Gabby probably isn't even awake yet; I texted her my news about Gavin, so she understands I'd be on the early bus because I was too hype to sleep in.

There has never been a dreamier dream prom date than Gavin Stackhouse. I can get lost in his hypnotic brown eyes. Imagining him in a tux leaves me weak. I wonder if he'd go classically dapper or next-level cool. Either way, he'd be flexin' on every other dude there.

I focus back on my phone and the promstyles hashtag. Our

Catholic school calendar is on a slightly different schedule than most schools. That means our prom happens in early May instead of late May. A lot of the prom fashion posts on social media are last year's. A few new ones are trickling in, but it's nowhere near as many as there will be in a few weeks.

Scroll. Scroll. Double-tap!

I rest my elbows on my knees, looking through the feed until my thumb aches. But I can't get enough of two-piece styles, classic long gowns, African prints . . .

We're talking heart palpitations every time I see a unique take on a trend, a standout silhouette, or the perfect color. Some designs have me stomping my feet and shaking my head, church-auntie style. It's that deep.

And when I do a #prommakeup search? I have to take deep breaths. Fierceness overload. I can't handle it.

Double-tap!

Judging from the most recent posts, girls are on beast mode. They are showing up and showing out, sometimes even making bold political statements with their gowns. One girl silk-screened photos of Black Lives Matter iconography on her skirt. And the guys? They are putting some *respeck* on the old-school tux. Swaggy accessories, like hats and walking sticks; cropped pants; and my favorite—bare ankles with moisturized skin, poppin'.

Double-tap!

Yup, I just know Gavin's ankles are shiny glowy.

The next hashtag I search is #promposal. Lately, people have been trying to one-up one another. Last week, a guy pulled up in front of our school and released a flock of doves. The girl, named Dove, said yes. Then some dude posted a rap he wrote and the video went Jersey-viral. Now "You & Me @ Prom" is a local hit.

I'm here for all of it—the wild promposals, the flamboyant self-expression, the pregame photo shoots. It's prom out loud.

Double-tap! Double-tap! DOUBLE-TAP!

I live vicariously through those moments, and there's some satisfaction in that. It lets me experience the rush and avoid the spectacle. Not everyone wants all eyes on them. So no, I don't mind that I didn't receive an elaborate promposal. I flipped it on society and asked Gavin myself because I didn't want to miss my opportunity.

"Lark Avenue!" the bus driver calls out.

I gasp out loud. I missed my stop!

I leap from my seat and dash out the back door of the bus.

Double crap!

My books shuffle in my shoulder bag as I jog across the street. Amita and Kira are waiting at the dollar bagel truck, Elevenies, that's parked in the paved lot a block away from school. They've nabbed one of the few garden tables set up there.

The shiny silver Airstream truck is a welcome sight. With its BLACK LIVES MATTER bumper sticker right next to a rainbow flag, we're in good company.

As soon as I sit down, Kira slides over the toasted bagel she and Amita ordered for me. I'm breathless and winded, but the aroma of chai latte and melted cream cheese makes me want to dance in my seat.

"Thank you," I say. "Sorry I'm late!"

Amita is studying me with a smirk. "See, Kira? The girl secures the prom date bag, then divas out on us."

"Girl." I play the role, cocking my head to one side to flip imaginary hair. "But I'll sit with you ladies, just this once."

"Uh-huh," says Amita, eyes flashing facetiously. "Just what I expected."

"But seriously, doing this together makes everything better," I say, taking a bite of my bagel. "I feel like this is a win for all of us."

"To the HomeGirls' victory," says Kira with her cup of coffee raised. There's some muscle in her usually thin voice. "One step closer to promancipation."

"Okay, so your texts left out the details." Amita leans in. The sunlight poking through the clouds highlights the light brown strands in her dark hair. "Tell us exactly how you asked him."

I take out my phone and read them the exchange verbatim so there's no mystery to how I nabbed my dream date.

"But . . ." I trail off.

"But what?" Amita asks.

"But we haven't spoken since." I put my phone down, nervously rubbing my fingers across the screen. I know it was only last night, but I can't help feeling antsy. It's all so unexpected—especially so soon after the arranged prom meeting. Gabby was right. Everything had turned in a snap.

"Oh. Are you *sure* he knows he's taking you?" Amita asks like a spokeswoman for the elephant in the room.

"Well, yeah—"

"I don't hear any doubt in his response," says Kira, adding a reassuring shrug.

But I'm stuck wondering if Amita has a point.

"What's going on with *you*?" I ask them, to distract myself. "Any progress on the Playlist?"

"Well," starts Amita. "I finally spoke to my cousin Krish about prom, and he says he'll have my back and step aside so I can go with Pritpal."

"How do you know he won't snitch?" I ask her, fascinated.

"He hates the idea of being my date as much as I do." She grimaces.

"Then let's toast to that!" I say. We fake-ding our coffee cups again.

"What about you, Kira?" I ask, eager to hear how excited she is about going with Ben.

"Um, let's see," she starts. "I got the cutest new collar for my dog. It's reversible sequins!"

Amita's eyes widen and meet mine. "Oh. Th-that's— interesting."

"I didn't know you had a dog," I finally say. "Lemme see a pic!"

140

We can't help but gush at the sight of Kira's corgi. The little guy really does look cute in his flashy new collar.

"Here's to finding that adorably sparkly accessory," Amita says without a hint of irony, her cup in the air again. "May we all have similar luck finding the right look for prom."

"Ding!" we all say.

Kira crinkles her nose and smirks with gratitude. "Thanks."

"My personal styling assistance for prom is still available." I point to myself and stick out my tongue like a rockstar. Then I swipe through my phone. "Check out the dress I'm going to have made. It's actually more of an outfit."

"I never figured you'd have styling skills." Amita leans in with faux concern, gesturing to my uniform. "I mean, you wear the same outfit every weekday."

Kira covers her mouth laughing. I play-act like I'm offended, and suck in my checks to make a popping sound with my mouth like Gabby does when she's about to clap back. "Well, I'm a fashion beast when it comes to prom, *thankyouverymuch*."

My girls gasp when I show them the long flowy skirt with the long split and midriff-baring top.

"Gorgeous. I can see you serving this look, yes," says Amita.

"Beautiful, Simone," breathes Kira. "So is this the pattern you'll be bringing to your meetup with Ben in Penn Station?"

"No, I have a couple of options, depending on what color you want to wear to the prom, Kira."

She sits up, loving the special attention of my stylist services. I smile at her and pull out the samples.

There's a food festival—*feastival?*—going on in midtown NYC today. It's the only reason Anne agreed to chaperone me to the city. She and her boyfriend are off sampling the street fare until Amita and I are ready to catch the train back home.

At the moment, Amita and I can't get around the throng of foodies in Penn Station that seems to share a collective mind. We cut left, and suddenly, we're swallowed up by a group that's hotly debating superfruits. We cut right and practically trip over *feastival-*goers in food truck tees. Still, this Saturday-morning crowd is way lighter than what we'd find here on a weekday.

Ben and I had agreed to meet between the pharmacy and the souvenir shop. That distinct smell of the subway wafting up the corridor takes me back to childhood, when Mummy used to shuttle us to the Flatbush neighborhood of Brooklyn every weekend to visit my grandma and aunties.

Amita has no such ties to New York City. Homegirl is straight-up Jersey, born and raised. I'm a Jersey girl with Brooklyn beginnings, which lands me in a sliver on a Venn diagram. Sort of like being a Haitian American who's never been to Haiti.

Fact: The only reason Amita was able to come today is because her parents are at a wedding. Yet everything about the bored, unimpressed look on her face would suggest that she comes here all the time. For added credibility, she sizes up the overzealous foodies like *they* are the New York newbies. I try not to chuckle when she starts chipping her old fingernail polish as we wait.

"Is that him?" Amita asks, proving she's been paying attention on the low. I whip around and wish I hadn't, because Ben is approaching. He's got his commuter face on. Despite his relaxed gait, his dark eyebrows hood his watchful glances.

"I remember him from that non-selfie he posted," says Amita, proud of herself.

And then she echoes the thought I'm ignoring in my mind.

"He's so much cuter in person."

I'm glad I don't have the chance to respond before Ben's within earshot. But it's not like he'd hear us over the Penn Station din.

"Simone, hey."

"Hey, Ben, hey . . . Ben," I parrot like I have no sense. I'm thrown off by his presence. This would've been so much easier over text. Keyboard courage and all.

"Hi, I'm Ben." He shakes Amita's hand like a sane person, and I'm immediately in a face-palm mood.

"Oh, sorry. Amita's a friend from school."

Ben nods his head. "Cool. Cool."

"How was your—"

"I just—"

We both stop speaking and laugh bashfully.

"Now let's just say what we were about to say, but at the same time." He grins. "You up for it?"

"Of course!" I laugh. "Three, two, one!"

"How was your ride in?"

"I just spoke to your mom!"

"Wait, what?" I ask Ben, my lightheartedness now weighed down by distrust. "You and my mom speak?"

"Lately, yeah."

Mole. *Mole!* I look behind me to shoot Amita an "Abort Mission" glare, but she's looking down at her phone. Suddenly, I'm seething. But I need to focus and pull that cord behind that emergency glass. I don't need this.

"Um, I didn't get a chance to tell you, but I already have a prom date, a guy who's coming with me to the prom," I blurt.

Ben blinks a few times and his bottom lip goes taut for a millisecond, but he doesn't show any emotion. "I understand what you mean by prom date."

"Of course," I stumble awkwardly. And suddenly, Amita's at my side.

"Ben, you are so perceptive. Yes, Simone is being redundant, but that's only because she's sorry to let you down. You've come all this way, and we really appreciate it," Amita goes on. "But I'm sure you understand the challenges of bucking tradition and doing things your own way."

Ben nods and then turns to look at me. It's like he's trying to figure me out. My, how the tables have turned.

Good, give him a taste of his own medicine.

"So, no swatch. No prom to attend," says Amita. She's right.

Something about her voice and the way she frames things makes it sound less harsh than it really is. It's like a gift. Or a spell.

I finally look up at Ben, and just like that day on Linden Boulevard, he looks no worse for wear.

"Are you sure you know what you're doing?" Ben asks me.

"What's that supposed to mean?"

"Nothing. It's just . . . I want you to know I get it."

"I have a date," I say very clearly.

"Okay," Ben concedes.

He looks like he's offered more of an opinion than he normally cares to. I can tell he's someone who opts for the diplomatic route to stay above the fray. He seems a bit disappointed in himself.

"So, if there's nothing else, I better get going. Nice to meet you, Amita. Take care, Simone."

When he heads down the corridor in the opposite direction, I feel his absence right away.

"You okay?" Amita asks me. "You look like you're second-guessing yourself."

I sneak a peek at the back of Ben's head and I check out his relaxed strides toward the uptown trains.

"Simone?" Amita sounds worried.

"Hold up, just one minute!"

I take off after Ben. *I want you to know, I get it!* Something in the way he said that felt like a hunch, like maybe I can trust him. If I'm right, this could help Kira.

"Ben, wait up!"

He looks back, surprised to see me running up to him.

"Thanks for waiting," I say, making things up as I go. I don't want him to know I'm outsourcing him to someone else just yet. "Listen, I was thrown off when you mentioned my mom. I just prefer she not know what we discuss."

"I respect that. I know it's not my place to divulge anything, and I wouldn't without your permission."

I exhale. "Thank you. Look, it doesn't make any sense that we shouldn't go to the prom together. But you know how I feel about this setup. It's not my wish. So, how do you feel about going as, like, a group of friends?"

Ben shrugs and the corner of his mouth comes down a little. "Okay. That works."

"Great." I'm so relieved, I hold up a hand for a high five. He looks at it for a long second, and then weakly slaps my palm. As I hand him the colorful swatch I hope will match what Kira ends up choosing, I continue rambling. "I can introduce you to my other friends. If you're free to hang out in Jersey one night in the next few weeks?"

He nods slowly. "Okay, I'll let you know."

"Good. Do that."

He glances at the swatch now in his hands. It's a hodgepodge of colors and patterns that work as well as I hope this thrown-together plan does.

CHAPTER THIRTEEN

I spent the rest of the weekend thinking about my awkward meeting with Ben and hoping to hear from Gavin.

On Monday, I still haven't heard from Gavin, and I didn't see him on the bus this morning. So I'm thinking the time is right to get back in touch with him.

At lunch, I send him a boomerang of the old wall clock in the senior lounge with the caption: *Countdown to prom. Can't wait!*

I start cringing as soon as I hit *send*. What if he's moved on? It feels like it's been a lifetime since we spoke. A new car can do wild things to a person. Especially to a fly, in-demand guy like Gavin.

Rewatching the video of the clock while keeping track of every second that tick-tocks by without hearing back from Gavin is admittedly ironic.

I crack open my laptop to tweak my senior thesis when a few girls walk in, talking about the same ol', same ol'.

Lately, there are two hot topics in the senior room: prom and college. It's all anyone talks about. The college chatter usually has to do with being away from home for the first time, finding that cool roommate, or just generally being excited about attending.

Yeah, but no.

I'm not interested in discussing college, because I don't feel like much will be changing for me. Rutgers's Newark campus is so close to my neighborhood, it'll be like going to the thirteenth grade.

So, hands down, I'd rather talk about prom. Talk to me about prom fashion any day, and I'm with it. I'm happy to answer styling questions and offer tips. Judging on how I flow on casual days, my classmates trust me with fashion advice, and I'm happy to offer it.

"Got your prom dress yet?" Kenzie asks me. Whew. I relax a little in my chair.

"Not yet," I say. "But a seamstress I know says she only needs two weeks to whip it up."

"A bespoke dress—how fancy." Kenzie grins. "Can't wait to see it. I think I'll have my prom date decide with me. I like his style."

"Oh, who are you going to the prom with?"

"A guy who plays basketball for Millwall High," she says with a nose crinkle.

My breathing switches off autopilot, which throws the inhale-exhale completely off rhythm.

Is *this* why Gavin hasn't messaged me back? Is he trying to avoid me because he's going to the prom with someone else? I don't want to hear any more details, so I pretend like I'm sending a text.

I look down at my screen and Gavin's written back. When did that happen?

Three minutes ago. Good. Now I won't look so desperate responding right away.

When is your prom? Gavin asked.

I message back the day, date, and time, so there's no doubt.

Then I wait, in doubt.

By the time the final bell rings for the day and I'm getting my stuff out of my locker, there are no replies from Gavin.

"How are you getting to my game?" Gabby calls out to me as she rushes down the hallway, already in her basketball gear.

"Amita is driving us," I say. Now that Amita's boyfriend has started filming his TV show, Amita happily has a few parental alibi openings already on the calendar that she can fill.

"Cool. See you there!" Gabby catches up to her teammates.

The game is in our town, so heading home after the game should be easy. Gabby's mom was going to try to come with my mom, but I'm not sure if they'll make it.

"Simone, come with me." Kira grabs my arm as I shut my locker. "There's someone outside I think you should see."

It's sunny and warm out, so there's more after-school activity than normal. Thumping music from someone's car stereo fills the street, which would be normal in my neighborhood, but not here.

"It's Gavin," says Kira, pointing to the driver of the music-banging car.

My belly does a happy flop when I spot him. He's at the wheel of his new-to-him car. The blond kid from the house party is next to him.

"What's that guy doing?" I ask Kira.

We watch the blond guy's slinky limbs climb out the passenger window—the *window*, not the door. We cringe. The move, however, seems to delight Kenzie, my beaming classmate from the senior lounge. She throws her arms around him in greeting. Then they both get into her parked car and drive off into the sunset. Oh. So *that's* her Millwall Prep basketball player date.

Gavin sees me and waves me over. I almost turn around to make sure he's gesturing to me. I cross the street to greet him as confidently as possible. He smiles. I smile. This is good.

"Congratulations on your new ride," I shout over the music.

"I love it, but it keeps acting up. I'm gonna take it to the shop."

I nod as if to say cool, but without meaning to, I nod to the rhythm of the blaring rap song.

"How're you doing?" he asks.

"I'm awesome," I say like a dork.

Not cool.

Recovery, Simone.

"Where're you headed?" I ask.

"What?"

"Where are you going?" I shout. Why won't he turn down the music?

The cop car on after-school security duty pulls up behind Gavin and throws on the emergency lights.

"Turn down the music," booms a policeman's voice out of the cruiser blowhorn.

Everyone within a three-block radius turns and stares at us. Gavin complies, but sticks his middle fingers up so that only I can see. I chuckle nervously.

"Hey, want a ride to the game?" Gavin asks.

I look at Kira. "I'll meet you and Amita there?"

Kira looks uneasy but nods at me.

"Sure," I shout to Gavin.

"Let's get out of here." He rolls his eyes in the direction of the cop car.

So, we're going to prom together, right? I mentally rehearse on my way to the passenger side of the car. Before I even buckle my seat belt, Gavin tears down the street. Once he turns the corner, he turns up the volume again. There goes my chance for bringing up prom in a casual way.

Oh, but who cares! I'm with Gavin. He's driving me around and we are hanging out in a small, enclosed space. I sneak a peek at his profile. Wow.

The music is so loud, we don't get to chat. But I feel like we're vibing wordlessly. Not five minutes later, we pull up to a barbershop and his friend Rashod walks up to the car.

"Do you mind hopping in the back?" Gavin asks me. "I would ask him, but his legs are too long."

"N-n-yes, that's totally fine," I say, poorly masking that I'm thrown off guard. "Sure."

But then, the most unexpected thing happens. Gavin runs around to my side to open the car door for me. I take his hand and practically float to a stand. *Swoon.*

"Thank you," I manage to say.

"Any time," he replies.

He holds on to my hand a heart-thudding moment longer than expected before he helps me into the back seat.

I don't remember anything else about the ride because I'm replaying that moment in my head over and over. When we get to the game, Gavin and Rashod go to join their teammates. I thank him and head over to join the HomeGirls.

Kira hugs me when I reach them.

"I was about to call you. Are you all right?" Kira holds my shoulders. "You look more than all right."

I sigh dreamily.

"Girl, what the—?" Amita hollers, leaping up from her spot on the bleachers. "Did we even have 'Go for a joyride with a boy' on the Playlist?"

The game starts, but I'm not paying much attention. I steal glances at Gavin so often, I could swear the dude throwing T-shirts into the crowd just shouted "Stalker" in my direction.

"Check it out, the guy from the hip-hop group Stalker is

behind us," says Amita, pulling out her phone to take a pic of him.

Whew. I need to get my paranoia in check.

I glance out at the court. The team is playing respectably, but they're behind by a handful of points. I wish Gabby could get out there; we're halfway through the first quarter and she's sitting on the sidelines, as dry as a whistle, while her teammates are already soaking from the intense game. A couple of times, she turns and gives me a nod and a smile. My being here matters to her, and I'm glad I came. It looks like my aunt and my mom couldn't make it.

I also love how much support the Millwall Prep guys show the whole girls team. Gabby's keeping busy chatting with some of the boys now, including Gavin.

Most of the time, Gavin is intensely focused on the game and listens in on all the huddles to hear what Gabby's coach has to say. Other times, he's checking his phone. He doesn't glance back to look my way.

I think about Mummy's childhood memory of playing a different kind of game in school. She and her classmate would stare at a certain part of the teacher's face—usually the ears or the nose—until the teacher scratched that area of intense focus. Mummy and her friends would muffle their laughter every time. It's accepted as fact that energy can almost materialize and take the form of a nearly real lightweight feather tickling the tip of a person's nose.

So, here goes. I take a deep breath and zero in on Gavin's chin. Someone blocks my view of him just then.

Ugh.

I'm relieved when Gabby's coach finally puts her in the game. I can now be happily focused on something other than a boy. *Shameful*, I scold myself . . . and then glance in his direction one last time. But he's focused on the court again.

Before the game-ending whistle, I get to see Gabby make some saves and rebound a few times. She looks good out there—a team player with control and style. St. Clare loses, but I can tell Gabby is still proud of how she played.

After the game, Gabby stops over to say hey to me, Amita, and Kira. She's not as sweaty as the other players, but she's got a work-out glow that's beaming from the inside out. We congratulate her and chat awhile until Gavin joins us.

"You good for getting home?" Amita asks me and Gabby.

"Yes, we live close to here," I say. "We're good."

Amita and Kira leave together, and it occurs to me that they're the ones who are a distance from home for a change.

"You looked good out there," Gavin tells Gabby. The stadium lights catch the gleam in his smile.

"Thank you," Gabby says. "And thanks for coming out."

The crowd gets a bit rowdy as folks chat and stomp on bleachers, but the three of us are suddenly enveloped in a bubble of silence. Uh-oh. Is this going to get awkward?

"It was fun," says Gabby with the save.

"Did you see that call the ref made, though?" Gavin asks.

"Oh yeah, yeah—that . . . call!" I say, just because I think I should. But full disclosure: I wouldn't have noticed if the ref made an actual call from one of those red British phone booths. Basketball isn't a sport I follow, so I'm pretty clueless about the rules.

"What did you think?" Gavin asks me.

My mouth dries up and I part my lips, willing the right answer to come out. "Uh, he was way, way . . ."

"Way on the money." Gabby for the save *again*! "That ref must see in slow motion, because I know I would have had to watch the replay before I called that move *for sure*."

"Word," Gavin chuckles. He's clearly not used to her emphatic hand gesturing and punctuated speechifying.

"For sure," I echo, and wonder if I'm playing this off okay.

Another silent beat. Gabby signals to me by raising her eyebrows a few times.

What? What is that code for?

Should I take a step toward Gavin? Okay, I just did! I'm standing a few inches from him. I can, like, smell the Gatorade on his breath. Fruit punch, is it?

He looks at me and then back at Gabby.

He must hear my thoughts because he asks if we want to get some drinks from the concession stand.

Gavin and I look like Gabby's security detail, flanking her on either side as we walk. The way we're positioned does help keep her personal space clear when people approach with daps and congrats.

Maybe I should bring up prom again? I wonder. But things are going so smoothly between us. If he's going to roll up to the prom with me, I can't be tense in his presence all night. No, I won't push the issue. For now.

"So, you a basketball fan?" he asks me.

"I catch a few games now and then." I take a sip of the water bottle he just got me. Gabby's opted for a candy bar, which she's devouring like there's no tomorrow. But like a pro, she catches the wayward crumbs that fall on her shirt and pops them back into her mouth.

"Ever go out to the Garden or catch the Brooklyn Nets?" Gavin asks.

"You kidding me? The Garden is like my second home," some strange girl in control of my tongue says. I can't stop her.

"Really? Where do you usually sit?"

"Um, where?"

"You were telling me how the mezzanine seats aren't as bad as they seem." Gabby uses her tongue to clean her cute buck teeth everyone loves. "Remember? You said you can see more than if you were courtside, and that's why it's a sweet spot."

I point at her and then back at Gavin, who's swirling the blue liquid in his new bottle of Gatorade.

"Nice, nice," says Gavin approvingly. "The Garden is a must-see, but you gotta admit, the Nets' home court is bomb."

Gabby spots someone she knows and turns away to give them dap. Thankfully, Gavin's comment is a softball. I got this.

"Even though it happened before I can remember, I still wish the Nets were New Jersey's own team." That part is true. "I feel like one of those old-timer Ebbets Field fans, getting all sentimental about what we lost with that move."

Gavin cocks his head to one side. "Where's Ebbets Field?"

"Oh, it's where the old baseball team the Brooklyn Dodgers used to play." I still remember when Papi showed me the plaque that designates where the field once stood. Gavin still looks perplexed. "Brooklyn Dodgers is the team Jackie Robinson integrated," I woman-splain.

No look of recognition is registering on his pretty face. You'd think I'd stop torturing him, but I take one more swing.

"In fact, Citi Field, where the Mets play, was built to look like Ebbets Field."

"Oh, sorry, I don't do baseball." Gavin smiles that dimpled smile I know well from the bus. "Finding a Black baseball fan is sorta like finding a Black Republican."

I'm not sure if he's joking or if he really thinks that to be true. One thing is clear: I won't be giving him the Etsy baseball cuff links I purchased on a whim in January, thinking they'd be the perfect accessory for whoever would be my prom date. Maybe I can still return them.

Gabby's finished gabbing with the people nearby. And it's just in time, because the mood has kinda gone a bit wonky after the Ebbets Field talk. *Really, Simone? You bring up baseball history that no one but stale old baseball heads would appreciate? Sigh.*

"What are y'all about to get into now?" Gavin asks.

"Now?" There's no need to bore the guy with the sleepy details of my home life. Coming to this game is the best it gets for my day, but he doesn't need to know that.

"Uh, I'm—"

"We're gonna go ahead home," says Gabby, making it sound cool. "It's getting late."

"All right, then. Congrats again on a strong game."

My own game is anything but strong. In fact, as far as I can tell, I got zero game.

CHAPTER FOURTEEN

I can sense the off mood in the house the minute my key clicks and the front door swings open. I wonder if my parents somehow *know* I was driving around unchaperoned with a boy earlier today.

Down the hall, my parents are speaking to each other in hushed tones. I can tell they're arguing. By the time I get to the kitchen and put my bag down on the table, Mummy turns to me.

She sounds frazzled. "Don't put that there. I just cleaned up! You know better than that." She shakes her head. "Your grandmother's coming over. She'll be here in an hour."

That explains it.

My mom always tenses up when her mother is around. Heck—we all tense up. Don't get me wrong, my Grandmère Rachelle is a lovely woman. Even at her golden age, the woman *serves* style and grace. Once, my mom and I took her shopping at the mall, and a customer mistook Grandmère for a mannequin. Her charm-school posture and poise keep folks doing double takes.

But she also has a way of getting under your skin. Every move you make, she scrutinizes and grades like an Olympic judge. No one is safe—especially not my mother, whom my grandmother holds to crazy high standards.

It's nothing like the relationship Mummy had with Grandmère's older sister, Ma Tante. Ma Tante, an easygoing, accepting, supportive soul, got along famously with Mummy, Anne, and me. She was like a second grandma, considering Papi's mother died before I was born. I think Grandmère was kinda jealous of the bond we had with Ma Tante, but Grandmère wouldn't dare admit it. Ma Tante sadly passed away three years ago, and I miss her every day.

Jumping out of the way as Mummy zigzags through the kitchen, I realize that with Grandmère in the house, all the women in the family will be lining up at our doorstep like Idris Elba is serving tea in here.

Great. What could possibly be next?

I head upstairs to my room and plop down on my bed to rest before Grandmère arrives. My phone dings, and I slide my thumb across the screen to read the text from Gabby.

Your mom knows about Gavin driving you to my game.

If my mouth wasn't so suddenly dry, I would gulp. *Damn.* I panic. Who told her? Was it Ben? No, it couldn't have been Ben. He knows about Gavin, but he wouldn't know about Gavin driving me anywhere.

It had to be Gabby's mom.

The Haitian network operates on 5G. It usually happens this

way—no matter the location of the incident in question, the info eventually funnels through Tante Adeline in Brooklyn. Next, Tante Adeline will pass this baton of information over to one of her sisters, who will then hand it to another sister, until it is finally delivered to my mom in what I like to call the "bell lap."

Did your mom tell her? I text.

My mom didn't make the game.

I'm confused. Is Gabby playing with me? My cousin has been known to switch to family spy mode when the balance of power shifts in her favor, but that was when she was younger. Could she be capable of that now? If she was, was this a confession?

My bedroom door swings open with a brute force. Startled, I look up, half expecting to see a SWAT team, but it's my mom. Her angry eyes are bulging and her lips are tightened. "I know all about what happened after school today, *mumzelle*," she snarls at me.

"Mummy, I . . ." I hold up my hands like a suspect under arrest.

"I don't want to hear it. I'll deal with you later." She doesn't bother stepping into my room, but she lowers her voice. "For now, get on downstairs to greet your grandmother. She's here."

My first instinct is to take deep cover like that other time Grandmère's visit coincided with a hot-seat moment. I was twelve, and one of the last girls in the seventh grade to get her period. A classmate of mine had started her cycle in the fifth grade, so hot topics like PMS, cramps, and maxi pads with wings had started to become old news. But at home, my first "visitor" from Red Bank was a huge deal.

161

It was bad enough having to tell my mom that it had finally come. But did she have to broadcast the news to my *dad* and everyone who came over to visit that summer day?

All I wanted to do was go outside and play catch with my neighbor, but my mom and Grandmère were bent on schooling me about how I was a "woman" now and that I should be aware that things had drastically changed.

They'd cornered me in the kitchen with their singsong voices and wagging forefingers to warn me about the unfathomable. ("You do know this means your body can now make babies.") I hadn't even kissed a boy yet! I thought I was safe when I retreated into the privacy of my room. But once I heard murmuring voices and approaching footsteps outside my bedroom door, I decided to hide. I stopped, dropped, and squirmed on my belly like a cobra until I settled into a cozy, covert spot underneath my twin bed. From there I watched two pairs of feet walk into my room—one was sporting leopard-print, strappy heels and the other pair was parked in red house slippers.

One of the high-society shoes balanced on one heel, twisting the pointy tip into my baby blue rug (I was in my Hello Kitty phase). "She's probably out running around with them dirty boys next door," I heard Grandmère say.

The slippers, aka Mummy, reacted by burrowing her toes deeper as if to withstand the sheer force of Grandmère's judgment-laden words. "The neighbors' boys are really very smart, well-mannered kids. I let Simone play ball with them."

She spoke quickly, just pausing for a quick breath before finishing. "But I plan to buy her lessons at the batting cage so she doesn't have to keep running over there."

If it weren't for that plane flying low overhead on its way to or from nearby Newark Airport, they would've heard me gasp. Batting cage sessions? Dopeness!

"I wouldn't encourage her." Grandmère sniffed, dissatisfied. "She's got to learn how to carry herself differently now. She'll soon grow that hourglass figure we Benoirs women are known for. She can't be hanging around them boys. They're gonna notice her blossoming and want to do other things than talk sports with her."

With that, the heels marched out, leading the slippers into the hallway, their voices trailing off, plotting my fate.

Did I have a say? Maybe I should've blown my cover to defend myself. But instead, I just lay under the bed feeling like a puppet on the run from its puppeteer's strings.

My mother eventually took her mother's advice and I had to stop hanging with my boy neighbors. They moved away soon after, and we didn't stay in touch. Mummy always let Grandmère veer her off course. Sometimes, I think she's as much of a puppet as I am.

Now I begrudgingly trail Mummy downstairs. She gives me the quick rundown: Grandmère is slated to undergo surgery—a procedure for her congestive heart failure—at the hospital where Mummy works. Grandmère will be driving into the city with my parents tomorrow morning for a presurgery physical. Once she has the surgery, she'll likely be hospitalized for observation for a few days. I nod in understanding but keep quiet.

By the time we get to the living room, Grandmère has already rearranged the throw pillows.

"Aren't you going to kiss your grandmother hello?" I feel my mom's bony finger nervously poke me in the small of my back.

I'm on a twenty-second delay because I am still replaying my mother's scowl in my mind. What kind of trouble have I gotten myself into? And where is Anne? She always seems to get off the hook. She should be here greeting Grandmère along with me. I etch a smile into my face and direct my puckered lips to Grandmère's cheek. They land just below her mountain-high cheekbone.

"Hello, ma chérie," Grandmère affectionately sings out. Her soothing voice calms my nerves. It has been months since I've seen my grandmother. I hadn't realized how much I've missed her until this moment. She tugs my hand to guide me to a spot next to her on the sofa. I exhale as I lean back on the smartly rearranged cushions.

"How's my jolie Simone? Eh?" she coos. "Simone, chérie, look how much weight you've gained."

"Aw, thank you, Grandmère." I know she's just saying this to make me feel good. I love that I've grown up in a Black neighborhood alive with that African American, African, and Caribbean appreciation of thicker bodies. But even though my struggle to keep meat on my bones means skinny is my default, my family always reminds me to feel good about my body, whatever shape it's in.

Grandmère's wide smile falters when her eyes scan my hair. She prefers when I wear it bone straight.

"Does Inez still run her salon on Main Street?" Grandmère asks my mother.

"Simone's been accepted into Rutgers, Manman." My mother ignores Grandmère's meddling question outright. I am surprised by her boldness. Being upset over the incident after school seems to fuel her. I feel strangely proud of her.

"I don't doubt that," Grandmère beams. "All of us Benoirs women are blessed with brains and beauty. Just look at that Gabrielle."

It didn't take long for Grandmère to jump to her favorite topic—Gabby. Apparently, my grandmother got in a visit with Gabby and her mom, Tante Nadine, before coming over here.

"How are you feeling, Grandmère?" I ask her and then immediately regret it.

"Just because they tell me I need surgery doesn't mean I'm not well," she corrects me.

"Of course not, Manman," replies Mummy.

I tease my grandmother about aging backward, and watch her respond with a playful chuckle. It's actually fun catching up with her.

But then our doorbell rings, and someone I don't recognize crashes our little party. She's a Haitian woman around Grandmère's age. I take it she lives in this neighborhood because everyone is weirdly calling her *Voisine*, the French word for neighbor. After I welcome her with a kiss on the cheek, Mummy sends me to the kitchen for extra coffee.

There's a touch of youthful excitement in Grandmère's voice as she and Voisine reminisce about old times. It's clear they go way back. In fact, I learn they used to be voisines in Port-au-Prince.

"Merci, chérie," Voisine says, accepting the coffee I'm serving. She's regarding me with a glint in her brown eyes. "Is this the lovely lady my little nephew will be taking to the prom?"

I nearly spill a steaming blend of Café Bustelo on her floral-print dress.

Mummy is quick to answer: "Yes, this is."

"You know, Ben was at my house when I left," Voisine says. "Let me see if he can come over and give his greetings."

"What a gentleman," Grandmère gushes preemptively.

I didn't realize Siri spoke Creole, because right after Voisine barks out a command, her phone is ringing on speaker.

"Hello?" Ben answers.

"Ben, mon cher," she bellows like a showman in a top hat. For sure, her performance captures Grandmère and Mummy's full attention. Their gazes are fixed on her. "I'm going to send you an address near the house, and I'd like you to walk over to meet the sweet girl you'll be taking to the prom. We'll wait for you."

I'm frozen in place, but my mind is reeling. In the span of a half second, I've already thought up (and shot down) my three emergency options. I can't seem to come up with something better than have a tantrum (I'll only embarrass myself), flee the scene (I live here), or pretend to be sick (nothing short of barfing would convince this crowd).

"Sorry, I would love to but I'm already on my way back to Queens," Ben says mercifully.

"Oh-oh." Voisine sounds like she and Ben have disappointed her captivated audience. But then she rallies. "I should've known—a busy, hardworking young man like you." Voisine sits broad as if fanning out invisible peacock feathers. "Okay, then say a few words to your future date."

"I—I'm not sure she'd want to speak to me," I hear Ben say, and I cringe.

"Nonsense. She's standing right here with her hand out, asking me to pass her the phone."

Voisine gives me that Haitian double-eye wink that signals one is joking around.

"Here you go, darling."

I don't even want to touch the phone while Ben's voice is piping through. It's as if it'll be too intimate an act.

When I don't make a move, Voisine takes my hand and places her phone in my palm.

Ben's voice comes through the speaker. "How are you, Simone?"

"Good," I say through clenched teeth.

Grandmère's eyebrows knit together and Mummy's lower lip

droops. In the silence that follows, I can hear their subliminal urgings for me to remember my Benoirs bloodline.

You'd think Ben would take the hint and hang up. Instead, he tries to make conversation. "I was at Rutgers for a class tonight."

"Oh . . ." My voice trails off.

Voisine's spoon clatters onto her saucer and Mummy glares at me, flames practically coming from her eyes.

I need to fix this, fast. "*Ohhh*, that's why you were in town," I add.

Voisine's shoulders relax, so Grandmère's and Mummy's do, too.

"Yes. Are *you* taking any college courses?" Ben is not fooled by my save and is clearly challenging me.

"I did that last semester." I almost add, "So eat it!"

"At Rutgers?" he asks smugly.

If our back-and-forth were a tennis volley, Ben scores a point with the question he's just lobbed. I have no choice but to concede.

"I chose an online course." Because Mummy would freak if I were roaming a college campus unattended.

"That's cool, too," he says, playing the role of the humble victor. "Good for you." Crowds love a classy winner. Plus, Haitians have been interested in tennis long before Naomi Osaka. Voisine and Grandmère look like they are on the verge of applauding. And I feel like I can really summon up that barf now.

Mummy, on the other hand, has clearly heard enough. Once

I've passed the phone back to Voisine, Mummy asks me to drive her to the supermarket. The way she manages to con me into doing something she's too afraid to do—which is drive—I'll always admire.

But I know Mummy only wants to get me alone so she can lecture me. If only I'd predicted this, I would've come up with an excuse to stay on the phone longer with Ben.

Behind the wheel, I look like the one with the upper hand. Mummy might as well be a tween who's just graduated to the front seat. It feels good. We ride in silence, walk into the store, and grab a cart. It's in the Latin American foods aisle next to a colorful array of dried beans that she starts in on me.

"I almost passed out in shock when Rose told me about you and some boy." She whispers the word *boy*. A few cart-pushing old ladies do double takes as they stroll past us. This causes my mom to put her lecture on hold until we are in the next aisle.

"You want to let some, some . . . *boy* sully your reputation so close to graduation? Is that what you want?" she asks over some eighties tune's emo sax solo. On the shelf behind Mummy, the Quaker Oats dude's Mona Lisa smile contrasts with her scowl.

"Mummy, it's not what you think. The police were just—"

My mother holds on to the cart to keep from blasting off into the stratosphere. "*Police?* What police?"

Oh no.

169

How could I be so sloppy? The eyewitness must have been at the game, not at my school pickup.

"Marie Simone Lamercie Thibodeaux," she fumes. "What. Police."

"His music was loud and the police asked him to lower the volume. That's all. They didn't even come out of their squad car."

Constance looks defeated, but after seventeen-plus years, I know better than to believe that. "Woy, Jésus qui est l'Éternel."

"The whole encounter lasted no more than one minute," I tell her, placing a calming hand on her arm. "And then it was over."

"Even still, it's not that boy being passed around in gossip, it's you."

"I thought we're not supposed to care what people think?"

"Don't get fresh! We didn't scrape together all that tuition money for you to be jumping into strange boys' cars. Who even is this *vagabond* boy?"

I tread carefully. I obviously can't say he's my prom date. If I say he's a friend, she'll start wailing over me going boy crazy.

"All he did was drop me off at the game," I say instead. "It wasn't anything more than that."

"What happened to your two flat feet? They don't carry you where you need to go anymore?"

Did she have go there about me lacking a foot arch? That's petty. I ignore her and pick up some oatmeal and try to keep us moving along.

"You better hope your grandmother doesn't hear krik about

this. She didn't come to this country and work long hours in housekeeping just to have a granddaughter tell the family what the donkey told the rooster on a Sunday morning! And while she was busy cleaning hotel rooms of rich Manhattan savages, do you think she had dreams of her future grandchildren tearing through the streets with *garcons*?" she spits out. "Non, *mumzelle*!"

When we reach the check out, Mummy is still fuming. In the midst of her eye-bulging, lip-pouting, eyebrow-furrowing fit, I pick up and flip through a celebrity gossip magazine. Sure, it's rude, but it's the clearest message that fifteen minutes of "how could you?" is long enough. I feel drained.

I just want the nice lady at the register to ring us up quickly so that we can leave.

But in the next second, Mummy snatches the magazine from my hands. I'm shocked. And apparently the cashier is, too, because the constant beeping that signals each scanned item has stopped.

I look up to see the cashier staring at us like there should be a Haitian reality TV crew shadowing us. That's when I realize that I have a piece of torn page between my fingers. The cashier is clearly embarrassed for me, so she speeds through the rest of our food.

"We'll buy the magazine," my mom huffs.

We drive home in silence and I don't object to that. I can sense my mom knows she may have overreacted.

When we get back, Grandmère clocks in at one thousand demands per hour from the comfort of our living room recliner. But I welcome it. With every fetched glass of water ("The bus ride dried out my throat"), throw blanket ("It's chilly in here"), tissue ("Now my nose is leaking"), and black ink pen ("Blue ink is not respectable") comes my cue to flee the deep disappointment in Mummy's eyes.

One thing my mother cannot resist is the opportunity to save face. When Anne gets home from classes, Mummy pulls Anne into the conversation and focuses all talk on Anne's recent acceptance into medical school.

"Too bad she can't already be a doctor today," says Grandmère, always willing to ignore the silver lining in any gray cloud. "I wouldn't have to see the inside of that doctor's office tomorrow."

"It'll all go well," says Mummy. "I'll be with you."

Grandmère is probably as agreeable a patient as she is a houseguest. Her biannual visit to her Manhattan specialist has come around quicker than expected. I see now it's more of an emergency visit. That's why my dad didn't pick her up from her Brooklyn home on a weekend morning, per usual. And it's why the house wasn't already stocked with all of Grandmère's faves.

Papi dutifully answers Mummy's plea to entertain us all with his butterfinger piano playing. At this point, Mummy would cut off the lights and perform hand puppet theater to keep Grandmère from asking me about my day at school.

As I lay down to sleep hours later, I think about the Playlist again. I realize that Grandmère's visit may be a very good thing. Mummy will be too preoccupied and wary of making a scene to come after me again, at least for a while.

I grab my phone and send a quick text to the HomeGirls' chat.

Morning meeting tomorrow? Time to discuss going clubbin' and our epic NYC trip.

I send it out with a GIF from the classic movie *Ferris Bueller's Day Off*. Kira and Amita text back confirmations almost right away. They seem just as eager to rock out the rest of this Playlist. Just wait until they hear my ideas.

A sly smile stretches the corners of my lips, and I finally drift off to sleep.

CHAPTER FIFTEEN

It's beginning to feel a lot like *spriiing*. I'll spare the good patrons of Elevensies my slipper dance, but I'm feeling good. I order my bagel and coffee and grab a table to wait for my HomeGirls.

Earlier this morning, Grandmère even took my side when Mummy questioned me about my group project meet ups with Amita and Kira for the next several foreseeable Tuesday nights. I was merely, nay, innocently informing her that I'd be clubbing—er, studying into the evening hours soon, and Grandmère took offense at all the pushback I was getting.

"My grandchild is enriching her life yet you accuse her of stealing from yours?" she snapped, staring her eldest child down.

Mummy started backpedaling. "No, Manman, if you knew what sort of things Simone has been—

"Pitit se richès malere," interrupted my feisty Grandmère, quoting the Haitian proverb that means *Children are the wealth of the poor.* "Did you forget that?"

She obviously did, Grams. Let her know! is what I said internally. But outwardly, I rubbed the supple brown skin on Grandmère's arm, tutting softly to keep her from getting too upset.

Mummy pursed her thin lips and cut her eyes at me before heading out to the car to meet Papi. Grandmère followed. They were all heading into the city to see Grandmère's doctor.

"See you later," I called out to them. And just like that, I am cleared to go clubbing on a future Teen Night Tuesday, whenever we decide.

Now a smattering of people are starting to arrive at the Elevensies seating area. I'm on such a high, I don't even overthink the text I send to Gavin.

I hope your car had a good check-up and is running great.

After a few beats, a reply bubble blows up and then pops with a *ding*!

She's running much better. Still in love. Happy together.

Omgomg! Is his romantic wording a hint? My heart thuds and I imagine my tattoo butterfly is flapping its wings right now, too. I wish the HomeGirls were here to vet what I write back, but I don't want to wait too long.

Think prom, Simone, I tell myself. *Bring up prom.*

Aw, you two. ❤ *It sounds like she'll be ready for prom.*

The moment I hit *send,* I wish I could edit the text to be a question, not a statement. It would be nice to hear more confirmation from Gavin about us going to prom. He doesn't reply, though this is around the time he'd be getting off the bus. Maybe he's distracted.

Ding! My breath catches. Apparently, Gavin's not too distracted after all. His reply is a short bubble.

Cool.

Not sure how to interpret that, but yay! Gavin and I are definitely text-compatible.

I spot Amita and Kira on line at the truck and I throw up jazz hands to summon them over to my garden table once they've ordered.

"Someone's in a good mood," says Amita as she takes a seat.

"Let's just say, my priority is making sure *you* ladies are cleared for hitting the club on a Tuesday night because my grandma's got me covered."

"You lucky duck," says Kira.

"That means you guys can visit my house last."

"Okay, then let's start with my house and get it over with." Amita fiddles with the metal stand holding her table order number. "Are you guys still able to come tomorrow after school?"

Kira and I nod.

"We need to go over some ground rules," Amita says.

"Should we arrive together?" Kira asks.

"No, did you read my email?" Oops. I didn't check my email last night or this morning. "I need you two to not act like friends—my friends, or each other's friends," Amita explains.

"Ugh. Does your mom believe friends can be bad influences, too?" I ask.

"Not exactly, but anything or anyone I'm on board with my parents are usually suspicious of."

I get that. "Okay, so we arrive separately, and we are not—repeat, *not* friends," I say.

"Just to be clear—when you two come over to my house, you can arrive together and you can be friends," says Kira.

"We'll get to your rules when we hit your house," I say. "Right now, I need to get into character because Amita got me shook about getting this right."

"My parents aren't going to seem frightening, but you should be very, very scared." Amita's eyes bulge a bit and she holds the stare. I swallow hard, until I see her break character with a giggle.

"Aw, you were just joking?" I ask, confused. "So, it's okay if we're friends?"

Amita stops chuckling and creeps us out with a cold hard stare in the next millisecond.

"That part was no joke."

"O-kay," I say. Kira and I look across the table at each other like we're not sure what's real and what's fake. "Under . . . stood."

The server comes over then with bagels and coffees for Amita and Kira. As soon as we're alone again, Kira rubs her hands together.

"What's our general progress on the Playlist been like?" she asks.

"Let's see," I say, pulling out the list for us all to revisit. Our eyes go wide like we're looking at something sacred. "So far, house party, check. Switched-up style, check. Clubbing, soon-to-be-check." *Tell parents about deepest-desire hope to go away for college,* I say in my heart. *Check.*

"And finally going on another date, soon-to-be-check for me," says Amita. She puts one hand on her hip and strikes a pose. "Pritpal will have some time off from filming, so we're going to hang out next week."

I wonder if getting a ride with Gavin, or our time at Karl Pool, counts as a date. Maybe?

"Before we get to planning our city hangout day," says Amita. "Kira and I were discussing using your stylist services for our prom dress hunt—"

"Yes!" I answer before she finishes. "When?"

"Well." Kira picks up the list and taps on number three: *Cut class*. "If we make up an excuse to leave school early one day, we can all go shopping together."

Amita opens up the notes app on her phone and starts tapping her screen. "If we're going to cut class, let's make it on a Wednesday. It's our easiest afternoon—study period, PE . . ."

"That works," I say. I like that we'll wrap up the house visits within a week or so. That'll be one less thing to worry about as we move on to our Tuesday nights out and more.

"And the following Friday is when we have that day off for teachers' conferences," Kira reminds us.

"NYC Day on Friday," Amita confirms, thumbs tapping. "Busy week."

"And then all we need to figure out is which Tuesday we goin' clubbin'," I say, seat-dancing like I'm already there.

Amita holds up a finger. "First things first. Start thinking of your excuses to skip out of school early."

"Whatever we come up with, facing our teachers will be easier than facing our parents," says Kira.

I'm not so sure. A mix of fear and excitement churns in my gut. "Oooh, we are so *bad*!" I say, looking around to make sure we're not being heard.

"Don't worry," grins Amita. "This is the good type of bad. Now what's your idea for our city hangout day?" she asks.

"I'm working on something fun," I say, unsure whether I should spill since I'm still looking into things. "How about if I share that with y'all closer to the day?"

Kira gives me a thumbs-up because her mouth is full.

Meeting accomplished. The best jams on the HomeGirl Playlist are about to turn up, and I can't wait.

The next day after school, as planned, I head to Amita's house alone. I take a different bus than usual from school and walk the four long blocks from the bus stop.

Amita lives in one of those subdivisions that from the sky must look like cornrows carved into the Earth's scalp. I know from Amita's Instagram that she's got a bean-shaped, in-ground pool in her backyard. I make the distinction that it's an in-ground, because if you have a pool in my neighborhood, chances are it's aboveground. My cousins had one put in two summers ago, and somehow today, it's just a drained oversized birdbath.

I can't see anyone in Amita's neighborhood letting their pool fall behind on maintenance. Every lawn is mowed to perfection and there's not a single person hanging out on the inviting front porches. What's the point of having such nice outdoor furniture setups if you're just gonna let it look like a showroom?

When I get to Amita's house, I ring the doorbell, and I don't hear anything. I expected elaborate door chimes, but nothing.

Maybe their doorbell is in disrepair or something. Or maybe I need to press it harder. Tatie Nadine had a bell like that once. You had to press it until you felt a tiny zap on your finger as it hit the faulty wire inside. That's when you knew the bell actually worked.

A few moments after my second ring, a man swings open the door with a mild scowl on his face.

"Yes, may I help you?"

"Hello, I'm Simone Thibodeaux from St. Clare Academy, here to work on a group project with Amita, please."

The lines on the man's face relax a smidge. "Ah, Amita mentioned this. Please, come in."

The inside looks like the lobby of a luxury hotel. Marble tiles line the floor, a mesmerizing chandelier hangs overhead, and the furniture is heavy and ornate.

"Amita must be an asset in your group, yes?" Okay, this is obviously her dad. I follow him into the foyer.

"Yes, she's very . . . dedicated." That's the best I can come up with. I can tell it's going to be hard to lie my way through a conversation with Amita's dad. He has a way of examining you as you speak. Maybe he can pick up on subtle cues that reveal someone is lying.

"Did you find your way easily from the bus stop?" he asks.

How does he know—?

"I can tell you've been walking because you're slightly winded," he responds to the question in my mind. "We'll get you a glass of water in a moment."

"Oh, yes, I found it just fine—thank you."

There are elaborately framed photos of Amita and her three brothers everywhere. They seem like they've been taken in a professional studio. There's Amita in what looks like a New Year's Eve party outfit. Amita's middle school graduation photo. Amita in a soccer uniform in an action shot, mid-game.

"These are great photos of your daughter," I say, keeping my references to Amita as formal and distant as possible. I hope she's satisfied with this. Where is she anyway? I don't know how long I can keep fooling someone who processes information like Sherlock Holmes.

"Yes, my wife is particular about photography, and thankfully, our Amita is very photogenic." He picks up a photo of Amita that looks like a headshot for a casting agency.

"That's nice," I say, with an eye on the large grandfather clock in the next room. And whoa, is that a life-sized Trojan horse statue in there?

There's a clippity-clop sound, but the horse isn't moving. *Thank the Lord!* But if it's not the horse, then who or what—

"Ah, speak of the angel, here comes my wife now."

Amita's mom is dressed exquisitely. She's in house slippers that look and sound like heels.

"Hello," she says.

"Lovely to meet you, Mrs. Nadar." I shake her hand and almost curtsy.

"The pleasure's mine. I travel so often for work, I don't often get to meet Amita's friends. Please, sit."

Uh-oh.

We take a seat on fancy furniture in a room that would surely be off-limits in Grandmère's apartment. My grandmother would cordon this whole area off like it was an active crime scene.

"Uh, I wish I could call Amita a friend. I'm afraid I've let high school zip by without much of a social life," I say with an exaggerated sigh, repeating Amita's prescribed reply almost word for word. It's not until the statement is out of my mouth that I realize how tragic I sound. I slump my shoulders forward to match the vibe.

"That's too bad." Amita's mother looks to her husband, a question in her eyebrows. "You must have noticed Amita's group of friends at school? Or maybe she likes sticking close to just one friend? Is that the third study member?"

Are they asking *me* about their own daughter? I search their eyes and get the confirmation I suspected. They have no clue about

Amita's moves. The CIA should definitely look into recruiting this girl as an operative. She's stealth.

"I—uh, wish I knew," I answer. I don't know whether to feel sorry for the Nadars or impressed with Amita.

"Oh," her mother says, deflated. "Tell me, will you be carving out enough of a social life to attend prom before you graduate?"

Amita's a lot like her mom. The woman wastes no time getting right to the heart of the matter.

"Um, actually I will."

Mrs. Nadar grins like a schoolkid. "Do you have a date yet?"

Here's my chance to impress them with my child-of-immigrants factoid. "Yes, a nice boy my parents have set me up with."

"Oh." There's that look of recognition in Mrs. Nadar's eyes that screams *She's one of us.* "As a happy surprise, my husband and I had a boy in mind for Amita, but we couldn't locate his contact information. He's someone Amita met at a wedding. At the time, we thought they made a lovely pair."

Where's that water Mr. Nadar promised me? My throat is getting more parched by the second. Unless dehydrating folks is their interrogation method . . .

"Oh yes, that talented singer," remembers Mr. Nadar. "He hopped off the stage to sing to our Amita and everything."

I cough and bite my tongue to stop myself from shouting out Pritpal's name like some game show contestant. Do they notice my struggle and are pretending not to, or are they that oblivious?

"We met him at your colleague's wedding, no?" Mr. Nadar asks his wife.

"It was at your cousin Sonu's wedding."

"No, cousin Sonu got married in Bermuda."

"Her honeymoon was in Bermuda, not her wedding."

Mr. Nadar chuckles sheepishly. "Too many weddings have blurred together."

"You see why our attempt has been unsuccessful," says Mrs. Nadar.

I am speechless. This is incredible! Amita's parents would be in full support of their daughter's relationship with Pritpal, the boy they've been yearning to reunite her with! In a desperate attempt to pull myself together, I focus on the question Mrs. Nadar's just asked me.

"Tell me, what are your college plans?"

Now the script I use is Mummy's.

"I am headed to Rutgers like my sister before me," I say. I almost give her the other line about going premed. But I guess I take pity on them or something, because I give them a peek of the real me. "I don't know what I'll major in yet. Still figuring things out."

Mrs. Nadar gives me a warm smile.

"You have time," she assures me. "I see you're a smart person, so I'm not worried about where you'll land."

I smile back and wordlessly nod my thanks.

When Amita finally shows up, she looks like she's half asleep.

I have to remind myself that Amita's in acting mode. In her email, she said she might play up or down her reactions, depending on what she felt the situation called for. Whatever she just dragged herself away from—even if she was watching paint dry—seems like it was hugely more exciting than meeting with me.

"Amita, your classmate has traveled here to meet with you," her father says. "The least you can do is get her a glass of water."

I almost look at her dad like, *Really, my dude?*

"The third person should be here any moment," I say instead.

The soothing sound of chimes ringing out makes for a pleasant interruption. I guess the doorbell really does work.

Amita comes short of rolling her eyes when Kira walks in. "Well, I guess we can start now," she sighs.

"Amita, where are your manners?" says her mother, before turning to me and Kira. "You just let my daughter know what it is you'd like to drink or snack on, and she'll take care of it for you."

I wonder if this is some sort of punishment, because this looks like the type of house that would have a waitstaff in the kitchen. Okay, I'm exaggerating. But suffice it to say a butler wouldn't seem out of place here.

"Right this way." Amita gives her mom a look, but she doesn't catch it. Mrs. Nadar is straightening the picture frame that Amita's dad picked up and moved out of place.

Kira and I follow Amita to the large kitchen in the back of the house. There is a gorgeous view of a patio, and beyond that lies the bean-shaped pool.

"You can stop acting like you think we're losers now, Amita," says Kira, chuckling to herself as we each grab a seat at the kitchen table.

"No, I will not." Amita unplugs the Alexa speaker device. "Just in case," she tells us.

I pull out my laptop. "Does this mean we can't ever come swimming when the weather gets nicer?"

"Sorry." Amita's answer might as well have come with a dead bolt.

This may not be the time, but I can't hold it in any longer. "Okay, if it's safe to talk, I'm *dying* to tell you something."

"What is it?"

I whisper-scream it all out before I burst. "Your parents told me that they tried to track Pritpal down to arrange your prom date with him!"

Amita's face turns ashen. When she finally blinks, I recognize that same desperate look that came over Mrs. Nadar's face when I couldn't tell her anything about Amita's inner life.

"You guys have to leave," she says evenly. "Now."

Kira is all types of confused. "Huh? But we just got here."

"I know, I'm sorry, and please don't take this personally, but you have to go."

I put a hand on Amita's forearm. "Because of what they told me? They seemed super sincere about it."

She shakes her head. "I know my parents. They must have found out about Pritpal and are trying to back me into a corner. I need to throw them off my trail, quick."

"How is getting us to leave all of a sudden going to throw them off? If anything, it could confirm their suspicions."

"But if you stay, they'll only keep digging. It's way easier for them to get info out of you both than out of me."

As if on cue, Mrs. Nadar clippity-clops into the kitchen.

"Girls, would you like me to order pizza?" she asks sweetly.

"Uh, actually, they were just leaving," says Amita, flashing us a back-me-up glare.

Mrs. Nadar frowns. "Already?"

There's an emergency stash of parental lies I keep stored in my brain for times like this. I grab one and run with it. "Kira and I have an online course we completely forgot about, and we have to log in from home soon."

"I'm sorry to hear that," Amita's mom says. And to me, it still doesn't sound like an act.

We sweep our belongings from the table, offer polite good-byes, then rush out the door and into Kira's waiting car. It's only as we're driving away that it occurs to me.

I never did get that drink of water.

CHAPTER SIXTEEN

It took getting to school extra early, but Amita, Kira, and I have the senior room all to ourselves. I didn't mind the crack-of-dawn bus ride because it meant I'd get all the details that were too long and confusing to text.

"Thanks again for dropping that smooth getaway lie," Amita says. "It worked, and my parents said nothing more about Pritpal or anything after you left."

"I almost believed I really did schedule an online class," Kira admits with a chuckle.

And I'm almost ashamed. Lying to parents is not my best attribute.

"I don't like to use my powers, but I will if they're needed."

"Oh, they were needed," sighs Amita.

Kira rubs Amita's back. "I'm glad you're no longer in crisis mode."

"Back to baseline for now," she says. "And the good thing is,

I think your visit did the trick. Now when I tell them we have another study group, they'll totally buy it."

I hold up my hand and Amita complies with a high five.

"You guys should come to my place when my parents have their get-together this Saturday," Kira announces.

"Wouldn't that make us party crashers?" I ask.

"It's okay. The more the merrier for my parents," explains Kira. "Plus, if any of their friends like you, they'll be more accepting."

"If you're sure it's okay," says Amita.

"It's okay, but I should warn you," Kira says. "They are *very* different from me. I can't even believe we're related sometimes."

"Oh, that's the story of our lives," I say. "That's why we have each other."

A warm smile spreads out the freckles on Kira's face. "You're right."

Amita's car is coming in handy. My parents can't afford to get me a car after the disaster with the lemon they were sold. Apparently, there are still people who think that speaking with an accent means you're dumb. But the bad thing about that incident is that my gullible parents played right into the dealer's hands. That is, if you, like me, believe he knew he was selling them a car with the life span of a hungry caterpillar.

Amita is a great driver. She just has absolutely no sense of direction. Thankfully, I make a good copilot.

I check the GPS. "This is the street," I say. "It should be a thousand feet down and to the right."

"Okay, let me know when I'm getting to like one hundred feet and I'll look for parking."

This is a quiet neighborhood, but somehow tons of cars are lining the curb.

"Someone is having a par-tay."

"Totally. I don't know how I'll find parking."

We're way past Kira's house when we find a spot.

"Um, I think all these cars are here for Kira's parents' gathering," I say with slow realization.

Amita cups her gaping mouth.

I shrug and shake my head at the same time. We're confused.

We giggle like grade-schoolers and try to outpace each other to the front door, eager to crack this mystery. Amita's never had to walk ten blocks under the threat of missing a bus, so I get there first.

A tall woman with a warm smile, wearing a V-neck shirt, answers the door. I can see a lot of people milling around behind her. The party looks to be in full swing.

I smile back. "Hi, we're not sure we've got the right house. We're looking for Kira?"

"Yes, I'm Kira's mother."

I almost stumble backward in disbelief. *This is Kira's mom?* There's a small tattoo of a zodiac sign above her left boob. I try not to stare at it.

"You're a Capricorn, too?" Amita says excitedly.

"Yes—the eleventh!" The woman smiles in that slow way that Kira does, and I can now see the family resemblance.

"Ohmygod, we're a day apart!" Amita and her new star-sign buddy beam at each other. "Oh, I'm Amita, Kira's classmate, and this is Simone. We're here to work on our group project."

"That's great. I mean—it's nice to have Kira's friends over." She invites us inside. People are gathered around a buffet table lined with appetizers and desserts. There are even live musicians taking a break while cradling their string instruments.

Two younger women who are the carbon copy of Kira's mom walk over to us.

"Did I hear you say *Kira's* friends?" one of them asks in surprise.

"Oh, these are my daughters, Kira's big sisters."

Kira's mother isn't the only one rocking a peek-a-boob top. Her older sisters, two curvaceous goddesses, are, too.

"You can feel free to join us at our little soiree if you like," says Kira's mom. "But we just ask that if you take any pictures, you don't post them anywhere." She holds out a basket filled with cell phones. "And if you'd like, feel free to drop your phones in here until you're ready to go. My husband and I host these gatherings to remind folks that the best interface is good old-fashioned *human* interfacing."

"And live music!" someone shouts from the kitchen.

Kira's mom is tickled and points to the heckler. "My husband back there. Wave, Bill!" Bill waves with a large serving spoon. "Yes, there's no *playlist* here."

I gulp when I hear our buzzword, but Amita nods and says, "I feel that. One hundred percent."

"Uh, thank you, but no, we couldn't stay," I say regretfully.

Amita turns to me to ask, "Couldn't we?"

I don't know how Kira would feel about us getting too cozy with her parents.

"Uh," I start. "We'll just wait for Kira and—"

"I'm right here," says Kira. She catches us completely by surprise. It's as if a column grew arms and legs and started talking all of a sudden. Amita has her hand over her heart, so I know she's as startled as I am.

"Kira! Honey, you're famous for sneaking up on people."

"You always say that, Mom. I was standing right here the whole time. I even announced my arrival."

"Okay, my bad," her mom says, holding up her hands. The many bracelets tumbling up her arm jangle in surround sound. "No need to get worked up."

Kira blinks wide-eyed at her mom for a few awkward seconds. I watch and learn how Kira opts to avoid escalating matters with her mom. It looks like it takes a lot of self-control. And a bunch of blinking.

Blink. *Seethe*. Blink. *Breathe*. Blink. *Shake head*.

And, just like that, Kira's good to go.

"Hey, guys." Kira looks happy to see us. "Come with me."

Kira takes us to her room, a quiet corner on the far end of their ranch home. It feels like we're worlds away from the party.

The door to Kira's room might as well be a front door. All that's missing is a welcome mat and a mailbox. There's a basket leaning against the wall next to her door.

"Is this where we drop our cell phones?" Amita asks, obviously trying to be respectful of house rules.

"Nope, no such rules in my room. You're safe to go online and post pics here. But that basket's for shoes. If you don't mind . . ."

"Sure, sure!" we say, happily obliging.

Kira leans against her neatly organized desk. Amita and I tour the space and pause to check out all the titles in her tall wooden bookcase. Even her room décor is different from the rest of the house. Everywhere else is farm style, and Kira's space is more boho eclectic.

"So, I guess you met my mom and my sisters," says Kira. She's got her arms folded in what for Kira passes as a mini tantrum. I know families can trigger us like no one else, but this reaction seems like it's about something specific. What's got her so upset?

"Yeah," I say.

"Yup." The *p* in Amita's *yup* pops a little too judgmentally. I elbow her and try to clue her into Kira's mood.

Amita and I swallow our reactions for now. Kira is clearly in her feelings about something.

"I told you they're different from me."

"I don't get the sense they wouldn't want you to take a date to prom," Amita says gently.

"Yeah, you mentioned they expected you to go solo," I say, taking a seat in an armchair.

Kira grabs a plush pillow and sits on her bed. "Exactly. That's because they lost it when I told them I was going to find a prom date online. I came across this Rent-a-Date app for eighteen-year-olds."

"Were you really going to do that?" I ask with fascination.

"Probably not, but it was fun seeing their reaction," she chuckles. "I mean, they're all right people, but don't you find their complete confidence in going analogue kind of annoying? It took spending a summer at my cousin's to make me realize how preachy and condescending my family can be toward people who live differently."

Amita takes a seat next to Kira on her bed and gives her a gentle shoulder bump. "I hear you."

"It's not like I'm trying to be difficult or anything . . ." Kira's voice trails off.

"You don't owe us an explanation, Kira." I stand up and sit by her other side. "We're your HomeGirls, remember? We know what it's like to feel different from our families. Just let us know however you want to rock the Playlist, and we'll help you make it happen."

Kira finally cracks the same smile her mother flashed earlier.

"Thanks," she says. "I'm looking forward to our club night . . . and the visit to your house, Simone."

I nod, suddenly feeling nervous about both things. Even though Grandmère helped me get Tuesday-night clearance, Mummy could still veto that if she picks up a whiff of our signature scent, Deception.

This might be harder than I thought.

CHAPTER SEVENTEEN

My stomach ties itself in a knot the minute I see my parents' car in the driveway. I'm a block away, but the white Honda is in full view, like a road sign that reads *Caution: Entering Parental Zone.*

Ever since our fight in the supermarket, things have been weird between Mummy and me. At first, I managed to stay out of her way by getting home before her and basically locking myself in my room all evening. But lately, it's harder to avoid her and my dad. Mummy's taken some time off to take care of Grandmère, who's been resting after her minor surgery in Ma Tante's old room. And Papi gets home early when he doesn't have to pick up my mom after work.

The HomeGirls are coming over today, so I should try to make nice with Mummy. I took the bus home alone; like Amita, I decided it would be better if we didn't all show up together. Coming in hot as a trio? We'd look too much like a unit. Like we were in cahoots. It would establish to Mummy that we were friends, not a study group. Insert "thinking man" GIF of the brotha fingertip-tapping his temple here.

I hear Mummy's laughter as soon as I walk into the house, which makes me smile. Mummy's got different kinds of laughs, and this one—where she's cracking up at the irony behind a joke—is my favorite. A balled-up fist on her hip, a lean to the left, and a scrunched-up face usually go with it. The smell of fresh-baked cookies stretches my smile even wider. Is she talking to Anne? On the phone with my dad? No way she'd be laughing that hard to one of Papi's corny jokes. I follow the sound to the kitchen with a bounce in my step.

What I see when I get there wipes the grin off my face. Mummy and *Kira* are sitting across from each other at the counter, eating chocolate-chip cookies like old buddies.

"And that was the last time he mispronounced my name," Mummy says. Kira lets out a sincere chuckle. She looks thoroughly enthralled by my mother.

"You need to try that when you need someone to get in line. It really works," says Mummy, giggling at their little inside joke.

Huh? Kira obviously has gone off-script, because none of the conversation cues I suggested to her would lead her down a path like this. I glare at Kira when Mummy looks away, and she gives me an apologetic shoulder shrug.

"Hi, Kira," I say, formally. "My bus got stuck in traffic. But I'm glad my mom has kept you entertained."

"Oh, my pleasure," says Mummy. This time I give her a look, like, *Really?* Since when does she take such pleasure in playing host to anyone who comes over who isn't named Her Sister or Her Side of the Family? "How was your day, darling?"

She sweetly holds out her cheek for a kiss, and I go over to greet her. I see talking to Kira has put my mom in a genuinely good mood. I'm at a loss as to why.

Thankfully, Amita arrives that instant. I rush to the door and return to the kitchen with her before Kira or my mom can swap another story.

"Amita, this is my mom, Constance Thibodeaux."

"Nice to meet you, Mrs. Thibodeaux. Lovely home you have."

Yay. Amita delivers a performance I approve of. She hits the right note, though she could be more natural with her delivery. But still, just like we'd rehearsed and I requested, she compliments Mummy's book collection. And bonus points for commenting on my good grades and knowledge of history.

I'm thrown off when I hear someone else at our front door. Gabby lets herself in with her key. Of all the different scenarios I played out in my head, I never factored in that my cousin would come through during the HomeGirls' visit. Gabby had basketball practice after school and caught a later bus home and still only made it here a few minutes after me.

"I came to check up on Grandmère." She helps herself to a cookie and takes a huge bite out of it.

Gabby's got a sixth sense for disruption, so I can't help but be suspicious. But I internally scold myself. Her visit is not about me, but about our grandmother.

"I didn't know you were coming," I can't help but say.

"I texted your mom," she tells me, and I give her a *C'mon, man* look.

Mummy laughs. "Ah. I didn't see it, Gabrielle. My phone is on silent somewhere in this kitchen."

Surprisingly, it takes my mom days, sometimes weeks, to check her texts. She treats texts like emails. "If it was an emergency, you would call me," she likes to say.

I turn to our guests. "Hey, you guys must know my cousin Gabby from school?"

"Sure. Hey, Sophomore," Amita says with a mischievous glint in her eye.

Kira introduces herself and formally shakes Gabby's hand.

Gabby sits down on a stool, looking in no rush to go check in on Grandmère.

I guess I'm the one who has to speak up here. "Um, we kind of need to start on our project, so—"

"So can't a sophomore get ahead by listening to what the seniors are learning?"

"Fine idea." Mummy is impressed. "I tell Simone to shadow her older sister sometimes for that very reason."

I try not to be too obvious when I glare at Gabby.

Mummy excuses herself to go tend to Grandmère, and I'm relieved. I know Grandmère will keep her occupied for a good while. We are now safe to drop the act.

"Okay, what are you doing?" I ask Gabby.

"What are *you* doing?" she asks.

Amita looks from her to me. "Can we trust her?"

"*Alla frekan.*" Gabby cops an attitude in Creole, eyelashes batting while she scowls. Yup, she's clearly talking about Amita in front of her face and wants Amita to know.

"I guess," I say to Amita.

Gabby sneers. "You *guess*?"

"Well then, there's no harm," says Amita. "You can stay."

Gabby claps her hands and does a happy dance in her seat. "What are you guys *really* working on?" she asks.

While the HomeGirls describe our Playlist, my cousin pops two more whole cookies in her mouth like they're movie popcorn.

"Pretty good," she says approvingly. "Let me see this list."

I dig through my wallet and pull it out. Gabby joins us in our starry-eyed stare.

"Isn't it pretty?" Kira asks.

Gabby nods but looks concerned. "How long ago did y'all start this list—in middle school?"

The paper *is* starting to have an aged look, which is actually cool. But Gabby's right. We need to preserve this piece of history a lot better.

"Here, let me take a picture of it and text it to you guys," volunteers Kira. She pulls out her phone and snaps the photo. "Aww, so fun!" Kira coos, eyes on her screen. She taps something and scrolls down. "Oh wow. You guys all show up on this AirDrop thingie."

Gabby whips around to look at me. "Is she for real?"

My head shake implores her to drop it. "It's a long story."

Our phones all go off in a chorus of alerts. Gabby's does, too. "Why'd you send a copy to me?" she asks.

Kira cringes. "Oops, my bad."

"Never mind that. Listen, you guys need me. Let me be your bucket list consultant," says Gabby.

"Aren't you a freshman?" Amita needles.

"Sophomore!"

"Let's say, for the sake of argument, you were our consultant," I posit. "What would be your first idea?"

"What I want to know is, when are you going clubbin'? Because I've gotta see this!" My cousin grins.

"Well, we were planning to go to LowKey some Tuesday night," I say. "Let me actually ask when Gavin's going to be there." It feels good to be able to text Gavin. I don't want to seem too needy, so I shoot him a short message asking him.

When there's no reply after a few long minutes, Gabby sucks her teeth and the sound is so sharp, I'm slightly afraid she's busted all the eardrums of the neighborhood dogs. She grabs her cell and sends a text of her own.

"Ta-dow," she says.

"What did you just do?" I ask.

By the time she puts her phone on the table, it dings. She picks it back up.

"Tuesday after next at LowKey, Rashod says he'll be spinning. You know Gavin's gotta be there to support his boy."

"Rashod's a working DJ?" I ask.

"Yup, you should listen to his stuff online. Bangin'." Then Gabby snaps her fingers. "Ooh. If we're all going to LowKey, maybe we should get a big group to come."

"A big group," I echo, because, of course!

"Let's do it. I'll even see if Pritpal can come!" says Amita, sending a text. "And maybe my cousin Krish would want to join us, too. That way you can all meet him before prom."

"What do you think about me inviting Ben?" I ask Kira.

"I'm down," she says. "It's way less awkward if I meet him in a group first."

"So, do I have the consultant job?" Gabby asks proudly.

"Whether we hire you or not, I know you'll be acting like you manage things, so why bother?" I tease.

Gabby winks. "Valid point."

"All right, then. Next Tuesday, we'll have some LowKey fun," I say, even as I low-key feel some type of way that Gavin still hasn't texted me back.

Before we go clubbing, the HomeGirls have another item to cross off our Playlist: cutting class.

We pick Wednesday to do it, and we have a very detailed plan. To make things less obvious, Amita didn't come to school today because she wasn't "feeling well." Thankfully, her parents bought her lie and left her at home while they went to work. Now it's just up to Kira and me to use two different excuses to each go home early.

Ferris Bueller may be our inspiration, but this is not like in the movies. At St. Clare Academy, you can't just walk out of the building without telling someone. The school is too small, and your parents will get a phone call before you even get to where you're going.

So, the plan is for Kira to say she has a doctor's appointment right before lunch, and for me to tell the nurse I'm not feeling well a period later. Kira texts me a thumbs-up when she exits the school, right on schedule. By the time I get to the nurse's office, I actually am experiencing stomachaches due to how nerve-racking this whole process is. I'm not cut out for this type of high-level lying. I almost start to freak out from the stress of it all, and the nurse rushes to get me water and some antacid. Once she's satisfied that I've stabilized, she sends me home in an Uber.

The Uber drops me off right at the train station, where I meet Amita and Kira.

"Whew, you made it!" Kira hurries over to me. "I was worried." She pauses and looks me over. "Are you okay? You're not really sick, are you?"

I shake my head. Amita can't hold in her cackle at my wussy behavior.

"I don't do this every day," I remind her.

It's not until we're seated on the train that I feel back to myself. And once we get to Jersey City, I start to really enjoy the day. The three of us scour the different boutiques and try on every prom dress. I actually have an appointment with my seamstress later that afternoon, but it feels like playful research trying out new looks and finding out which silhouettes work best.

In one store, I spot a flowy, floor-length emerald-green dress with a high neckline. It looks like it was made for Kira. When she tries it on, she feels this way, too.

"I love this look, and especially the color, so much," she says, spinning around in front of the full-length mirror.

"Kira, you look freakin' fantastic, girl," Amita says.

"Freakin' fantastic," I echo, because it's true.

Kira takes in every detail of her reflection, and Amita and I snap a few pics. When we ask Kira how she feels, she turns to the camera, throws up two fingers, and shouts, "Freakin' fantastic!"

Amita tries on a bunch of dresses, too, but nothing speaks to her like the dress she already has her eye on online. When she shows us a picture of it, we agree that it's perfection. It's a sleek black gown with a diagonal, off-the-shoulder neckline, and I just know Amita will slay in it.

We leave that boutique with Kira's prom dress in its bag, and it's the best feeling.

On the train home, we can't stop looking at pics and dreaming up what hairstyles and accessories we should wear. Amita and

Kira get off at their respective stops, but I stay on the train and head straight to my seamstress's house.

"Haaa! Simone, is that you?" calls out Auntie Victoria, letting me inside the house.

"Hello!" I say, happy to see her.

She leads me down to the showroom/workspace in her basement. It's a much different setting than the boutiques in Jersey City, but one may argue that these seamstresses are just as popular. Wooden-slat stairs and a low ceiling make for a careful descent. But once the workroom comes into view, there's a lot that catches my eye.

The entire space is no larger than my bedroom. Stacks of beautiful folded fabrics in every possible color and pattern line the walls. Hanging on any free space of wall are fashion images—dozens of them: magazine clippings, old wall calendars, posters, all featuring full-sized models in gorgeously unique designs. In the middle of the room is a cluttered table with a shaded light bulb and, of course, Auntie Victoria's magical sewing machine.

I stretch my arms out as Auntie Victoria expertly takes my body measurements and I show her how long I'd like my skirt to be.

"Nice length."

I grin. "I want to show off my shoes."

Auntie Victoria scribbles all my measurements down with a pencil in an overused spiral notebook. She doesn't bookmark the page before placing the pad atop a pile of fabric strips. My head aches wondering how it is she'll recover the info ever again.

"Do you mind if I—um, take a pic of my measurements?" I already have my phone out, and I'm zooming in on the curly figures listed under my name and phone number. "Just so I have them," I add.

"Excited?" Auntie Victoria asks after I pay her the deposit and thank her.

"Very!" I bounce on my tiptoes.

She tells me to come back in two weeks for my fitting. I can't wait to see my dress come to life.

Just as I'm leaving I get a text. It's from Ben.

Hi there. I found a good tailor not far from my house. He said he can get started once I get him more of the material you gave me.

Perfect timing, I write back. *On it. I'll be in the city Friday and can bring you the material.*

Perfect timing indeed. I'm on spring break! When can we meet?

I text Ben a suggested time, then return to Auntie Victoria to get an extra yard of a different material. Now that I know Kira's wearing emerald, this tan-and-green motif is a better match. It works out, because it looks similar to the pattern I'll be wearing. I love how everything is syncing up nicely.

And even after all that, I'm still on the train and back home before my parents arrive from work.

Whew!

CHAPTER EIGHTEEN

On Friday, it's time for our next adventure: the trip to NYC. There's no school today because of the teacher conferences, but my parents don't know this. And for best practices, neither does Anne. It's better to share these things with Anne after they've already happened. She has a way of trying to talk me out of stuff, just because she'd always rather play it safe.

I get up at the usual time, and after my parents and Anne have left the house, I change out of my uniform. But I carry it with me, folding it up and storing it neatly in a big backpack.

I catch the bus and meet Kira and Amita at the train station again. This time, though, we're not going to Jersey City. We're going all the way to *the* city.

"So will you tell us what your idea for today is?" Kira asks as we walk to our track.

"You'll see." I grin.

"No, we won't see," protests Amita. "We'll hear it from you. Like, now."

"Now see this is why I love this girl so much," I tell Kira. "She's the lion to my Dorothy. All growl."

"Why do you get to be Dorothy?" Amita asks.

"You can be Judy Garland Dorothy. I'm Diana Ross."

We're still laughing when we get on the train, and to put Amita out of her misery, I tell her my surprise once we're all seated.

"Okay, I'm making this way bigger than it is, but we are going bike riding—"

Kira instantly gasps with excitement.

"Across the Brooklyn Bridge," I finish.

"No freakin' way!" Amita shouts.

"Yes way." I pull out the Playlist and hold up my fingers as I name the selections we are rocking today. "That's number five, *Hang out in NYC*, and number seven, *Ride a bike!*"

"And on my favorite bridge, no less," says Amita. "It's like a triple-word score."

We are the loudest people on the train, cheering and talking up a storm right until we arrive in Penn Station.

New York City, as always, is vibrant and noisy and thrilling. But it feels a lot different without Mummy ushering me through the streets or Papi pointing out traffic offenses. It feels a whole lot bigger. This city is my parents' stomping ground, but today I'm making it mine.

I've plotted out our route, thanks to a trusty subway map app I downloaded—and thankfully we'll be nowhere near Mummy's job or her favorite shopping area.

We take the subway to downtown Manhattan and walk to the nearest Citi Bike spot. It's a bright-sky day, and the weather is not too hot. The streets are crowded and full of conversation and energy. When we get to the Citi Bike stand and select three bikes, I whip out three Goodwill-purchased helmets from my backpack.

"You really came prepared," Amita says, impressed.

The three of us get on our bikes and pedal onto the Brooklyn Bridge. It's pretty windy, so I get practice steadying my bike. I want to take in the impressive views, but focus instead on dodging pedestrians in the bike lane and all the cars swishing by below. Amita can't stop waxing poetic about how this is as sensational as she imagined it would be. And Kira seems to be in heaven, pedaling along with a huge smile.

We reach a spacious area along the path where there are a few benches and an art vendor set up against a tower structure. There's a crowd here, but we stop to take pictures: selfies and shots of the amazing views. I gasp at the sight of the lower Manhattan skyline and the Statue of Liberty in the distance.

"This is so unbelievable." Amita looks like she'll get emotional, and Kira and I stand by with tissues and back rubs just in case. But Amita's as steely as the bridges she loves so much. She holds it down and continues sharing factoids about the bridge's features and its architects. A few people nearby mistake us for a guided tour group and listen in.

At one point, I go off to take photos of Kira as Amita answers tourists' questions. Kira looks like a kid in an Apple store.

"Why don't you make a plan to go bike riding with your family?" I suggest. "You guys could even come into the city like we did and do this."

She nods, suddenly too choked up to speak. This time, I'm ready with the tissues and back rubs.

We all get back on our bikes and continue on across the bridge. We pedal the rest of the way in meditative silence.

I get absorbed in a historical memory that Tatie Nadine gifted to me. She's reminded me of it so often, it feels like my own. Tatie was a few years older than Anne in the spring of 1990 when she marched this bridge, shoulder to shoulder with an estimated 150,000 mostly Haitian people, in protest of the FDA's ban on Haitian blood donation. The bridge shook with Haitian outrage then as it vibrates with history now.

When the three of us reach Brooklyn, it feels like an accomplishment. We reward ourselves with pizza from the famous Grimaldi's and then ice cream cones from Ample Hills.

"Thank you so much, Simone," says Amita.

"This was the best," adds Kira.

A group hug and a selfie later, we're headed in different directions. Kira, inspired by our bike ride and the promise of family time, has texted one of her sisters, who works in Midtown, and they're going to grab coffee. Her sister is surprised Kira's in the city, but she's so touched Kira's reached out that she's promised not to snitch to their parents.

Meanwhile, Amita is off to visit Pritpal, who happens to be filming in Greenwich Village today. I tell the girls I want to check out the Haiti exhibit at the MoCADA, the Museum of Contemporary African Diasporan Art, which is true. But for some reason I can't quite explain, I don't tell them who I'm supposed to meet there.

Which is weird. I *was* going to ask Kira to come with me, but I remembered how she'd said it would be less awkward if she met Ben in a big group. Then she texted her sister, and it really was too late. Right?

I hop on the bus and head to the Fort Greene address Ben texted me.

From about half a block away, I see him standing outside the brick-face museum, waiting for me. He's wearing jeans and a concert tee, so I don't feel underdressed in my black leggings, ankle boots, white tee, and denim jacket.

"So cool that you're in town during my spring break week," he says, smiling wide once I'm face-to-face with him. Something tickles my heart when I see that smile, but I clear the feeling away with a forced cough. "I'm glad you could come. I've been planning to check out the Haitian exhibit for a minute," he adds.

We walk into the airy, modern space and head for the exhibit. My parents have Haitian art on their walls, and a good number of Haitian households do, too. We are world famous for our art, and we are raised to know that. But I don't know as much about the artists behind these works as Ben does. It's pretty special, getting to see his excitement over the vivid pastoral scenes on display.

I notice one painting is titled after a famous Haitian proverb. "I'm pretty sure my grandmother used this proverb against my mother the other day," I say, chuckling.

"Rude," he wisecracks when he reads the insult the proverb is. "Well then, my sympathies to your mom."

"Oh, I'm sure she's counting down the six weeks my grandma will be staying with us."

We share an easy laugh as we make our way around the gallery, and just as easily, our hands brush together.

My smile melts and I slide my hand away, embarrassed. Ben looks at me, as if trying to catch my gaze, but I turn my head and pretend to get lost in another painting. We're quiet for an awkward moment when I hear a soft rumble of laughter travel through the gallery. I turn around to see a group of people filing in. It looks like a guided tour has just begun.

"That's the museum's executive director," Ben whispers, gesturing to the stylin' young woman with long braids. "She's Haitian American."

The director catches our stare. "You're welcome to join us," she says with a wave.

I'm grateful the tour is about Haitianness. As we pause in front of a painting of a bustling marketplace, the director asks the group how it feels to be Haitian. Even though I'm not one for public speaking, I raise my hand and find my voice.

"To me being Haitian feels like this Venn diagram of experiences that overlaps many cultures," I say, nervous and hoping that I'm explaining this clearly enough. And then I remember the Brooklyn Bridge, and I go on. "Even though I catch anti-Haitian prejudice on the regular, it's the dynamic culture that makes it easy to build bridges to other people. I find so many different cultures relatable and I see us and our ways in other people and their ways. It's like everyone is a little Haitian, and they don't know it."

"I love that observation," says the director. "We only hope one day the world will appreciate how the Haitian cultural experience reflects all humanity."

I shrug my shoulders and smile wickedly. "And if they never do, we'll keep marching in our awesomeness, and shaking things up once in a while."

The rest of the group backs me up with "that's right"s and "amen"s, and Ben reaches out and squeezes my hand.

After the tour, Ben and I thank the director for an amazing visit. We leave the museum together and breathe in the crisp air outside.

Still feeling the imprint of Ben's touch on my hand, I busy myself with chatter as Ben walks me to the nearby subway station. If I want to be part of the after-school rush in New Jersey, I have to head home now.

"You should come meet me and Kira and our friends next Tuesday night," I say, my words tumbling out my mouth one after another.

Ben raises an eyebrow. "Kira, huh?"

"Yup. We're hitting Club LowKey on their teen night."

"Oh, there's a teen night," Ben says with a lip curl. "That's cute."

"And how old are you?" I throw back at him, pretending to wait for his reply.

He grins. "All right, all right, I'll come to teen night. And hey, I'll be in Jersey most of next week, so if you want, we can meet up on Rutgers's campus sometime, too."

"Maybe," I say, noncommittal. We've reached the Atlantic station, and I search inside my backpack. I pull out the African print fabric for his prom look.

"Before I forget," I say. "Here you—"

Our fingers brush when he reaches for the fabric, and I forget what I was saying. What is going on with me?

"Here you go," I recover. "And here I go. Train to catch."

"Cool, yeah," says Ben, like he's just snapped out of a daydream.

I throw on my best pinch-faced-commuter expression and turn all my attention on travel.

"Get home safe," Ben calls out.

"I will," I call back, heading down the stairs.

CHAPTER NINETEEN

Finally, it's Tuesday night, and the HomeGirls are about to go to LowKey. But first, we're gathering at Gabby's place to get ready.

Anne was nice enough to lend me her car tonight, so I drove here, even though Gabby lives within walking distance from us. But the plan is that I'll drive Gabby and myself to the club, and then back home at the end of the night. Kira and Amita will take Kira's car.

This meetup location was Consultant Gabby's idea. With my aunt being way cooler than my mom, we HomeGirls feel like CIA agents reporting to a safehouse. Here, we're free to look one way when we arrive and another when we leave. Except for Gabby, who has the green light to leave the house in black pleather leggings, a cute African-print top, and a pair of classic Jordans.

"Great outfit," I tell my cousin as she welcomes us inside. Amita and Kira compliment her as well, and Gabby eats it up.

To add to the safehouse mystique, Gabby's place is undergoing construction.

"You guys are still doing renovations?" I ask Gabby as we all pass various tools and paint cans left in the hallway. Looking around, you wouldn't suspect only two people, Gabby and Tatie Nadine, live in this house.

"Yeah, my mom fired the last crew because of their shoddy work."

"Oh."

Just then, I hear my aunt's voice. "Hello, ladies! And good-bye, ladies—I'm heading out soon."

Tatie Nadine breezes into the foyer on a cloud of perfume.

"Hi, Tatie!" I go greet my aunt with a cheek kiss. "Love your skirt."

Tatie Nadine takes two handfuls of her flowy skirt and starts sashaying around while kicking out her legs this way and that in a dance.

I'm instantly her hypewoman, egging her on rhythmically, in sync with her two-step.

She freezes with a hand-on-hip pose and we all crack up. I give her a hug and introduce her to the HomeGirls.

"Momone, you braved your way over to this house of madness?" she asks me.

"The place is going to look amazing when the reno's done," I say.

"It will. I just want the inconvenience to be over," Tatie Nadine says. She grabs a brown leather handbag from the cluttered counter and starts rummaging through it. "*Wooo*, if I misplace one more thing, I'll scream."

She literally has screamed. I've witnessed the hilarity. I love my auntie, but the woman would call the fire department with her personal problems if she could, like, *Umwaaaay, send a rescue team—I'm late for work and can't find my keys!*"

It's the only time she shows the dings in her armor—when something forces her to slow down or wait. Otherwise, my Tatie keep things moving, whether it's flying off to business conferences, attending fancy grand openings, volunteering for shifts at the pantry, or kicking her ex-husband, Gabby's dad, to the curb for bad behavior. It's like stillness is her kryptonite. Even the walls in her house are constantly moving. This is not her first home reno in recent years.

"Welcome, welcome," she says to Amita and Kira. "Please make yourselves at home. You'll have to use the bathroom upstairs if you need it. The one down here is being worked on."

Gabby pokes me with her elbow. "Let's go upstairs." We follow Gabby up the stairs. A college-aged girl wordlessly strolls out of Gabby's room as we're walking in. Gabby doesn't even flinch.

"Who was that?" I ask, because my cousin clearly isn't about to address this.

"She's a distant relative staying in the guest room until she gets back on her feet," she says. "My mom and her bleeding heart."

I still don't get it, but Amita asks the burning question.

"But why was she coming out of your room?"

"The hallway bathroom entrance is blocked off because of the reno, and the only way to get there is through my room."

For the first time, I notice the new bathroom door in Gabby's room.

"This is a cool upgrade," I say, inspecting it.

"Having an en suite bedroom is smart," says Kira.

Thinking back to Kira's room that has a whole-house vibe, it's no wonder Kira is into real estate.

As Amita and Kira admire Gabby's shiny new bathroom, I set my small duffel bag down, right next to an abandoned pair of jeans and a sweater lying like shed snakeskin on the floor. Then I unzip the bag to reveal the treasures inside.

"What's all this?" Kira asks.

"I told you I'd coming bearing gifts," I say with a curtsy. "A few key pieces and accessories to wake up any outfit. You're all free to borrow anything you'd like." I'm hopeful someone will let me style them. And okay, if I have to beg for the chance, I'm not above that either.

"Poor thing," says Gabby, rubbing my shoulder. "Someone please give this girl a shot at her dream."

"Don't rub too hard," I tell her. "My tattoo is pretty faded, and I want to show it off at least this one night."

"You're hired," Kira tells me, smiling. "Do your worst."

"Are you serious?" I squeal. Kira has been stepping out of the box lately.

"Yeah, I'm finally meeting Ben tonight, aren't I?" Kira says.

My breath catches in my throat, and Amita notices. She gives me a funny, knowing look, and I ignore her.

"Might as well try something different," Kira says. "But not too different."

"I promise to keep your style, only punch it up a bit," I tell her.

I've watched enough "day-to-night" YouTube tutorials to know how to choose a style that allows for easy changeup when it's time to head home. The plan is for Amita, Kira, and me to duck into the club bathroom for our quick make-under at the end of the night.

Over the next hour, I do everyone's makeup according to their evening look—shining star shimmer for Amita, a smoky eye and glossy lip for Kira, a wild-child, playful palette for Gabby, and rockstar chic for me. Gabby blesses me with a runway model hairstyle—a chunky twisty cornrow worn to one side and cascading into a fishtail over my shoulder.

We all squeeze together for a group selfie.

"Did you lose your glasses, Simone?" Gabby asks through a frozen smile pose.

"I'm wearing contacts," I reply without moving my lips. "Test run for prom."

"Switching up your style, and I love to see it," Amita says, flapping her lips and not bothering to hold any smile.

I take a bunch of pics, and then we review them.

"We look amazing!" Kira says.

"But look at Amita in that third pic," Gabby can't resist mentioning.

"Hey!" Amita protests.

I shake my head, grinning. "Y'all are so messy."

We do look fly. Kira's in a flowy floral romper that's classic and classy. Amita looks super sophisticated in a white tunic over jeans. And I'm wearing distressed skinny black jeans with a black sleeveless top that shows off my temporary butterfly.

Gabby checks us each out and shouts, "Let's get it, HomeGirls!"

CHAPTER TWENTY

There's no velvet rope, but tacky orange cones keep all the teens outside LowKey in a neat, long line. Gabby, Amita, Kira, and I are in the middle of that line, and we got here a little after 7:30, when the club opened. The mood from our dress-up party is still with us, and there's a comfortable silence as we check our text messages, refresh our lipstick, case the crowd for familiar faces, and, if you're me, get lost in thoughts about seeing Gavin.

I start calculating how many hours I have before needing to head home. Anne let me borrow her car tonight, so the plan is to leave at 9:30 p.m. That means I'll barely be here for two hours.

"Come on, Simone." Gabby tugs my arm.

Yes. They're letting us in.

We roll in like *"gang, gang, gang"* and make our way through the wallflower crowd bunched up by the entrance.

Dance floor lights on the ceiling are flashing, bass is

thumping, and everyone is buzzing. It feels like a Saturday. People are hugging one another in excited greeting as if they didn't just see everyone earlier today at school.

Full disclosure: I catch this bug, too.

"There's Ben!" I shout, doing a little hop. I wave him over when he catches my eye.

"Hey!" He gives me a wide smile.

Ben is looking cute tonight. He's wearing a red Toussaint L'Ouverture shirt that I recognize from the Queens vendor, slim blue jeans, and a retro track suit jacket. *Nice.*

I look behind him in search of a friend, a brother, anyone.

"Is it just you?" I ask him. "You here by yourself?"

"Just me," he says, like he's answering a simple math problem. Again, the puzzle pieces aren't fitting, and I feel an itch I can't scratch.

"I'm sorry," I say. "I didn't realize. I would've tried to meet up with you before so you wouldn't have to wait alone."

"Don't be sorry, I don't mind my own company," he says. "I was just taking in the Jersey scene. Fascinating stuff out here."

We both chuckle.

"Yeah, well, it grows on you after a while."

"The *people* or the places?" He smiles, and I smile back.

I shouldn't be staring at him this long.

"Okay, so let me introduce you to my girls," I say just as the DJ drops the beat and some EDM sound effect screams out through the speakers.

"What?" he asks, gesturing me closer to his ear. He cocks his head toward me and I lean in.

"Let me introduce you to my girls!" I repeat.

He nods and meets my eyes in understanding. Now that we're in each other's orbit, there's a serious gravitational pull happening. I remember our non-hand-holding from the MoCADA museum, and I try not to blush. What's with me?

"Hi again!" It's Amita. She surreptitiously pinches my elbow, as if to reel me back in. I'm kind of scattered right now, and I'm pretty sure it shows.

"Hey," Ben says to her.

I turn around to see where Kira is. I spot her deep in conversation with a short, cute, brown-skinned guy who's just joined our group. I realize that must be Amita's cousin/designated prom date, Krish; I recognize him from Amita's Instagram.

"Okay, we have Amita, my lil' cousin Gabby, back there is Kira, and Amita's cousin—"

"Krish," says Amita.

"Waddup, Krish," I call out.

Ben waves at them, and they wave back.

Amita unleashes a squeal and runs up to a suave-looking guy who's just walked in the door. He's wearing a crisp white button-up and has salon-coiffed hair, and I instantly recognize him, too.

"Everybody, meet my boyfriend, Pritpal."

Pritpal's smile momentarily dulls the club's flashing lights.

Gabby whistles when she sees him. "Ooo, somebody gave you

a five-star scrubbing," she says. "You do know Amita's prom isn't tonight, right?"

Pritpal bashfully lets his head drop.

My eyes couldn't get any wider. "Gabby."

"No, it's cool," says Pritpal. "I'm just coming back from a taping and didn't have time to go home to change."

Still giddy, Amita links an arm through her boyfriend's. "Pritpal has a pretty big role in a Netflix movie."

"Amita told us," I say to Pritpal. "That's awesome."

"Congratulations, man," says Ben.

"Thank you," Pritpal says with a shake of his head in disbelief. "I've been on set since five a.m., so this is the break I needed. Let's ball out! Drinks on me!"

We follow Pritpal to the bar, where sodas and mocktails are on offer, and Pritpal asks everyone what they want. Then he and Amita flag down the bartender.

Just when I start wondering where Gabby went, I see her bobbing and weaving through the crowd toward us. A tight huddle of kids freestyle rapping to the music scatters as she slices through and comes rushing over like Paul Revere's horse. "I got us a booth!"

There are only like three booths in this place. Man! Gabby makes it happen wherever she goes. And as her crew, we benefit.

She heads back toward the booth, and Kira and Krish follow her. "C'mon, hurry up," she calls out to me and Ben. "We can't hold off the crowd too long."

"We'll meet you there," I say. "Amita and Pritpal may need help with the drinks and finding everyone."

Ben and I are alone together.

"Your friends seem cool," he says. "Prom night should be fun."

"I'm glad you think so." I'm worried that he hasn't spoken to Kira yet. "Hopefully you'll get a chance to talk with them some more. "

Ben nods and our eyes meet again in that gravitational pull.

I blink first and take a breather. What is even going on?

"Let's see if Amita and Pritpal are ready with those drinks," I say as the perfect distraction.

We help carry the sodas and mocktails over to the booth, where Gabby, Kira, and Krish are seated and chatting. Amita and Pritpal slide in beside them, passing out the drinks.

Ben and I stay standing with our drinks and face the dance floor. It's looking like Eastern Parkway in Brooklyn on Labor Day, which is to say, all turnt up.

"So, what have you got planned for *your* prom?" I ask Ben.

Ugh, should I not have said that? I hope Ben doesn't think that I'm hinting about his date situation. He should NOT feel pressured to invite me to his prom just because he's coming to mine.

"That's a topic that's nowhere on my radar," he says in that even delivery I recognize as his subtle way of either joking or moving on.

"Um, no, that answer is not gonna satisfy me. As my mom would say, sa manke sèl," I tell him. That phrase is Mummy's way of getting folks to slap some more seasoning on whatever bland dish of news she's being served. "What's the story? Aren't you going to your prom?"

"Actually, no, I'm not."

I cross my arms, and with a turn of my neck, I whip my fishtail. "What are you? Too cool to go unless it's a favor?"

Ben takes a sip of his drink. "I didn't plan not to go; it just happened that way," he says. "Months ago, I bought tickets to Haiti for this big fundraiser I helped plan. I didn't realize my prom would be on that same day. All the Haitian kids I've been working with are dedicating so much time, so I can't let them down. Plus, I convinced a few deep-pocketed New Yorkers to contribute to the cause."

"Wow, that sounds like something you cannot miss." It's incredible to stand face-to-face with a teen activist. I hold up my palm and he joins it in a high five. "I'm proud of you."

"Thank you. So, now you know why I didn't really resist our moms making this suggestion," says Ben. "Because, well, I'm curious about prom and this will give me a chance to say I've gone."

"That explains a lot," I say. "At first it was weirding me out how freakishly accepting you seemed."

"I'm freakishly accepting, and you're oddly big on high-fiving." He smirks. "So, we're even."

"Hey, I'm not above being corny." I shrug.

"I see you're fully committing to that, so go off."

"Hey, our ancestors defeated the world's mightiest armies and won independence. So, I figure no amount of corny could ever-EVAH cost me a fraction of cool points."

Ben holds up his drink. "Thank you, ancestors, for making us eternally cool—even those of us who live in Jersey."

I give Ben a playful shoulder nudge and shake my head.

"So, I see how Jersey does it," says Ben. "Teen night, huh?"

"Yup." I can tell Ben is in a mood to poke fun, and I chuckle before he even drops his punch line.

"How sweet," he jokes with a sneaky smile and a deadpan delivery.

"What? You don't have stuff like this in Queens?"

He smooths down the front of his shirt with one hand. "No, because Queens isn't a fictional setting of some Disney musical, but real *skreets* in real life."

"Oh, these *skreets* get real here, too." I buck up and raise my arms like I'm prepared to fight, but then dab instead. "Only thing is you settle things with a dance-off."

Gabby joins us, teeth shining from having noticed my move. "Once upon a time she was too scared to hit the stage and dance," she squeals, throwing her arm around me. She gives me a hip bump. "Look at my baby girl now."

"Whose side are you on?" I bump her back.

"Who's the older cousin again?" Ben gives us a quizzical look and points from me to Gabby and back again.

I raise my hand. "Um, driver's license, college acceptance, soon-to-be graduate over here."

Through fits of giggles, Gabby forces down my hand and I try to force down the one she's raising. "Ahem," she says. "Wise advice, bold moves, first to lead, last to follow over heeere."

"Ouch!" Ben is laughing openly now. And so am I.

"Okay, I will give Gabby that," I say. "The girl is ahead of her time."

"And you?" Ben asks me.

"I admit I'm somewhat of a late bloomer," I say. Then I strike a pose to the beat. "But *fashionably* late."

"Yeah, get it, cuz!"

The DJ is spinning a soca and reggae mix that's got people losing their minds. How did this go from EDM to island beats so fast?

I look up at the DJ booth and notice the neon-shirt dude that was there earlier is now replaced with a young guy in a baseball cap and a black shirt. I think I know him.

"Is that Rashod up there?" I ask Gabby.

"Oh yeah, it is!" Gabby starts jumping up and down and waving, but Rashod is too focused on spinning to notice us. But someone else does.

"Gabby, I thought that was you," says Gavin. "Simone, hi!"

CHAPTER TWENTY-ONE

My prom date is on the scene, and suddenly I don't know how to act. I bite my lower lip because it gives me something to do.

"Hi. Gavin," I say, just like that. Two words. Two full sentences. With a pause in between. As in, the furthest thing from a normal person's greeting. Every time Gavin's around, I act like there's a text bubble over my head with three blinking dots that never quite lead to the right words.

"How's it going?" he greets Ben.

"Ben, hi. Gavin?"

"Yes."

Gavin and Ben don't know what to make of each other. Gavin may be wondering if Ben's with Gabby, and Ben could be wondering why I'm suddenly the blinking-dots girl. Neither Gabby nor I give them an explanation.

"Hey, come meet the gang, gang, gang," says Gabby, gesturing to our booth.

"Pritpal?" Gavin recognizes Amita's boyfriend. "Yo, wassup? You performing tonight?"

"How do you guys know each other?" I ask.

"Our moms are friends," says Gavin.

"I hear you guys are coming to dinner soon," says Pritpal.

Gavin nods. "That's what's up."

"Small world," shouts Amita before asking Gavin, "so, you perform, too?"

A sneaky smile spreads across his face. "Naw, but maybe I *should* be up there performing," Gavin jokes. "Performing stand-up."

"Oh no, don't do that," says Gabby. "Because I'll be the first to heckle you if you dare make fun of my friends. It's not their fault they're corny."

We all start heckling Gabby, tossing *boo*s and balled-up napkins at her, and Gavin steps in front of her like her personal Secret Service agent.

"Wait—she meant that as a compliment!" Gavin faux-pleads. "Corny is the new badass!"

"Look up there!" shouts Gabby. Her attempt to distract us works. "Y'all see Rashod doing his thing?"

"Yeah, he's killing it, and he'll be there for another hour." Gavin's tone is not without a hint of pride for his friend. "I'm about to head up and see him. Simone, Gabby, you want to come?"

If there's one word I'd use to describe Gavin—besides fine

and fly—it's generous. I haven't spent a lot of time with him, but he is always offering a ride somewhere, a seat someplace, or access to something.

"We'll be right back," I say. I feel like I'm leaving Ben hanging, but he seems fine. He's got his back to me and is talking to Krish. Maybe he'll get more acquainted with Kira next.

Gabby and I follow Gavin to the DJ booth. Rashod's got control of the mic and is in charge of passing it to whoever wants to spit rhymes. When he spots Gabby, he calls her up and hands her the mic. I lose my mind as Gabby riffs and vocalizes like an R&B goddess. When she hears Gavin rhyming to the grooves she weaves, she moves closer to him, and the two of them share the mic and perform together.

It's amazing how in sync they are. You'd think they'd practiced this whole routine before tonight. I watch, mesmerized, like they're in a music documentary.

The whole time, Rashod is spinning all sorts of music. Afrobeats, reggaeton, hip-hop, pop, rock, and even some country make it into the sounds that blend so well together. I get caught up in his flow. I can't even help it—it's a part of who I am.

"Dancing queen, she's a dancing queen. Move up out of her way when she steps on the scene," Gavin raps, and I fall out of step and almost trip over my feet.

Wait. Gavin is rapping about me? I lose my cool for a minute, before the crowd hypes me back into a zone.

As much fun as I'm having, I look out into the crowd for Ben.

Is he watching me? What does he think? And most importantly, why do I care?

Something in my gut tells me it's time to go. And being Haitian, I've learned that when "something tells me," I better listen. I notice the time on one of the big screens playing some nondescript music video. It's getting late. We've got to get out of here anyway.

I motion to Gabby that we should head back to our booth. Gabby and I say bye to Rashod and Gavin, and though I want to have a moment alone with Gavin, he's soon swallowed up by the crowd of guys who've just entered the DJ booth.

Gabby and I walk back to our table and announce to everyone that we're leaving. This starts a domino effect, and one person after another says they'll walk out with us. I'm still on schedule to get home at a decent time, but everyone who asks me to wait up makes me an extra minute later. Then we get pulled into one conversation after another on the way to the exit. Either someone recognizes Pritpal or Gabby. Plus, Amita, Kira, and I need to duck into the bathroom for our make-unders.

By the time we're outside the club saying our extended goodbyes, that "something tells me" feeling is still stirring. Just as we're about to go our separate ways, a car pulls up in the street. The driver rolls down his window and shouts in our direction. I wouldn't expect a man to be so bold as to catcall us when we're in such a large group. But hey, what do I know? I don't hit the streets at night that much.

This particular catcaller did his homework. He knows us by name.

"AMITA!"

Amita looks like that melting Dalí painting. It's like she's traded in her human card for a ghost pass.

OMG, it's her dad! She clutches my hand and I clutch back. *Whatdowedo?*

"Um, Pritpal, maybe you should head home," Amita says.

Pritpal looks like he's in a paper towel commercial reacting to a kitchen spill.

Amita's only course of action is to walk over to her dad before he comes for her. And he's a-comin'. Dude's got his car parked vertically in a parallel parking street and he leaves his door swung wide open once he exits his car.

"I was on my way to the college library to surprise you, and I see you here?" he calls.

He scans our side of the street in search of the name of the establishment we're in front of. I show him the back of my head, but Kira is a deer in headlights, staring in his direction. Great.

"Here I am." Amita tries her best to subdue the situation, speaking in a calm tone. "Everything's fine; I'm here. Let's go and we'll talk at home, please."

Amita manages to come off more like an adult than her dad. He snaps out of his mini rage, looks at the state of his parking, and joins Amita, who's already in the car. They drive off with way less drama than when he arrived.

"Whoa," Kira finally says.

CHAPTER TWENTY-TWO

The whole way home, I keep checking my rearview in case my parents are tailing me in an unmarked car. Maybe they were on a stakeout to catch me clubbing tonight. I wouldn't put it past them.

At the last red light before home, I check the mirror once again, but this time, to make sure my make-under is holding up. My mom knows I usually step out of the house with a little makeup on, so I have to have on just the right amount. Too little and she'd be suspicious, too.

But when I step in the house, I'm relieved I don't have to face anyone. I go upstairs, and I hear the TV playing at a soft volume in my parents' room. As I'm creaking down the hallway to my room, Mummy does her roll call.

"Simone, ou la?"

"Yes, I'm home," I say.

"Okay, amen." She's now peeking through the crack of the door. "There's dinner for you in the Tupperware in the fridge."

"I'm not hungry, thanks."

This is how it's been between Mummy and me. We've moved on to being formal with each other so as not to go at it in front of Grandmère. We hold obligatory conversations like this, and then move on. Barely asking how each other's day went. I suspect it'll be like this until Grandmère leaves. Or maybe until prom.

As soon as I get to my room, I text Amita.

You OK?

That was a disaster, she responds.

No kidding. But I don't tell her that.

You handled it so well. We were all impressed. Is your dad still upset?

Surprisingly no. He bought that we were celebrating a major academic victory and we lost track of time.

Note to self: That excuse needs to go into a sheltered life survival guide.

How did Pritpal take it? I ask. *Sweet how concerned he was.*

Yeah, he's been texting me.

Have you answered him?

No. I can't. Too embarrassed.

But he must understand, no?

I never told him about my parents. He didn't know.

Oh. But still, no reason to ignore him.

I'm glad Krish agreed to be my backup date because now I need him. I'm sorry—I think my promancipation goals are scrapped.

You'll feel differently tomorrow. Just sleep on it.

No, I'm sure about this. Less complicated this way. Thanks for checking in.

I don't nudge her anymore. For now.

It's time I come clean with Ben, I realize the next day. It's not fair that Krish knows of his floater date status while Ben is none the wiser. He's too good a guy for me not to speak up.

Thanks to a St. Clare tradition, school lets the seniors out early today. The idea is we use the time to work on whatever we've been slacking on—namely, our research papers, which are due in two weeks. It's like an annual Senioritis catch-up day. The HomeGirls plan to be head down getting their papers done—especially Kira, who switched her thesis subject last minute. She's a lot more invested in her new topic, which she's titled "Luddites, Then & Now: From the Industrial Revolution to the Information Age."

Thankfully mine is almost finished, so I'm not as pressed to use this time constructively.

As soon as I get home, I shoot Ben a text.

Hey, free to chat when you have a sec?

He writes back a few minutes later.

Want to chat in person? I'm still in your hood, Jersey girl.

An hour later, I'm in downtown Newark on the grounds of Rutgers University.

Check me out, flexing like a college student. I'm on campus and I feel like I belong. I'm wearing my biker jacket, buffalo plaid button-up, black leggings, and black ankle boots.

As much judgment as I throw at this campus, I don't think I actually ever visited while it was bustling with people. I'm actually loving the vibe and the *ah-mazing* level of diversity in the students strolling the place. Here, no one knows me as sheltered Simone. Here, there's nothing boxing me in.

I walk into the Dana Library and find the carrel off the lounge area. Ben is supposed to meet me somewhere in this section in a few. I get dibs on a carrel next to the window with a view of the main campus.

Times like this I wish my parents would roll up and catch me doing exactly what I told them I'd be doing. It would restore some of that credibility I'm constantly losing.

Matter of fact . . .

I open my sleeping laptop, angle it, and place a notebook and a few pens beside it. Next, I pull out my phone and FaceTime Mummy. I watch the screen while it rings, looking for the sign that she's picked up on the call. Swiftly, in the second or two I have before her face pops up, I stuff my phone in my back pocket.

"Hello? Allo? Momone, you there?" her muffled voice pipes through.

I slide my phone out and answer with my eyebrows fixed in a pleasantly surprised positioning.

"Mummy? Hi, I can't talk right now," I say on the low.

"You called me."

"I did? Oh, I'm sorry." I shake my head.

"Where are you?"

"School got out early today, so I came to the Rutgers library." I shift so she sees my cubicle—staged to perfection—then move again to place her in full view of the library space.

"It's my daughter calling from the college library," Mummy says to an off-screen work colleague, who *wah-wah-wah*s her approval.

"Mummy, I should go. I don't want to disturb other students."

"Yes, okay. God bless you, darling."

I press the red button to end the call.

And . . . scene.

I look around to make sure the call did *not* in fact disrupt anyone's flow. There's polite chatter a few yards away that's well above a whisper. It sounds like staff answering questions. *Good. I won't get kicked out after all.*

And, *word*! This video chat decoy was a perfect idea on an Earn Goodie Points Now & Cash in Later level.

After a few minutes on YouTube, I feel a soft tap on my shoulder. I yank out my earplugs and whip around to see Ben standing there. He's got a young scholar vibe going on, and I like it. He's in a tweed sports jacket, a denim button-up, and khaki pants with the hem slightly rolled up.

"Fancy meeting you here," I say.

Ben looks at me sideways. "Let me guess—you've always wanted to say that to someone."

I flutter my fingers against each other in a soft clap.

He pulls over a wooden chair from the neighboring carrel. He cranes his neck to look at the video playing on the screen behind me.

"What you got going on back there?"

I shut my laptop.

"Was that an episode of *Drunk History*?"

"For your information, that show has plenty of factual elements that are inspiring my senior thesis."

Ben makes a face and pretends to be disgusted with me. "Plebeian," he scoffs. "And what is your thesis on?" he asks.

"Teen heroes in history. Do you know author Mary Shelley started writing *Frankenstein* when she was eighteen?"

"I did *not* know that," Ben says.

"Stick with me, and you'll learn all the things." I grin.

"So what are you now, a superhero chronicler?"

"Wearing *tights* doesn't get you on my list, but being a *ti-tan* in history will," I recite like I'm in a poetry slam.

Ben points at me and I playfully wince at my wack performance.

"A historian." Ben studies me. "Cool. At the museum, I picked up on your passion for big-picture things, so being a history buff makes sense."

I nod. "I don't know what that passion will translate to when it comes time to pick my major," I say, looking around us. "But whatever that major is, I'm sure my mom will report to everyone that it's premed."

Ben does something I've never witnessed him do before. He mocks. And pretty well, because his Haitian accent is on point. "I can hear it now. 'Pick *any* career you want, chérie: doctor or lawyer.'"

We catch ourselves laughing a little too loudly now. When Ben speaks again, there's a lower hum to his voice. It's nice.

"I can't believe I've been coming here all semester, but now that it's almost over, we've just started hanging out," he says.

He's in such a good mood. Hopefully that means he'll take what I have to say in stride. It's best to get the awkwardness out of the way now.

"Hey," I start. "I think you're a cool person, and I want to be truthful with you."

"I appreciate that," Ben says cautiously.

"Well, it's no secret. I didn't want to have my prom arranged by my parents." My chipped nail polish demands to be picked, so, while addressing Ben, I comply. "And I know I mentioned that we should go as part of a friend group."

I look up to make sure Ben is paying attention. I'm used to people interjecting or *Uh-huh*-ing me every step of the way. But he's listening. Wordlessly.

"I've been looking forward to prom for months," I go on, "and every time I imagine myself on that night, I imagine a guy *I* pick by my side."

"A guy like Gavin," says Ben with a half smile.

I nod. His jaw clenches, and he shifts the positioning of his feet.

"You could tell?" I ask.

"Have you asked him to go with you?" Ben asks.

"Yes, and—"

"No need to say more." Ben gets up to leave. I touch his wrist.

"I still would love for you to come to our prom, just like we planned. And I know it's super awkward, but Kira is in need of a date, and she's happy to go with you."

"I don't know, Simone," he says, suddenly sounding fatigued.

"There's a pair of Mets tickets in it for you as thanks for being so flexible," I say, my voice light to lift the mood.

I reach in my bag and pull out the two slender paper tickets and playfully fan my face with them.

"Great seats," I singsong. "Tough to turn down."

"Where'd you get those?"

"I got them for my birthday."

"I'm not taking your birthday gift," he says, incredulous. "I'm not taking a bribe, either."

"Wait." I stand up. "I didn't mean it like that. I'm just sorry I didn't tell you about the Kira setup right when I thought of it. Here, take at least one. It would be nice to see the game with someone who actually appreciates the Mets."

"You know what? Fine, I will take it. Thank you very much."

Ben carefully picks one ticket from between my fingers like he's drawing straws. From the look on his face, he's got the shortest one. In his steady gaze I catch a flash of disappointment. Could it be because of this perceived "bribe"? I get the sense he's calling my bluff. He pauses, as if waiting for me to whine for my ticket back. But I stand there, matching his calm, cool demeanor.

"All right, I'll think about Kira," he says before he walks out. "Check you later."

That was unexpectedly quick. I pause there, wondering how it is that I'm all dressed up, with hours to spare and no one to hang with. Nothing else to do but sit back down and dive into my senior thesis. I guess I really will be spending my early dismissal day working at the college library.

Touché, Mother. Touché.

CHAPTER TWENTY-THREE

Speaking to Ben, as difficult as it was, gives me the moxie to talk to Gavin about the prom. I want to show him a few fashion posts I've saved. Maybe it'll spark some ideas for what he wants to wear.

Gabby's at basketball practice today, so I'm on the bus going home by myself. I take a deep breath, step off the bus outside Karl Pool, and watch it leave for East Orange without me. Even if I miss the next bus, I'll be home at a decent time if I catch the bus after that. I'll just pop into Karl Pool and see if Gavin's there. No harm in me just happening by. It's not entirely unusual. And if he is in there, I'll take it as a sign that this is the moment to get results. I set some imaginary timer and tell myself I can seal the deal with Gavin in thirty minutes.

I take a swing and I don't miss. Gavin's at Karl Pool, but it looks like he's leaving. Rashod isn't with him.

"Simone, hey!"

"Hi." I smile at his beauteous face. "Have a few minutes?"

"Nothing planned," he says. "What are you about to get into?"

"I figured we could . . . grab coffee and talk about prom?" I say.

"What about prom?" He sounds clueless. *Um, is he serious right now?*

"Well—"

"Just messing with you. You mind if I check on something at home first? I live just a few blocks away."

I feel a flutter in my stomach. *I'm going to Gavin's house!* Oh my God. Are we going to kiss?

But wait, is this a ploy to get me somewhere private so he can be alone with me? To do more than kiss? When Mummy's "Boys only want one thing" refrain pops into my head, I swat it away and picture it disappearing over Citi Field's centerfield wall.

I reverse the camera on my phone and sneak a peek at my face. Nothing gooey in my eyes, nose clean, lips moisturized, nothing in my teeth. I'm good. If Gavin steps to me for a kiss, I'll be ready.

I wonder how I'd react. A few weeks ago, that would be a dumb thing to ask. The me of a few weeks ago wouldn't hesitate in this moment. The me of a few weeks ago would slap me to sleep for even waffling like this. But I can't help it. I'm feeling kind of uneasy about going to Gavin's house alone.

When in doubt, call on family. I text Gabby to see if she's nearby, and it turns out she's braiding a friend's hair a few blocks away and just finishing up. She was planning to browse the racks at her favorite boutique; her next hair-braiding client lives in our neighborhood.

"Great news," I tell Gavin. "Gabby can meet up, too. She'll be waiting for us at the bus stop around the corner."

"Cool." Gavin seems totally unbothered by the extra company. I'm realizing how out of character it would be of him to ever say no to someone he considers a friend. For the first time, the thought occurs to me that this same friendship code may apply to him accepting my invitation to prom.

"Nice ride," I say once I've slipped into the leather passenger seat of his car.

"Mèsi, Thibodeaux."

"Ah, you're keeping up the Creole." I smile a mile wide. "I'm impressed."

Gavin steers though the streets. "Of course!" he says. "I told you I love the language."

It's sweet to be alone with him in close quarters again. But that's all we get to say to each other before we pull over to let Gabby hop in. My ever-zippy cousin chats her way into the back seat. "Y'all just saved me a few bucks."

I reach an arm back and extend my hand in greeting until her fingers make contact with mine.

"Why? What happened to your bus card?" I ask her.

"I left it at home. I thought today was May first and I switched out my April card."

"Yikes. You're a few days off," I wince. "Good thing you had money on you."

Gavin looks in his rearview at Gabby. "I'll give you my number so you can text me if that ever happens again," he says.

He is so giving.

"Thank you," says Gabby with all sincerity.

I check my phone and see a new text. It's Anne, with one of her periodic warnings. This time, apparently, I need to beware of my parents, who are home and wondering where I am. *Already?* I check the time and realize it's been half an hour since I got off the bus at Karl Pool.

I instantly have what my Italian American grade school teacher would call *agita*. The anxious knot in my stomach is replaced by annoyance when I tell myself that I'm not doing anything scandalous. *Mummy and Papi can take two chill pills and check me in the morning.*

We arrive at Gavin's house, and he collects the mail and a package before we enter his home. The inside is like the neighborhood—neat, affluent, nicely maintained. The fresh flowers in the foyer blow my mind. They seem to have been engineered to bloom on cue, right when we step into the house.

In the sun-bathed kitchen, fragrant air wafts over in greeting, but so too does the faint sound of a video game in progress. It's coming from the lower level.

A short row of carpeted steps off the main living space leads us to what looks like a sophisticated playroom. The TV is on, but there isn't anyone in sight. *I guess the TV is on a timer, just like the entryway flowers.*

The space is furnished with two brown leather armchairs that are large enough to swallow anyone who sits in them. A huge flat screen that's about half my height hangs low on the far wall, and a Ping-Pong table anchors the center of the space. The Ping-Pong major leagues, if there is such a division, would play on this table. That's how legit it looks. And trophies that look like they've been spit-shined proudly line the built-in nooks in each corner.

"Yo, B, meet Simone and Gabby."

Who be this B?

"Who're you talking to?" asks Gabby.

I almost jump out my skin when a shadowy figure pokes his head out from the cavernous armchair, like a groundhog checking for winter's end.

"Simone, Gabby," he echoes in a video-game trance, but he sits up to reveal himself to be an older teen boy who resembles Gavin. He's handling a console and barely looks behind him to acknowledge us face-to-face.

"Oh. I didn't realize anyone was here," I say, my hand still over my heart.

"This is my big brother, Garvey. You hungry, man?" Gavin asks him.

"Yeah."

"I told you you should grab something from the fridge. Did you?"

"Naw."

I wonder how long Garvey has been camped out here. From the looks of how firmly rooted his bottom is in that chair, probably hours.

Gavin points a thumb at Garvey and affectionately shakes his head. "*This* dude." He hasn't given up getting Garvey to engage. "Bro, Simone and Gabby go to St. Clare Academy."

"I have a friend named Claire." Garvey perks up, his eyes still on the screen. "Her birthday is the same day as mine."

"Yeah, buddy," says Gavin, giving his brother's shoulder a squeeze.

Gavin's phone rings, and he takes on the upright stance of a track star at the starting block. He answers the call on speaker.

"Hello, Mom?"

"I need you to come outside and get these bags. I have to run *right* back out to a meeting. Did a package come for me? Is your father home yet?"

My head spins just listening to all the stuff the woman throws at Gavin in the span of a split second.

"I'll bring the package out," says Gavin, his back stiffening. "I'll get the bags, and I think he's on his way."

"Good, see you then," she says and hangs up.

"Be right back," he says to me and Gabby as he heads to the stairs. "Hope I remember where I put that package."

"On the kitchen counter by the fridge," says Gabby, hastening behind him as if she's answering the call of duty, too. "I saw you put it there."

I kick back with Garvey and watch him play his game for a few minutes. And then without warning, he stands up.

"I'm going to get a snack. Want a snack, Claire's friend?" he asks.

"Um, sure," I tell him. We head up to the kitchen and Garvey grabs a bag of chips. I pop open the bottle of iced tea he hands me. "Thanks."

"No problem." There's a little pride mixed into his joyful smile. "Say hi to Claire for me when you see her."

"Okay," I call at his back before he disappears downstairs.

I'm swiveling in my seat at the kitchen counter, wondering how I came to be in Gavin's house. *Gavin, my dream prom date,* I remind myself. *Gavin, my dreamy dream prom date.*

Then why am I sneakily checking my phone to see if Ben texted?

Gabby's loud voice breaks into my ill-timed thoughts, and for the second time in this house, I get startled.

"Your mom seems like a boss," she booms from the front hallway.

"Not a lot of people like that about her." Gavin sounds a bit wounded. "I'll never follow her footsteps into politics. Too many trolls."

Hearing their conversation, it occurs to me that I don't even know much about Gavin.

"Well, she must be doing something right if the sexist trolls are calling her unlikeable," says Gabby.

Gavin's laugh sounds bubbly. "I like the way you put that. You two would get along."

Gabby and Gavin enter the kitchen, and Gabby sits beside me at the counter. I fire up the prom pictures I'd like Gavin to look at.

Gabby sees my screen and gives me the kind of look I normally give her when she oversteps. What's with *her* all of a sudden? She seems to be thinking things internally instead of saying them out loud. *How odd.*

"Are you seriously going to do that right now?" she finally whispers.

I nod.

"I have to meet my client in a half hour. It may take us a while to get back to East Orange, so we need to be leaving soon."

As annoying as it is to admit, Gabby's right. She's the one doing me a favor by coming here, so it wouldn't be fair to make her late. But it sucks that I've come this far, only to have my plans unravel.

"I guess we can talk on the drive back?" I ask Gavin.

"Sure."

But there's not much talking over Gavin's thumping car stereo. Soon after we get into the car and program the GPS with our addresses, Gabby and Gavin's bop (apparently they share a favorite song) comes on. It's hip-hop karaoke the whole way.

Gavin lowers the volume when Gabby hops out of the car in

front of her client's apartment building. Mercifully, he doesn't turn it all the way back up on our ride home.

Wait. Gavin's about to drive me home? My parents are going to freak if they see us. I clearly didn't think this through. If I had, I would've switched seats with Gabby and asked him to take me home first. Rolling up in the back seat with Gabby also in the car would not look nearly as damning as this looks.

"You know, my mom grew up in East Orange," says Gavin, looking around the streets with reverence. "It must be cool being from a city where so many old-school legends passed through—Whitney Houston, Queen Latifah . . ."

Just ask him to drop you off a few blocks from home.

"Lauryn Hill, Naughty by Nature . . ."

But how is that going to look? Anyone who asks that is hiding something. And he'll want to know the backstory, which is too humiliating to tell. I'm a year older. He expects some sophistication.

Gavin's GPS has our ETA in three minutes. *Think. Think.*

My phone is going nuts with alerts. A call from Anne, which I promptly send to voicemail. A couple of texts, none from Ben. Mostly it's Amita and Kira fishing for updates on my afternoon with Gavin. I text them my current situation and ask the HomeGirls what they advise.

As he's rolling to a stop sign, open your door and roll out, stunt-woman style.

Amita's got jokes. But a second later, she's back with something more practical.

It sucks giving him the facts, but it'll suck way more if your mom catches you.

Too late. We're already on my street.

"Yo, is that your moms?"

My heart thumps in my ears at the sight of my mom outside, standing stiff as a Buckingham Palace guard in her pink floral robe and fuzzy slippers. Her arms are crossed and she's fuming.

This is bad.

CHAPTER TWENTY-FOUR

I get out of the car, fast, hoping Gavin will smell danger and flee, but he rolls down the window to greet Mummy.

"Get in the house," Mummy growls in Creole between clenched teeth. She's tapping the ground with one foot, and embarrassment edges out horror for control of my brain. It's like, *Woush,* if you're going to come outside in a bathrobe, do you have to wear it with house slippers? Couldn't she have paired it with flip-flops?

"You, sir." She points to Gavin. "Come on out so I can speak to you."

"Mummy, no," I plead. "He's just doing me a favor because I forgot my bus pass." It's reflexive, the lie. I make up whatever story I can think of on the spot.

"I'm not going to put up with some boy dropping you home this *late,*" Mummy says evenly.

"It-it's barely six o'clock," I stammer, my temper flaring.

"Go inside and tell it to your little list!'"

I freeze. "*How* did you—"

"You didn't think I knew about that, did you?"

I storm inside the house in desperate search of the nearest portal to the multiverse.

My dad is playing piano. Classic Papi avoidance tactic. He stops mid-melody when he hears me race past him.

"Simone?" he calls, alarmed.

My legs carry me up the stairs lightning quick and not without a thunderous rumble. And there in my bedroom, my street-facing window reveals the ongoing saga outside. Mummy's arms are still crossed and she's speaking while Gavin is listening respectfully, nodding his head. Anne comes into my room, followed by Papi's worried face peeking in. I run right into Anne's outstretched arms and Papi softly shuts my door, leaving us alone.

"How can she do this?" I sob into my sister's shoulder.

"It'll be all right, I promise," she says gently.

Water droplets fall like rain on the side of my face that's not buried in my sister's neck. I know I can't be crying that hard. Is it Anne? I look up to see Grandmère in my room, reaching her hand into a container of water and dousing me with a flick of her hand.

"Be calm, child. Cool down. No need to put yourself en colore. That's right. Joy comes in the morning. The Lord is all powerful."

Is she performing some kind of exorcism? I'm not possessed. I'm hurt and angry.

But somehow, my anger starts to subside, or at least settle a bit.

"Merci, Grandmère," I tell my grandmother, and she leaves my room, satisfied.

After what feels like hours, Mummy finally walks back in the house. She doesn't come find me, and I wonder if Grandmère intercepted her. I hear them talking in Ma Tante's room, and the low rumble of their voices sounds calm.

Anne stays with me as I wipe my tears on the sleeve of my uniform cardigan and plop down on my bed.

"I still can't believe it," I say, pulling my legs to my chest.

"Please don't take it to heart. Mummy just wants you to be more careful."

"What does careful have to do with anything? Mummy already treats me like I'm reckless, and I'm more careful than anyone I know. What she calls a pileup is a fender bender to just about everyone else."

At least, I have been careful, until the Playlist. But was that really so wrong?

"Well, things between you might be less strained if you didn't lie to her so much," Anne goes on.

Maybe I'm paranoid, but that sounds like a dig. "What's that supposed to mean?" I ask Anne. "How did Mummy even know about my list? Did *you* find it and show it to her?"

I stand up, waiting for her answer. But the one she gives is not cutting it.

"Mummy's seen it. That's not on me."

I know it's not fair to Anne, but sometimes I want to lash out at her for making such tame choices that I'm then expected to make. She picks up on my vibe, and she doesn't like it.

"You know what," says Anne. "It sounds like you want to be alone. I'm close by if you need me." She gets up, turns on her heel, and exits my room.

Everyone retreats to their corners of the Thibodeaux house. Papi's resonant piano notes build the perfect sound barrier to muffle the sounds of our private worlds. In mine, it's rapid thumb-tapping as I send urgent messages to the HomeGirls about the Gavin disaster and the Playlist breach. In Anne's room, it's prob-ably furious keyboard clicking as she works on an assignment. Grandmère must be asleep by now. As for Mummy, I can bet she's leafing through and tabbing the pages of some paperback novel, still fuming at me.

In the midst of all this, a text from Ben comes through. I can't lie, I'm excited he's reached out. Until I read his message.

Hey. Ordering flowers. Should I get Kira a corsage you pin on the front or the type you wear like a bracelet?

I feel so alone and crowded in at the same time.

Mummy knocks on my door a little later. I can hear the TV blar-ing CNN downstairs, so my dad must be back to his old self after the drama. I sit up, and I start clearing my uniform and my back-pack off my bed.

Mummy can speak freely. I have no plans to talk to her, but I want to hear what happened between her and Gavin.

She pads over to my window and leans against the wall. "I'm not going to get into how disappointed I was tonight, you asking a stranger to the prom and lying to me about it," she begins. "I don't even know who this boy is, but I can see he was raised well. For him to want to do you a favor when he's interested in a different girl let me know you are only friends."

My lower jaw swings on its hinge. I am in shock from everything my mom has said.

Gavin is interested in a different girl? He thinks we're just friends? I'm confused, but oddly, I'm not cut up by this. I don't feel the hurt I was expecting.

So, all this time, he was just being . . . nice? No, he was being himself. In fact, the only person who wasn't being themself was me. I flashback through all the times I put on airs around Gavin. Being authentic didn't come as naturally in his presence.

But maybe he was just telling my mom we were "just friends" so she would back off. I may have not always been in sync with Gavin, but I don't think I misread his flirting with me. I know I was flirting right back at times.

I'm so confused. Was he telling my mom the truth?

Just in case he was, it would be wrong to continue to make him feel obligated to take me to prom.

I have to de-promposal him.

Mummy studies me, processing what my face is revealing to

her about me and Gavin, and I look away to lock her out. That's privileged information.

"Sometimes challenges can show you the face of a true friend," she continues. "And although I don't believe in friends who are boys, I understand why you felt like he was a good choice. But the choice is yours. I will have to tell Madame Honoré your decision soon, so let me know if you'd like me to cancel the plans with Ben."

It's my second shock wave in the span of five minutes. Mummy is willing to cancel the arranged prom. I never imagined that would happen in a million years. I'm so bowled over, I don't even notice her exiting my room until I hear my door meet the frame.

I sit there processing what just happened. And I realize that I didn't even get a chance to ask Mummy how—and what—she knows about the Playlist. I'm wondering if I should muster up the courage to go after her and ask, when I get a text from Gavin.

You alright?

I should be asking you that. I am so so sorry.

Don't sweat it. Mama bears gonna mama bear.

I take a deep breath and type:

The good news is, you're now free of your escort duties.

I wait for him to respond and say that no, he still wants to take me to prom. But then his reply comes.

Sorry that didn't work out.

I sigh. So he wasn't lying to Mummy after all.

It's ok. Thanks for being so cool about everything.

Keep your head up. And hey, if you still wanna ride to prom in my car, let me know.

"Aw, what a stand-up dude," Kira says the next morning at Elevensies when I show her and Amita the texts.

I let out a ragged sigh. I'm still reeling from how fast everything changed in a snap. I'm in a funk, but at the same time, feeling . . . lighter than I have in a while.

"Yeah," I say. "I'm glad he took the whole thing so well. That wasn't fair to him."

Amita reaches out and rubs my hand. "It's all good. I'm sure he'll still find a way to reach out to you if he wants to be your boyfriend," she says. "But we're sorry about your prom dreams."

"Well," I say, looking up from my cream cheese bagel. "At least there's a chance we can still have Pritpal join our table?" I ask delicately.

If I can't have my dream prom date, I'll be damned if I don't get the dining dynamic just right. Everyone knows your prom table crew is as important, if not more important, as your date.

Amita's face drops. "We broke up."

"What? Why?" Kira and I are screeching like two alley cats.

Amita shakes her head. "He keeps texting and calling, but I just wanted to spare him the drama. Thank goodness for my safety date, cousin Krish."

Kira starts fidgeting in her seat like a preschooler about to be served cake pops. "Oh, so Krish *is* coming."

"Yup, and he was kinda excited when I asked him to suit up."

"But Pritpal wouldn't be reaching out to you if he didn't want to see you again," I say.

"Same goes for you and Gavin," says Kira, who is clearly still impressed with Gavin's texts. "Maybe there's still a chance you can take him."

"It's different with Gavin than it is with Pritpal," I admit out loud for the first time. "It seemed like Gavin was on board with everything because he's ride-or-die, not because he's *my* ride-or-die."

I pause.

"At least Ben seems committed to being your date," I say to Kira. My attempt at finding a silver lining only makes me feel guilty that I'm feeling some kind of way about the Ben and Kira pairing. *You can't have your cake pops and eat them, too*, I scold myself.

"Ben's another nice guy." Kira nods. "He messaged me asking if I'm allergic to any flowers."

"That sounds super nerdy but cute, and I wouldn't expect anything less of him," Amita says, managing an amused smile. She looks over to me and there's a flash of recognition in her eyes.

"But, Simone—I can't take Ben, knowing that you have no date now." Kira leans in and touches my arm. "You should go with him. I was on track to go solo anyway."

"That's sweet of you, but no, that wouldn't be fair."

"Well, let's handle one problem at a time." Amita cuts us off before Kira and I go another few more rounds. "Tell us more about your mom and the Playlist, Simone. How did that *happen*?"

She and Kira look as alarmed as I've been feeling.

"I have no idea," I say. "And I was too afraid to bring it up with her last night."

"She must have seen it somewhere," Kira says.

I shake my head. "I never leave it lying around, and it's still snug in my wallet as we speak. My sister, Anne, might have seen it at some point, but she wouldn't do something so cold-blooded. And neither would Gabby." I meet my friends' eyes with my own. "It's a mystery."

No one has anything funny or comforting to say after that. We pick at our bagels and sip our coffee in silence, a cloud hanging over our collective heads.

Do I have any reason to doubt Gabby? I'd heard from my cousin first thing this morning. She sent me a "How're u doin'" text, which I thought was her way of tracking my estimated departure time for the bus. I responded that I was already on my way to the early bus. But now I realize she might have meant "How're u doin'" as in *How are you doing after yesterday's humiliation?*

But how would Gabby even know what had happened with my mom and Gavin? I hadn't texted her last night after the incident, partly because I'm not ready to laugh about it and Gabby definitely doesn't respect the "too soon" code. And partly because Gabby's not about that life. The HomeGirls understand, though.

As Amita, Kira, and I clear our table and walk over to our school, I fill them in on the Gabby conundrum. "How did she find out about my mom and Gavin?" I wonder aloud.

Kira holds the heavy entrance door for Amita. "Maybe your mom told her mom? Didn't you say there's a whole network there?"

"True," I sigh.

"Just ask her," Amita says matter-of-factly. "Text her now."

The choice sounds so clear when Amita says it. And I suppose it's better than asking Gabby in person. If she makes a joke over text, I can just delete it, because I can't deal.

As quick as I text the question, she responds with the answer.

Gavin called me. I'm so sorry. Everything will work out.

I blink. *Gavin* called her? Great.

"*Ugh*," I tell my friends. "Now my name is ringing out on the gossip circuit. Pretty soon, every corner of St. Clare Academy and Millwall Prep will be whispering about this."

"Don't worry about that. Now you know, so one less thing to wonder about," says Amita.

She's right.

Think positive, I tell myself. *The bright side: You're not that important. No one cares as much as you do, and nobody's checking for you.*

"Are you okay?" Amita asks at my locker. "Do you want me to talk to her?"

"To who?"

"Your mom." Amita thinks she's Mummy's absolute favorite, but clearly we all know that Kira is the fave.

"Outside of, like, the governor calling in a last-minute pardon, there's nothing anyone can do at this point," I say. *I'll go to the prom alone,* I think, but I haven't accepted that fact enough to say it aloud.

The day is a blur. Between my workload and the load on my mind, I don't remember much about who I speak to or bump into in the halls and in class. But one thought lingers . . . Gavin called Gabby. Not text. He called. Curious.

By the end of the day, the only thing I care about is catching the early bus. Over my years at the Academy, I've learned if you leave school immediately upon dismissal—meaning no stopping at lockers or tracking down Gabby—and you speed-walk, you can make the early bus.

When I settle into a seat in the back, it feels like I won a prize. My speed-walking paid off and now I'll get home early. Though, yes, home is the scene of the crime, it's also where my little piece of the world is. And today, all I want to do is find a cozy nook and stream a funny movie. It'll be hours before anyone else gets home, so I'm especially looking forward to having the place to myself.

But as soon as the bus pulls away from the curb, I can tell something is off. There's a louder-than-normal rattling that just won't quit.

When we coast down the hill, the rattling isn't as loud. But on a small incline, or when the bus turns a corner, it's back on full blast. The bus driver keeps going, but I suspect the only reason she does is to find a busier area to break down. We're still deep in leafy suburbia, where there's no chance to hop on another bus route.

Kuh-kuh-kuk-kuh-twhaaaap . . .

"*Shhhhh—!*" The bus's final hiss comes from the driver's lips instead.

I guess this is my stop. I guess this is all our stops.

"Um, ladies and gentlemen—"

The groans and shuffling of the departing passengers drown out the rest of the driver's announcement.

It would be too expensive to rideshare from here. But if I hustle down six or seven blocks, I'll have more options. The main ave there is bustling with activity and transportation.

No use sulking over how much this sucks. I still have a chance to get home within the hour. Three long street blocks later, I arrive at a quiet intersection and spot a familiar car. *Gavin's* car. At least, I think it is.

He's at a stop sign, but he's heading in my direction. I bend down, duck my head, and pretend to tie my shoelaces. I stay low. Thankfully, Gavin swishes by without noticing me. *Phew,* I think, when one sharp glance confirms it is in fact Gavin behind the wheel. But in the next breath, I recognize the girl in the passenger seat.

Whoa, that's Gabby riding with him.

No doubt about it.

CHAPTER TWENTY-FIVE

I don't answer Gabby's *Where you at?* texts that afternoon and evening. And she doesn't follow up by hounding me with calls or swinging by unannounced. She gets the hint that I want to be left alone. She probably thinks I'm still stewing over Mummy.

At home that night, I *am* still dragging out my silent treatment toward my mother, even though she keeps trying to spark conversation with me. I know it bugs her that I'm hanging out with Grandmère and chatting, but she needs to know I'm not a little kid and she just can't wreck my life like that.

And now seeing Gabby with Gavin has added another layer of *what the hell* on my confusion cake.

It isn't until the next day at school that my cousin appears at my locker.

"Gavin and I were looking for you yesterday after school," she says.

I gotta give it to Gabby. "Bring It Up Before They Ask About

It" is a pretty brilliant tactic. But she owes me more of an explanation if she's looking for permission to date my dream prom date.

"Oh, you were, were you?"

Gabby gives me a once-over that lets me know she doesn't like my tone. *Good.*

"We thought it would cheer you up to hang out at Karl Pool again, so he came up to St. Clare to drive us there."

Gabby is dropping that "we" in a French rather than a Creole accent, like she's bougie. But her excuse is classic "Tell Her You Did It For Her." *Respect, cuz. Another smart tactic.* Somewhere inside Gabby's brain, a fired-up neuron is slow clapping.

"Tell me again," I say, closing my locker to face her. "How exactly did you find out what happened with Gavin and my mom?"

She pauses a beat. And then, with her usual Gabby gusto, spits fire like she's been sipping on hot sauce. "Wait a minute. I don't think I like the places your mind is taking you. What type of answer are you looking for here?"

Gabby steps back to give my locker neighbor access to her keypad. My cousin and I make our way through the crowded hall and duck into the nearest bathroom.

"I just want to know," I go on. "Did you bump into him someplace? When did he tell you?" I was genuinely curious.

"He texted me when he left your house."

"Oh." Boy, they wasted no time.

"He was worried about you and wanted me to check up on you."

I see we're back to "You Did It For Her."

"But you didn't text me or come by later that night." Something's not making sense. Too many holes.

Gabby folds her arms. I don't take the bait. She's not going to turn the tables on me. Nope. She's the one who has to speak up right now.

Come on, Gabby. You're so close—bring it home.

"I didn't come by because I finished with my client so late."

Good one. I can see the train pulling up to the station. I resist the urge to lean forward for the strong finish to her closing argument.

"And, *okay*—after that, Gavin and I stayed on the phone until late. I knocked out before I could call you."

*ish just went completely off the rails.

"There it is," I say. "Just when I was wondering if you'd say it out loud."

"Say what?"

"Say that you're checking for Gavin."

Gabby opens her mouth, then closes it until it's gathered into a tight pinch. She holds her face like that for a few moments, and then releases the built-up tension with a head shake.

"I wasn't always checking for him." She sounds measured and defensive at the same time. "At least I'm sharing what's going on with the people I'm closest to." She speaks faster with every word she utters. "You'd rather talk to girls you hardly know."

"So, this is jealousy warfare? You envy the HomeGirls so you try to make me jealous of you with Gavin?"

This ranks up there with some of the wacky theories Mummy usually hurls at me. I'm immediately embarrassed I said it.

Gabby shakes her head. "Why you gonna make up stories when you have access to the truth? You know I don't hide anything from you. If *my* mom went buckwild in these streets like that, I would tell you. But I had to hear it from someone else."

"Some things need to sink in before I feel comfortable talking about them," I say.

"By that logic, that means you told no one, correct?"

"No, that means I told no one who wouldn't get it."

"Just when I was wondering if you would say it out loud," says Gabby, turning my words against me.

"And what does all this have to do with you getting cozy with Gavin?" I ask. "Just because I don't move as fast as you'd like?"

"Just because you're realizing that you spent your high school years pining after guys but never dating any of them doesn't mean you have to take it out on me."

I almost feel physically winded from that gut punch. But I firm up my core and say as strongly as I can, "Nice try making it sound like I'm blaming you for all the evils in the world. I'm just calling you out on your shadiness."

"Gavin told me you two aren't going to prom together anymore."

Oh, so somehow that makes everything okay for her to shoot her shot with Gavin? I don't think so.

"One ride home doesn't mean you're dating," I say.

Gabby storms out, leaving me alone with my ruffled reflection.

The sound of a toilet flushing alerts me that I'm not alone. When the person comes out, I freeze in my embarrassment. It's the same girl who'd witnessed my conversation with Amita, way back when we first decided to form the HomeGirls. She looks a bit freaked out at the sight of me. I think I've solidified a reputation.

"Hi," I say weakly. She attempts a painful smile back. I wordlessly wash my hands and get out of there.

Honestly, I don't understand why I'm in my feelings over this. Especially when—if I'm completely honest with myself—Gabby and Gavin are clearly a perfect match. I have to admit it. They're kinda like the pop culture couple you never knew you needed in your life.

Plus, the truth is, I've been thinking way more about Ben than Gavin.

As I sit at my desk in my bedroom, printing my finished thesis, I try to ignore the echo of Gabby's words in my mind. When I replay the part where she called out my preference for HomeGirls, guilt sets up camp in my chest. It's not a good feeling. My cousin is important to me. Now I'm wondering if I make that clear enough to her.

Sure, Papi overshares, Anne overanalyzes, and Mummy overprotects. It's embarrassing, annoying, invasive, and unnecessary.

The thing is, that's the worst they get. But when they cause scenes like Mummy's Gavin gotcha, I have trouble remembering that.

And they get *stuck* in their overreactions. It makes things drag on and on. Lately, the mood in the house has been so heavy. Bu it's getting tougher to make out who's the one dragging things out—them or me.

The ironic thing is the HomeGirls—once my trusted escape and source of fun—are becoming reminders of our failed mission. Seeing them at school just reminds me of my sheltered life. Another reason to feel like the only thing I can lay claim to is my academic success. My social achievements are not remotely as stellar.

Scrolling through prom fashion happens less often now. Planning takes a back seat. I haven't even identified what earrings and accessories I'll wear, which is so unlike me. I would've loved everything to play out differently, but Mummy. But Mummy . . .

I can't help but feel that this is all my parents' fault. I stay on my side of the emotional wall I've built between Mummy and me, until later that week she breaches it and asks, "Ride with me to the supermarket?"

Grandmère is sitting in her favorite lounge chair and looks encouragingly at me. And that's the only reason why, once again, I'm following Mummy down the bright aisles of our local supermarket.

She parallel-parks her mini cart next to the shelves of dried beans. "Are you in the mood for pwa rouge or pwa vé this weekend?"

Suddenly, I can't keep my frustration in anymore.

"I don't know. Do I get a choice?"

"*Oh-ohhh*, that's what I'm asking you."

I shrug my shoulders. "Well, I can't be sure. Lately it seems like I have no freedom to choose what I want."

"What is this girl standing before me saying?" Mummy says in Creole, the bag of red kidney beans suspended in her frozen hand like she's a robot on low battery. The only things moving are her eyebrows and lips, really.

I have to try extra hard not to stomp my foot in a fit of temper. "You can't lead my life for me!" I blurt out.

Mummy's thin lips get even thinner. They are so taut, they don't even curve to form her next words. "So lead—lead by lying your way through life like a politician!"

I can't believe I want to laugh at a time like this. But what she said was so unintentionally funny. And the way she said it made her look like an elaborately drawn character on an animated show.

"Go ahead and kikiki," says Mummy, tossing one bag of beans after another in the cart. "Wait and see if you think it's funny one day when you're a mom. You and your lists."

I tense up. The Playlist again. "If my friends and I lie, it's because that's the only way we get to do anything." *Ugh. Why doesn't she get it?* "Like our list you keep mentioning."

"What things from the list did you and your friends do, any-way? Cut class?" She raises her voice, before sidebarring with the

Lord. "Father God, look at the poor unfortunate soul I am. How did I wind up here?"

I look to the heavens but all I see are warehouse rafters. My mother is such a worrier, she'd turn all her wigs gray if she owned any. "Figures you would start with that one, and not ask about the enriching experiences we had instead."

"Enriching? Enriching is l'école," my mother snaps with wide-eyed incredulity. "Enriching is what your father and I wish we had in the bank. We invest all we earn in you for you to be in l'école, studying. That's all the enriching I know about."

"Okay, if it makes you feel any better, I was so nervous about cutting class I was literally sick to my stomach."

"Eh bien, good for you," Mummy spews, her head cocked to one side, a menacing finger jabbing the air like it's my feelings. "You act like somebody was paying you to look for trouble. Who sent you, anyway? Wha-who-who-ki-ki . . . *woush*," Mummy stammers.

I clutch imaginary pearls and stare in disbelief at my saintly mother's malfunctioning spiral. *Have I broken Constance?*

Yes, I could lip-synch to everything she's saying—it's the same ol' Haitian parent song, down to the rhetorical "Who sent you?" classic. I'm pretty numb to all that. But seeing the wildly disappointed look in her eyes cuts deep.

We're silent as an elderly man in a motorized shopping cart rides through the chasm between my mother and me.

When Mummy lets loose a sharp chupee, I'm actually grateful.

It's the release valve that relieves her tension. The chagrin fades from her gaze, and I act quick to change the subject.

"How did you even find out about the list?" I ask.

"Your friend Kira texted it to me," says Mummy.

What? Kira texted Mummy? When? Is *she* a mole? But then it hits me: That afternoon in my kitchen. I remember Kira accidentally using AirDrop to send the photo of the list to everyone—not just me and Amita, but Gabby.

And apparently Mummy, too.

I want to pull out my phone and text Kira an all-caps IT WAS YOU! but then Mummy goes on.

"I want to confess something." Mummy's tone has shifted. We no longer are on opposing sides, and that brings me so much relief. I listen with an open heart as she continues. "When I saw the list, I thought you wrote it to get your friends to laugh at me and your father, because you think we're such a big joke."

Is that what she's been thinking this entire time—that, as some sort of sick sport, I was making my parents the laughing-stock? When I think about how this must've made Mummy feel, it hurts. I deflate and let my arms go limp at my sides. My eyes well up. I can't remember a time beyond my toddler years when I cried in a supermarket, but here I am.

"Mummy, I wasn't laughing at you. None of us were," I start gently, and catch the tears at the corner of my eyes before they're able to stream. "It's just that, I hear a lot of nos from you. There's always a no blocking my way, even for the simple asks. After a while I started saying no to myself. No to my dreams." I take a breath. "Well, this list is my yes. I took a stand for what I believe in and started saying yes to myself, to my desires and my dreams."

My mother's face softens and there's a glint of recognition in her eyes. The tenderness I see there tugs at my heart. I steel myself and slide my hand to the spot where I'd placed my temporary tattoo. "A butterfly that doesn't break out from its chrysalis can't survive. You've prepared me for this next stage in my life. I aced high school, I got into Rutgers, early decision. I'm smart, I'm strong, and I'm ready to use the tools you gave me."

"Yes . . . you are," Mummy breathes, barely above a whisper. Her words speed up my tear production factory, so I can barely make out that her eyes are watery, too. We use what we have—a shirt sleeve, an old napkin—to stop the flooding.

"Attention, shoppers," a voice announces over the store PA system. "Super-soft two-ply facial tissues are on buy-one-get-one special offer. Shop this deal today in aisle sixteen."

Mummy and I bust out laughing. It's a good kind of laughter. Not the PlayList mockery Mummy imagined. It's the kind that literally moves you, until the shaking you do vibrates your spirit and recalibrates your mood. Mummy's shoulders bounce and my side aches.

I always want to laugh this way with my mother, and I never want to make her feel ridiculed, just because she experiences life differently from me. What's old-fashioned to me seems positively à la mode for her.

"Mummy," I add. "That list was sent to you in error. Your phone must've been in the kitchen when Kira AirDropped it to the group. I'm sorry seeing the text made you feel that way. You know I love and respect you," I say soberly. "You're my hero."

"And you're my pride and joy," she says. "I know I'm hard on you, Simone, but I only want to protect you. The world can be cruel to girls."

"I know," I say, stepping toward her just as she steps toward me.

"Especially Black girls."

I bow my head, overcome with the anguish in Mummy's words. "I know; I really do," I whisper.

The arms that wrap around me are warm, and loving, and hers. Wonderfully hers.

"Our mother is impossible," I tell Anne when I get home. She's in her room, surrounded by piles of new clothes she bought and smiling at her phone screen. "But I still love her."

"FaceTime you later?" she sweetly asks her boyfriend, Max. She blows him a kiss and hangs up. "What happened?" she asks me.

"We got into another fight in the supermarket," I groan. I pick up one of the new shirts draped over her bed frame and size it up against my body. "But I think we made up. Sort of."

"I'm glad I wasn't there," says Anne, snatching the shirt from me. "Getting caught in the cross fire when you two are going at it is *not* fun."

"It's not fair, either," I say, picking up the next shirt, which looks more like a long dress. Would she dare wear it like that, though?

"No, it isn't. But you can't expect someone to change her stripes overnight."

"Oh yeah?" I singsong, holding up a striped minidress from Anne's purchase pile. She snatches that away from me, too, and I laugh.

"Mind your business," she scolds. Anne walks the dress over to her closet and I'm not at all surprised when she pulls out an identically striped hanger for it. "Okay, so maybe I'm Haitian-level extra with the whole dress-hanger matchmaking. But I swear that's not why I bought this particular dress."

"Whatever makes you happy." I heave out a sigh before belly flopping onto Anne's firm bed. "At least I helped my friends all get set with their prom dates, so thinking of that is what keeps me happy these days."

"*You* did?" she asks.

I nod and explain how I arranged it so that Kira can have a date, and Ben can still get to experience prom.

"That's . . . interesting." Anne walks back to her bed, resting a knee on it.

I prop myself up on my elbows and ask Anne sincerely, "How do you do it? Your life has been dictated for you and you just . . . go along with it."

The minute the words are floating in the air and stinging our ears, it's too late to take them back. Anne's got this familiar look on her face. I'm pretty sure I wear the same look when Gabby says something to make *me* feel like an overprotected fool.

"I—I'm sorry. I misspoke. I didn't mean it like that at all, Anne, believe me."

The words tumble out of my mouth, and I wait to see if Anne will pick them up. But her stiffened back is unbending. In her posture I see the girl who did, in her own way, engage in a form of resistance during her arranged date those four years ago, by wearing protest black to her prom when Mummy and Madame Honoré pictured her in cheery yellow.

"You know, Simone," Anne says with a flavor of bitterness in her voice. "With all the prom date arranging you've been doing for your friends, it looks to me the apple hasn't fallen far from the tree."

Anne's revelation yanks me upright, and it serves me right.

Have I turned into a mini Mummy?

CHAPTER TWENTY-SIX

It's been a week and there's been no communication from Ben. I'm not sure what to tell Kira.

When the day of the Mets game arrives, I decide to go in case he shows up. I wear my V-neck Mets tee. It's heathered blue with an orange-and-white-striped trim along the neckline and short sleeves. I pair it with distressed jeans and my bright white sneakers.

My mom insisted Papi drive me to the stadium. I thought it would be awkward, but Papi was fine with me giving away his ticket. When I told him I'd shared it with Ben, he was all smiles and approvals. While I'm at the game, he plans to watch it on TV at his brother's place in Brooklyn, where he secretly prefers his sister-in-law's cooking to my mom's.

The minute I step out of the car and navigate the sea of blue-and-orange jerseys, my phone rings. Mummy's Haitian intuition is on point.

"Yes, I'm here safely," I answer.

"Is your phone charged?"

"Yes."

"Did you find your seat?"

"Not yet."

"I'll wait while you find it."

"Not possible. I have to go through security, and I can't be on the phone when I do." I say good-bye to Mummy and walk ahead.

Citi Field on a clear Sunday afternoon is like a piece of heaven on Earth. The sun has the baseball diamond sparkling like a real diamond. The players are casually fielding balls like I imagine they did as kids when it was just for fun. It does take me a few seconds to get used to the dizzyingly steep stadium seating, though.

Is that the Mets dugout straight ahead? Sweet!

I check the row and seat number on my ticket to make sure I haven't passed it. *Down farther?* How close to the front will these seats be? My excitement is accompanied by a pang of guilt for not choosing to bring my dad. He really got me great seats.

With the crunch of peanut shells underfoot, I step down even closer to the field and finally to my row. I see him before I see my row number. Ben is in the second seat, wearing a vintage Mets cap, white tee, and jeans. He's leaning forward, elbows on his knees, eyes on the field. He doesn't notice me until I've slipped into the aisle seat next to him.

"Hey, Ben," I say hesitantly.

He snaps out of his focus and looks at me.

"Hi." He leans back. There doesn't seem to be a trace of resentment in him. "Thank you for inviting me. These seats are incredible."

"I know, right?" I sit there taking it all in. *Whoa*. I could act like I expected to be right above the dugout, but then I'd have to play down my excitement, which I cannot do.

"Let me get you something to eat," Ben says. "It's the least I can do right about now."

"Okay, but I'll buy the next snack. Nine innings is a long time."

While Ben is off getting food, I take a few selfies with the dugout behind me. I text my Mummy a pic, and before I can hit *send*, she's calling me again.

"Check your phone," I tell her. "I'm sending you a picture."

"What picture? Ou rive?" she asks, wanting to confirm that I got here safely.

"Oui, I'm here. Check the picture." Ben is back now with our snacks, standing in the aisle and waiting for me to get up. "I gotta go. All is well. Bye-bye."

"Good. Bye. Get it? Good-bye?" Mummy chuckles, and it tickles a smile out of me. I shake my head.

"Corny," I tease her. "Okay, gotta go."

"Sorry," I tell Ben, standing up so he can pass by. But my seat gets caught on my thigh and never folds up. As a result, I don't give him much clearance as he makes his way to his seat.

We're face-to-face, inches apart. There's not even room for the cardboard tray he's carrying between us. I've reentered his orbit, and the gravitational pull is strong. He reaches for my arm to steady himself, and I hear him breathing.

"Hi," says Ben with a slow smile. He's looking at me like I'm the only queen in Queens.

"Hi," I whisper back.

"Yo, kiss cam couple—have a seat!" someone shouts from a few rows back.

I close my eyes and slink down to my chair, feeling as exposed as if our moment had aired on the jumbo screen. Ben clears his throat, then continues to his seat. After that, it's like we've crossed an invisible line. Now we touch without awkwardness. We brush arms, legs, and shoulders without apologizing. We don't pull back when we both lean on the same armrest. We elbow-bump in conversational laughter.

"So, what's your story, Simone?" Ben asks.

"What exactly do you mean?"

"Why are you scheming so hard for prom?"

I let his question linger, and let it pull out that deep-seated reason for feeling the certain drives we feel. "What can I say? I'm into milestones, rites of passage, all of that."

He nods. "That's cool."

"How did you get involved with helping the kids in Haiti?" I ask.

Ben doesn't hesitate before he answers. "Through an uncle who is a teacher out there. I wanted to get involved because I know how it is to be in their shoes, and I know that any one of them could just as easily be me."

"Yeah, my mom often tells me stories about what folks have had to endure, but how they do it with such grace."

"Their faith and resilience are off the charts. I'm learning so much from them."

I pause. "I love that you know Haiti so well."

"Yup. I lived there until I was about five, and I love visiting."

Wow. But wait, one little detail pops to mind, which has me slightly confused. "But I remember your mom saying she left Haiti in the nineties. That's before we were born."

"She's not my biological mom."

"Oh. I never realized. So, you were adopted?"

Ben opens his mouth to say something but then closes it. That's enough of a cue for me to stop prying. What have I been doing?

"You know what? You don't have to answer that. I don't know why I'm being so nosy, gosh."

A crack of the bat sends a ball hurtling high into the sky. Ben and I instinctively stand up with the crowd. We watch the ball hit an imaginary ceiling in the sky before it barrels down.

The crowd lets out a collective groan when the ball lands on the wrong side of the foul line. Ben and I sit back down.

"No, it's okay," he says, swatting the air. "I don't mind talking about it . . . with you."

"Only if you feel comfortable. And please know that what you say is safe with me." I feel like taking his hand or—for some strange reason—high-fiving him.

"My mom died when I was four years old and my older brother was eight."

"I'm so sorry."

"From what I can remember, she was a loving person. I felt adored around her. My brother remembers a little more about her, so . . ." His voice trails off.

"Was your dad around?"

"My dad flew back and forth from the States, so in those days, I didn't feel much of a connection to him. Now things are more relaxed between us."

"That's a good thing," I say, perking up a hopeful notch. "Do you visit him when you go to Haiti?"

Ben looks at me as if he's realizing for the first time that I'm not following. "I live with him. Here in Queens."

"Monsieur Honoré?"

"Yes. He's my biological dad."

"And Madame Honoré is not your biological mom."

"Correct."

Oh. Wait a minute. *Ohhh.*

Ben takes off his cap. He fiddles with the bill and puts a fist in the lid like he's breaking in a new baseball glove. I listen to his story with my whole body, and sit still.

"Yeah, now that I'm older I can appreciate how messy that situation must've been. My dad with his frequent trips to Haiti to visit a secret family while his wife stayed in Queens. And then after my mother dying, my dad faced with the choice of taking me and my brother to the States or leaving us behind in an orphanage."

Wow, that must have been godawful for a little kid to bear. The tear ducts in my eyes start production against my orders. I lift my tongue to the roof of my mouth to stop from crying. So far, it's not working. Thank goodness Ben is too focused on figuring out the design structure of his baseball cap.

"Madame Honoré seems to treat you and Jude like you are her world," I manage to say. "She couldn't be prouder of you."

"She's been amazing to us. She grew to see us as a gift, I think because she always wanted children."

"I can imagine how tough it was for women of her generation not to have kids."

"Exactly. So, she embraced us in a genuine way and raised us like her own."

"She must have a big heart, because I know that had to be hard," I say.

"Are you calling me hard to love?" Ben stuffs his hat back on his head and narrows his eyes at me like he's offended.

I look at him through my blurry vision and giggle. The tears welling up have subsided a bit, and I manage to keep them from journeying down my cheek. Hopefully, Ben doesn't notice.

His smile has a touch of sadness to it, and he pats my knee. "It's fine. Look at me—I'm fine."

You are *fine*, I think. I'm realizing it more and more.

Wait, am I really thinking that?

"Oh, this?" I point to my eyes. "It's probably just . . . allergies or something."

"As in, you're allergic to sad life stories?"

I chuckle again. "Haitians always got jokes, no matter what the hardship. That's what I love about us—our ability to laugh about life, good or bad."

"You got to." He sighs. "Even Mom has to pause and laugh things off now and then. No doubt all this was tough to deal with, but she never directed any of her anger against us."

"That's because you're special, and she knows it."

"I think you're special, too, Simone," he says softly.

For once in a long time, I don't judge his words, fight my feelings, or plot my next move. I just take in this moment and enjoy every second of it.

We smile at each other, and somehow we get closer, and closer. I can feel the warmth of his face as it edges toward mine. *Is this really happening?* I feel the shea-buttery warmth of his skin, and finally the softness of his lips.

Our hesitant lips don't connect but for a second, and then we gently break apart. Cheers erupt in the stadium, and I imagine they're all for us.

CHAPTER TWENTY-SEVEN

I kissed Ben.

Ben and I kissed.

Ben.

The boy I vowed I'd never be linked with.

I like this boy. Like, a whole lot more than I ever imagined.

I spend practically all of Monday thinking about Ben and our kiss. By Tuesday, I'm starting to lose track of a few things—namely, the printout of my thesis. I'd added notes and a few edits on it, and I need to make those changes in my document. I search all over my bedroom, frantic, because I need to leave to catch the bus. How can I be this messy, this late in high school? Maybe it's a good thing I didn't have much of a social life to juggle before now. I probably wouldn't have handled it so well.

Finally, I find my paper in the unlikeliest of places—in Papi's hands. He's sitting at the kitchen counter, a steaming cup of coffee in one hand and a page in the other. The sight of him reading my work takes my breath away.

"Mummy told me how interesting your paper was, so I was curious to read it," he says, his reading glasses hanging on the tip of his nose. "Thank you for including Anacaona on the list."

"Of course," I say, my voice cracking as I accept my paper back from him.

I give Papi a kiss, tuck my paper into a folder, stuff it in my bag, then run out to catch the bus.

Gabby's not on the bus, and I feel a pang of guilt. We haven't been in touch since the Gavin blowup. I tried to make her feel guilty about liking Gavin, and the whole time, I'd been falling for Ben. Talk about foul.

In school, I avoid Kira and Amita, which also makes me feel guilty. I love my HomeGirls, but ever since I talked to Mummy about the list—and ever since Anne made me realize how controlling I've been with my friends—I haven't felt ready to face them. Besides, with the senior thesis deadline looming, we all went underground to get our papers done. We still texted each other, but I've spared Kira from telling her how my mom got the list—I don't want *her* feeling guilty as well.

The one good thing I accomplish is turning in my senior thesis. My history teacher thanks me and seems impressed when she sees the topic is "Teen Heroes in History." Funny to think that the HomeGirls might not have even existed without my paper.

I wonder if Ben might be interested in reading the paper one day, given that he seems to stay civically engaged. Maybe I'll email it to him—but for now I'm avoiding him, too.

The heft of the guilt I'm carrying around becomes unbearable the next afternoon, when I look into Gabby's sad puppy-dog eyes. And that's not just because I put too much charcoal eyeliner on her. No, it was seeing her walk into my home with that overnight bag slung over her shoulder, looking like a kid planning to run away.

I guess the renovation going on in her home has reached disaster zone proportions. The good news is that according to Tante Nadine, this is usually the turning point, after which the reno gets more tolerable and more beautiful.

But for now, Gabby's spending the night and she's indulging me in a makeup session. She's sitting at the kitchen counter and I'm trying out all sorts of fun prom colors on her eyes. It's just like Gabby and me to ignore the big chunk of awkwardness hogging the space between us. Or rather, it's just like *me*. Gabby usually forgets about stuff right after she unloads on you. While you're still stewing or replaying her last biting words, girlfriend has moved on. She'll greet a person like she didn't have a shouting match with them days prior.

But apparently not this time.

"Close your eyes," I instruct Gabby, and I rub on some eye shadow.

But my cousin flings her eyelids open and blurts out, "I'll stop seeing Gavin if it means we can be cool again."

I can feel my mini Mummy coming on. On purpose this time. "You better not," I fake-scold. "I forbid it!"

It's obvious Gabby's eyes would be sparkling even without the shimmery eye shadow she's rocking. "What do you mean? I thought you'd feel better if Gavin and I didn't—"

"I'd feel better if we face facts." I stop busying myself with the eye shadow brush and its accompanying colors. The palette case clinks against the marble counter as I put it down. "You and Gavin are super cute together," I admit out loud for the first time.

"For real, for real?"

I nod. "He's a good person. And you guys vibe, like, organically."

"No, like—seriously?"

"Yes, Gabby, don't make me have to spell it out."

"Wow, thank you, Simone. That's real big of you."

I scoff. "You'd think it would rub off on you, but not every-body can be classy."

She ignores me, but grabs hold of the counter and twists her bar stool to face me.

"To be real with you, I was trying to pass off my feelings for him as some stupid crush, but it just wouldn't go away," she says quietly. "It wasn't until you invited me over to his house with you that I realized how much I . . . get him. Being around him is the easiest, most comfortable thing."

I nod in understanding. "Yeah. I didn't realize Gavin wasn't the one for me until that day at his house, too. It's like he was more of this . . . vision for me. Like a prop in my prom dream world. And I made myself as this prop, too, playing a role I didn't recognize. It didn't work."

"So you really don't want to date him anymore?" Gabby asks.

"Gavin?" I shake my head. "You can be yourself around him. I just . . . couldn't."

She scrunches up her nose. "I kinda noticed."

"Ugh. Did I make it obvious?"

She shrugs. "I also kinda noticed how comfy you are around Ben."

Just the mention of his name draws up the corners of my lips.

"Ohmygod!" Gabby shouts.

"I know, I know." I lean in close and lower my voice. "I think I—I really like him." I don't tell her about our kiss, though—that feels like something I'm not ready to talk about . . . yet.

"You see?" Gabby beams at me. "Maybe your parents were onto something with that setup."

I laugh, shaking my head. "I refuse to give them credit. Besides, Ben is going to prom with Kira, remember?"

"Oh yeah." Gabby looks disappointed. "Are you sure you don't want to just tell him how you feel?"

"No. It'll just make everything more complicated," I say firmly.

"You know," Gabby says, sounding wiser than I ever did as a sophomore, "it's not so easy to find someone you feel at home with."

I take in her words, fiddling with a tube of mascara. She's not wrong.

"Speaking of home," she says with a deepening frown. "Being at my own house doesn't feel so comfy right now." She drops her chin into her palm. "I think a big part of my mom actually likes the chaos."

"Well, you're welcome to hide out here anytime," I offer, uncapping the mascara. "And if you ever get homesick, we'll stick you in the hallway or some place with a high traffic flow."

Gabby sucks her teeth, and I grin at how far from her face she stretches her mouth. But mostly, I'm grinning because the tense air has cleared and my cousin and I are best friends again.

Gotta love a make-up makeup session.

When someone checks you on your misstep, you have to consider the source. And there are no other sources as brutally honest with me as Anne and Gabby. Having been properly checked by my most trusted homegirls, it was time to come clean with the HomeGirls.

I meet with Amita and Kira where it all began—in the empty classroom at school. I spring for their fave bagels from Elevensies. When we're fifteen minutes from the morning bell, I know it's time to stop stalling and start 'fessing.

"Nice meeting up like this again," says Kira, scrunching up

the last of the napkins and stuffing them into a brown paper bag. "I've missed you ladies."

I play with the crumbs I've gathered into a pile on the table. "Me too," I nod. "Congrats to us on getting our papers in, HomeGirls!"

We touch our fists and give a little cheer.

"But that's not the only reason I called this meeting," I say, belaboring the issue like a goofball.

"I was waiting for you to get to it," says Amita. She shifts out of her seat and plops back down on her folded legs. "It's getting boring watching you agonizing. Just spit it out."

"Well—" I shape the pile of crumbs into a triangle. Like a diner waitress on a mission, Kira sweeps my pile of crumbs off the table into her brown paper bag.

"Nice move!" I compliment Kira, impressed with her gumption.

"Just when you think you have HomeGirl Kira figured out." Amita slaps the table.

"No, no—this isn't about me." Kira giggles softly. "You were saying, Simone?"

"Okay, here it is," I say, clearing the shame from my throat. No crumbs to babysit, I meet my friends' eyes. "As much as I hate to admit it, I think I've done to you what my mom did to me—I meddled in your prom arrangements and I'm sorry."

"All you did was make sure I'd go to the prom with a date you . . . trusted and . . . selected . . . for . . . me . . ." Kira's voice trails off and a brief silence follows.

"Nah, you're *nothing* like your mom, Simone," Amita jokes.

I half playfully bury my head in my hands and wail, "How did I become the very thing I resisted?"

"It's a slippery slope." Amita shrugs. "Kinda like when you hide one thing after another about yourself from your parents, and then eventually, without intending to, you hide even the harmless stuff or the important things. Pretty soon, your parents learn to play detective just to find out the smallest info about you."

I'm surprised to hear Amita admit to this. Kira gives her hand a pat. "You can reverse that by letting them in on one harmless fact at a time."

"They seem like the type to appreciate that," I say cautiously. "I'm sure they'll be so happy, they'll insist you invite your study group over for a swim in the pool."

Amita's sly grin is back. "Nice try."

"So, where does this leave us with our list?" Kira asks.

I pull out the original list to the HomeGirls' exaggerated *oohs* and *aahs*.

Amita does the honors, reading out loud. She adds a "check" whenever at least one of us has accomplished a goal.

"Go to a REAL house party—check. Go clubbin'—check. Cut class—check. Go on a date—two-thirds check. Hang out in NYC—check. Sneak a boy over to your house or go over to his house"—Amita gives me a knowing glance, and I shake my head at the memory of being at Gavin's house—"*one*-third check. Ride a bike—check. Switch up style—check. Resist arranged proms . . . one hundred percent, check!"

"That's incredible," I say, flustered.

"We really did it." Kira wipes her eyes, and I marvel at how emotional we've all become lately. Maybe it's senior year. Or was it this mission we set out on together?

"We should be proud," Amita says. "Even if there were some bumps along the way."

"Sure I wish my mom hadn't been AirDropped the list, but I don't blame you, Kira," I tease.

Kira points to herself, mortified. "Wait. It was me?"

Amita pats Kira's back, and I nod and chuckle softly. "But it's all good. I look at it this way: Sometimes taking action can't stay a secret. Sometimes we have to shine a light on things we keep in the dark." I check out the list again. "I mean, if the powers that be don't know about our resistance, can real change even happen? Maybe part of resisting is learning that we don't always have to do things in hiding."

Kira nods. "Are you sure you're okay with how prom worked out, though?" she asks me. "You won't have a date now."

I nod. "So what if we're not going to prom with our desired dates? This is about *us*. We should go to the prom and own it."

"After that speech, you almost make me want to cancel Pritpal as my on-again prom date," says Amita.

"What?" Kira and I squeal at the same time.

"How did you guys get back together?" I ask, elated.

"He came to my house," Amita blurts before stacking her

hands over her mouth. "When I wouldn't answer his calls, he got concerned and showed up at my doorstep."

My eyes widen. "And your parents didn't trip?"

"No, the opposite," she says. "Remember when they told you they were seeking the out wedding singer for a prom setup for me? Turns out it was *true*. So they thought it was kismet that we found each other."

"Wait, they think he just showed up out of the blue?" Kira says.

"Pretty much." Amita grins. "And I didn't correct them. Let them think their prayers had something to do with it."

"I love it," I say.

"Looks like cuzzo Krish just became your prom date, Simone," Amita tells me with a hand flourish. "If you'll have him. And with Ben as Kira's date, that means most of the gang will be back together again, minus Gavin and Gabby."

"About Gavin and Gabby," I say. "Breaking news: They are an item."

Kira gasps, but Amita doesn't seem the least surprised.

Not everything should stay secret, but I decide to wait to tell them about kissing Ben until after prom. I wouldn't want Kira to feel weird about the prom arrangements.

"So is the list done, then?" Amita asks.

"I have an idea," Kira announces.

We turn to her and listen to her explain. And her idea is awesome. The three of us agree to create a new list—one we don't have to hide or keep secret. And one that will carry us through our college years.

THE HOMEGIRLS' PLAYLIST
1. *Go out and play*
2. *Don't be afraid to get a little messy*
3. *Don't hide who you are*
4. *Shed light on the dark*
5. *Keep your friends & fam close*

And what do you know? When I share the new list with my family that evening, Mummy asks for a printout to keep in her locker at work.

CHAPTER TWENTY-EIGHT

"How is it possible to look so glum and so glam at the same time?" Gabby asks.

For once, my cousin isn't exaggerating. When I stare into my full-length mirror, I see what she means. How can I look this amazing yet feel so very nervous? Not even the aroma of fried plantains climbing up from the kitchen is enough to snap me out of my existential crisis.

Today is prom—the event I've been waiting so long for. But the boy I wish was my prom date is someone else's. Ben and I have texted each other since the Mets game, but we haven't discussed the kiss at all. And now it's just too awkward to bring up again. At least not until prom is over. Tonight, I'll just have to pretend like everything is status quo.

Anne stands beaming as Gabby takes pics of me from a few flattering angles.

"Come on, Simone," says Anne. "It's your prom night. You've

been counting down to this forever. And you look gorgeous."

"Thanks," I tell my sister.

Scanning myself from head to toe is pretty trippy. *Is that really me?* Brown skin poppin'. For this special occasion, I got the best hand-whipped, most-shea-buttery goodness I could find. Gabby had me sit under her hooded dryer with a million corkscrew rollers in my hair, and the result is divine. The high bun. The cascading ringlets. The light from Mummy's mini chandelier catches every zig and zag of each shiny strand. Plus, the seamstress did a fabulous job with my two-piece, which I picked up from her showroom just a few days ago. And Anne did wonders with my makeup. So much talent in one 'hood.

"Give a little twirl, girl," says Gabby.

I pivot away from my cousin, and the vibrant colors of the African print on my voluminous high-waisted skirt practically glimmer. The colors perfectly match my strappy open-toed shoes, not to mention my nail polish. My outfit is slaying in all the right ways.

Somewhere, some girl is going to find my picture online and pin it to her faves list. And this same pic is going to spark in her a small goal or a tiny dream, and the thought will make her heart soar. It's my own way of contributing to the cause—if the cause is being fashionably fierce.

There's a slit in my skirt and I can't help notice my ankles.

They're glowing!

I've been searching so hard for glowy ankles on guys that I

hadn't once considered my own. I beam with the dizzying realization: I'm my own dream prom date. *This* is something to celebrate.

As if I've just surfaced from water, I can now hear the Haitian konpa grooves floating from downstairs. I sway to the music, appreciating how unexpected and super sweet it is of my parents to throw me a surprise pregame celebration. I'm happy that I took action, even if it didn't lead me to the place I imagined. And I know what I activated in me will carry me through college and beyond.

"Yes, Port-au-Princess," Gabby says, raising her phone to record my konpa moves. I extend my long arms toward her and Anne.

"Come on, y'all," I beckon with a giggle. "I've saved my first dance for the both of you."

My girls join me and we all hold hands and do the poised two-step. So happy for me, Anne rocks with it and dips on the off beat. She raises our hands above our heads and throws her head back. My sister stretches her body so far out that box I've placed her in, I catch a wave of both regret and pride. It's amazing to see her feeling the moment. In just a few months, she'll be out of the house, killing it in medical school. I dance to the rhythm of my pride.

"Aay! Aay! Aay!" Gabby chants to the beat like the world's best hypewoman she is. She's studying my moves and starts copying the way I flex. I smile and switch up how I whine my hips until she has trouble keeping up.

Could it be my baby cousin is learning something from *me* for a change?

"*Woy! Woy! Woy!*" Gabby flips to the Creole version of that chant and we all crack up and pull it in for a group hug.

"Y'all are gonna mess up my makeup before my big reveal!" I say, dabbing at an errant tear of joy.

The chime of the doorbell fills the house, signaling Ben's arrival.

Gabby happy claps, her eyes wild with excitement. "Wait! Let me go down first and announce your hair's grand entrance—uh, I mean, *your* grand entrance." I give her a playful nudge.

In the end, it's Anne who announces my arrival while Gabby beatboxes the drumroll. Mummy and Papi are at the bottom of the stairs, holding up their phones and wearing huge smiles. The rest of the family gaze, starry-eyed, as if watching me on a movie screen. For people who seem at a loss for words, they are not short on reactions.

Mummy's eyes pool. "Oh la la."

"Whoooa," intones Papi, in that familiar Haitian singsong.

"Ayayay mwen," sasses Tatie Nadine.

"A la bèl," adds Grandmère approvingly.

My mom's bestie, Terrence, shakes his head. "Stunning, my dear."

Ben is the only one speechless. He stands there in a tailored retro black suit, just emanating strong classic Motown singer energy. The vibrant African print bow tie pops against his stark white shirt and beautifully complements his deep brown skin. His eyes follow me as I make my way through the small crowd of relatives and friends greeting me with hugs.

Terrence's husband, Jeremy, Voisin, Ben's aunt, with her adult son, and a couple of her toddler grandchildren are also here. I wish Ma Tante could be a part of this, but I know she's here in spirit.

"And voilà!" Tante Nadine sweeps her arm across Mummy's prom night tablescape. Our dining table is all dressed up for the occasion. I put my hand over my heart as I scan the elegant presentation of mini veggie and fruit trays alongside an array of plantains and griyo skewers.

Mummy is watching me and my reaction so intently, she gets choked up when I rush over to give her a huge hug.

I keep one arm around her and point at the top of her head with the other. "My mom may not be the best dresser, but when it comes to décor, she can throw down!"

Mummy breaks free from me and calls me "fresh" in Creole. "Frekan! You try to act so fancy. We'll see how fancy the rooms are when we tour the dorms with you next month."

I keep laughing, until her words play back in my mind. "Sa blan an di?" I ask in a daze.

"Mummy, you were supposed to mention that at graduation," Anne reprimands her. "Do you want her to ruin my masterpiece makeup job?"

Okay, yes. Mummy has only committed to a dorm tour and not campus living. But trust me, what may seem like baby steps to some is a huge deal to me. My mom and dad sandwich me in an embrace, and though I'm not crying, I feel droplets of water showering down on me. I look up to see Grandmère flinging water from her container again.

She calls out her blessings for the family. "May they stay healthy. May they stay safe. May they stay together."

It takes both Gabby and Anne to pry me out of there. I turn around and finally find myself face-to-face with Ben. And then he speaks for the first time tonight.

"You look—wow," he says tenderly. "Like, truly."

I look away from his mesmerizing brown eyes and notice the incredible bouquet of pink roses he's holding. As Ben hands them to me, he leans over and kisses me on my cheek. And it's not the type of air kiss given to elders. It's a full-on soft lips on tingling face kiss. The memory of our Citi Field kiss rushes back, and I melt inside.

When he pulls away, it takes me a second to catch my breath—which, to hide my true feelings, I immediately puff out in a joke.

"I really don't think I can fit this entire bouquet around my wrist," I tell him.

"Can't a brotha play the gentleman?" he jokes.

I wonder what other roles he's playing, standing there looking like the prom king at Wakanda High School. He makes it seem like he really wants to be here and is not just going through the motions. A big part of me can't help wishing those googly eyes he's making right now are really meant for me.

"Not to worry—I got your button-ear, too," he assures me.

"Um, don't you speak French better than I do? It's boutonnière—or really, it's a corsage if it's for me."

"My bad." Ben hangs his head in mock shame. He looks so adorable doing this, I have to restrain myself from leaning over to kiss *his* cheek as he places the sweet-smelling corsage on my wrist.

"I've got something for you, too." I pull the Etsy baseball cuff links from my purse and hand them to him.

Ben's face does that light-up thing that goes along with his smile. "Simone, these are amazing. Thank you so much!"

"I got them before I met you—which is kind of psychic of me, because they are totally meant for you."

"Not psychic," says Ben with a chuckle. "Just Haitian."

Anne takes the flowers while I help Ben put the cuff links on. Then we pose for a gazillion pictures alone, together, and with different relatives.

"You guys make such a cute couple!" claims Gabby.

Ben and I eye each other with bashful smiles.

"Don't they?" Tante Nadine coos.

They don't know that Ben is only keeping up his part of the bargain. He's expected to be here and play the role of the arranged prom date. It's his final act in this charade we're pulling off on my parents. Yet somehow, I don't feel like I'm the one having the last laugh.

"You look beautiful, just like I imagined," Mummy says before wrapping an arm around my waist for another photo.

"Merci." I angle my head toward hers until her forehead makes contact with my chin. It's a closeness we haven't experienced in a while, which makes me realize how much I've missed her. "And thanks for this party, Mummy. I love it."

"Anything for you, Simone," she says. Her index finger affectionately boops the tip of my nose. "Even things you don't approve of."

The first notes of the next song drop, and it completely throws us off our train of thought. We wild out and throw our hands in the air. It's a popular old-school konpa hit that's an ode to our island nation. The lyrics paint a vivid soundscape, until you're visualizing Haiti's mountainous peaks, vibrant culture, and survival spirit. Everyone pairs up or dances in groups in front of Grandmère's perch on her favorite recliner in the living room. It's good to see her fully recovered from her surgery. I've got to think maybe a little of her holy water had something to do with that.

As we two-step to the song, I pick up the same bliss in the singer's voice in this room.

The love and support around me keep my heart and my flat feet light. It reminds me that while being sheltered has been somewhat stifling to my independence, no one here is out to stifle my joy.

The St. Clare Academy senior prom takes place every year at The Mayfair, a sprawling venue in Millwall Cliffs. The place looks like a country estate you see in Hollywood, gated and glamorous. The fountain right outside the entrance spouts in elegant formation, and once we walk into the marble interior, the sound of running water fades into the familiar bass thud of our favorite jams.

There's still a dull pang in my belly that reminds me I am here with Ben but *not* here with Ben. Like tearing off a Band-Aid, he and I part the moment we enter The Mayfair. He's off to the restroom and I'm off in search of my friends.

In the main ballroom, the fierce prom looks are front, center, and wall to wall.

"You look amazing!" I squeal between selfies with different classmates.

"What about you, queen?" Kenzie points at me. We promise to save each other a dance later.

As I cross the ballroom, I make my prediction on who deserves the prom queen and king fashion title. In this case, they are prom queen and queen Alexa and Stacie, who match fabulously in an all-checkerboard pattern and are wearing roses like they're from some avant-garde production of *Alice in Wonderland*. I have no choice but to stan. I give them air kisses and pose with them for yet another dope selfie.

Finally, I find my HomeGirls at our very own prom table. When Amita stands up to greet me, that one-shouldered black gown she bought online is in full view, and she's stunning. And just as I suspected, Kira looks dazzling in the emerald-green high-necked dress we bought together in Jersey City.

The three of us hug, toss flattery bombs at one another, and take the requisite selfie or two hundred. When we're done, Amita and Kira pull me aside. Kira mimes like she's putting something in each of our hands.

"These are your coffee cups," she explains. "Just go with it."

"O-kay." I giggle, wondering what this is about.

Amita holds up her empty hand. "We'd like to make a toast on this momentous occasion of our promancipation! The HomeGirls found each other and came together in a time of desperation, not knowing exactly what to expect. But in the end, we found something we didn't know we needed the most—friendship. And let me tell you, girlies, there has been no better company to my misery."

"Cheers to that," Kira says, a hand to her heart. I raise my invisible glass higher in the air.

"Oh, and cheers to the HomeGirls for crushing our research papers and collecting all the A's we deserve," I say, holding a pinch of my skirt and fanning it out with a bow.

We celebrate this news by bringing our hands together and saying, "Ting!"

"Um," I say a moment later, glancing around. "Ben should be here any minute, Kira. He just went to the bathroom." I pause and ask, "Where are Krish and Pritpal?"

Amita and Kira exchange a glance.

"What?" I ask, feeling suddenly worried.

"Simone, we have a surprise for you," says Kira.

"Uh-oh." I give them the side-eye.

Kira grins and faces me, placing her hands on my arm where my butterfly tattoo used to be. "After being the beneficiary of all your tireless prom date rigging, we decided to repay you by personally arranging your prom date for the night."

"But I apologized to you guys for all that. Didn't I?" I ask, searching both their faces. "Ugh, I should've known there'd be more to pay."

"Quit your whining, close your eyes, and turn around," Amita says.

I close my eyes. I assume it'll just be Krish standing there waiting for me, but what if I'm about to get clowned in prime time? "Oh no. There's going to be the Millwall High mascot in a tux, I just know it."

Kira spins me around. I open my eyes and standing there before me is . . .

"Ben?"

A shy, cautious smile comes across his face. Is he wondering, as I had earlier, if my feelings were just for show? Is he wondering, as I am now, how amazing it would be to be together, for real, for real?

I tear my attention away from him and turn to Kira. "But what about you?"

"I'm never solo with my HomeGirls around me," she says. "*But* Krish and I hit it off, and I'm starting to really like him. It's been super sweet hanging with him. So he's my date tonight."

"Ohmygod, Kira, that's great!" I give her a quick hug.

"How did you guys even know how I feel about Ben?" I ask, looking from her to Amita. "I wasn't going to mention it until after the prom."

"We had our suspicions," Kira answers. "But we weren't sure until we DMed Ben and had an emergency video chat with him."

"Once he confirmed everything, we were pretty sure you wouldn't mind if we arranged one last prom date," Amita says with a wink.

I just stand there and beam because I'm looking too cute to bust out the slipper dance. Pritpal and Krish come over and greet me with hugs, and it's a Kool and the Gang celebration all over again.

Amita whispers to me, "Ben's still waiting."

I turn to face him again, but this time, I can't stop smiling.

"What do you say?" Ben asks with a glint in his eyes. He reaches into his pocket and pulls out a super-cute set of dangling earrings in the shape of baseball bats. "Simone Thibodeaux, will you be my prom date?"

I'm breathless, my heart is thumping, and it's the best feeling. "I accept!"

In the blink of an eye, I cross the distance between us, and Ben wraps his arms around my waist. And right there, in front of a much smaller audience than the one at Citi Field, we kiss. But it's not unsure and tentative like our first kiss. This time, our kiss is deep and sweet. Our lips meet each other, slow and deliberate, locking us in this moment in time, here on the dance floor, surrounded by our friends.

"What is it with us and PDAs?" I ask when we finally pull apart.

"I don't know," whispers Ben, his fingers brushing my cheek. "But if we keep up this kiss cam challenge, maybe we'll finally get on a stadium jumbotron somewhere."

"As long as it's where the Mets are playing," I say.

A smile opens up his whole face, and I smile back at him. I can't wait to kiss him again.

"I really like you, Simone. I think I've liked you for a while now," Ben says, his eyes studying every inch of my face. Heat rises to my cheeks. I try to keep a steady balance on my heels, hoping there's no missing plexiglass behind me this time.

I guess there are no secrets with Ben. So I decide to give truth a try.

"I really like you, too," I say, looking right back at his handsome face. "I think I have for some time—but, definitely not before you liked me."

Ben smiles. He pulls me close and we kiss again, until there's another commotion.

The DJ starts playing "You & Me @ Prom" and our whole crew floods the dance floor.

Ben and I join them and I watch him do the two-step while I throw my hands in the air; Amita and Pritpal spin each other around and shout out every word to the song; Kira can't stop cracking up at all the goofy moves Krish shamelessly tries out.

After the song is over, I tug the HomeGirls by their wrists and lead them to the center of the dance floor, where we can hold a mini dance party to celebrate our Playlist wins, highs, and lows. In true Jersey fashion, the DJ blasts a song from the Bon Jovi canon and my HomeGirls and I sing along. *"Take my hand, we'll make it I swear!"*

As the night goes on, our dream dates take breaks to sit down and have some water, but the HomeGirls stay on the dance floor. We stick to the business of partying our hearts out, like it's the top goal on our Playlist. This is our moment, for now. And we make the most of it.

After all, we still have to be home by midnight.

ACKNOWLEDGMENTS

I'm the third born of four girls, but my mom once lamented I was her first teen-acting teen. Yes, there were restrictive rules (on her part) and lies of convenience (on mine), but thank goodness there was also lots of love, laughter, and journal ~~venting~~ writing.

Writing, for me, has always involved capturing what's in the ether and sculpting it into letters. The influences I've turned to for this book are many. I only hope my characters give off even a whiff of their dauntless spirit and dynamic energy.

To my family, friends, and community: Thank you for living so fully. Your essence leaves imprints everywhere, which I can see, interpret, and weave into stories so that young minds can perceive the message to live life wholeheartedly and express the self in its fullness.

To my dad, the New Jerker (translation: what I call a New Yorker living in New Jersey). He says his umbilical cord is buried in Brooklyn. But New Jersey is where he rests his brainy head.

Thank you, Papi, for selling an organ for me that one time. Relax, y'all—he's an organist.

To my whip-smart agent Laura Dail, who protects my space to create, nudges me when needed, and knows my worth and works dang hard to make sure everyone knows it, too. I am so pumped to be on this journey with you!

Thank you, Team LDLA, especially Samantha S. Fabien and the interns who pored over early drafts of this book.

Aimee Friedman, we get to do this again? Hashtag blessed. You are a discerning editor who sifts through the organic for gold until what was once dull and grainy shines. Thank you.

To the talented Yaffa Jaskoll: Thank you for designing this stunning cover. And to the gifted artist Erick Dàvila: Thank you for rendering Simone so vividly and soulfully! P.S. I am still not over this cover!

Scholastic is such a perfect fit for my voice, and I've been blown away by their kind welcome. All-around hugs and utmost thanks to the Scholastic village, including David Levithan, Taylan Salvati, Rachel Feld, Erin Berger, Olivia Valcarce, Caroline Flanagan, Janell Harris, Lizette Serrano, Danielle Yadao, Michael Strouse, Irma Jarvis, Julia Eisler, Emily Heddleson, the @IReadYA crew, the Book Fairs and Book Clubs teams, the Sales team, the Power of Story video series team, and so many more.

Mesi anpil to Professor Cécile Accilien for your feedback on the Creole in this book. You are a gem, and I am so grateful for your work.

Extending so much gratitude and thanks to librarians and booksellers, especially at Columbus Library branches, Westerville Library, Cover to Cover Bookstore, and Watchung Booksellers.

Thank you to Brown Bookshelf, Vanesse Lloyd-Sgambati, My Very Own Library team, and SCBWI-Central Ohio. A heartfelt merci/mesi to bloggers and bookstagrammers and reporters. Loving thanks to my Rutgers University (Newark campus!) journalism professor, George Davis. Thank you, Kimberly Jones, for the coolest book launch parties.

A special thanks to the generous authors who have invited me to panels and book fests, provided encouragement, support, advice or, most recently, blurbs. Thank you to Edwidge Danticat, Ronke Idowu Reeves, Sylvia May, Julia DeVillers, Sarah Mylnowski, Ronni Davis, Jennifer Baker, Stephan Lee, Christina Soontornvat, Justin A. Reynolds, Alicia D. Williams, Gayle Forman, Maika Moulite, Maritza Moulite, Ben Philippe, Tami Charles, Jasmine Guillory, Nic Stone, Zoraida Cordova, Carlotta Penn, Debbie Michiko Florence, and Varian Johnson.

To the Essex County, New Jersey streets—including the cities of East Orange and Newark. And to the "bugged-out" girls I caught the bus with during high school—Courtney, Celeste, Kofi, Jackie, Kisha, Yolanda, Kasanu, Wilita, and all. Thanks for the laughs, the companionship, and the bus stop dance breaks to keep warm. And much love to my true HomeGirls Myrna Perez, Desiree Jones, Tamra Wilson, and Yvy Joseph.

Extra, extra special thank yous to my family: to my beautiful sisters who helped to shape who I am and to my brothers-in-law who introduced me to Shea Stadium and took me on my first visit to Haiti. Shoutout to my sister Golda, my North Star/Zero-Got-No-Higher, to my cherished cousins who faced the world alongside me, to all my nieces and nephews who amaze me every day, to my aunties who lift me up and cover me in prayer, and to my wonderful in-laws who have given me not only my husband but also two additional amazing sisters.

And finally, to my love, Bernard. Thank you for clearing a path to this life. I am eternally grateful for you. A brotha who thinks fast and turns on an episode of *The Office* during intense labor is definitely the man for me. To my heaven-sent kiddos, Olivia and Lincoln . . . getting to know you two has been my greatest joy. Y'all crack me up! I love you both. And, oh, hey Rosie! 😊

ABOUT THE AUTHOR

Debbie Rigaud is the author of *Truly Madly Royally* and the coauthor of Alyssa Milano's *New York Times* bestselling Hope series. Debbie grew up in East Orange, New Jersey, and started her career writing for entertainment and teen magazines. She now lives with her husband and children in Columbus, Ohio. Find out more at debbierigaud.com.